As part of the

Go Indie now!

Library

Changing the literary world
by storm

J.Z.N. MCCAULEY

This book is a work of fiction. The names, characters and events in this book are the products of the author's imagination or are used fictitiously. Any similarity to real persons living or dead is coincidental and not intended by the author.

Published by White Moon Press

Illustration by Mélanie Delon | www.melaniedelon.com
Edited by Kiele Raymond

ISBN: 9781619845312
eISBN: 9781619845329

Library of Congress Control Number: 2016953022

Printed in the United States of America

To The Lily of the Valley–Thank you for your pure fragrance and graceful beauty.

To my husband and children–My best friends, soulmates, and loves of my life.

CONTENTS

PROLOGUE

CATHERINE WAS ABOUT to tell Kathleen to shut up when the pilot announced that the plane was about to land. Her sister had been pestering her nonstop for the last hour about their plans.

"Kathleen! Please!"

"I don't understand why you're getting so riled up!" huffed Kathleen as she sat back, invading Catherine's personal space.

Danny made it back to his seat just as the stewardesses walked down the aisles for a last check.

"You took an awful long time," Catherine said as he buckled his seat belt.

"I wasn't gone *that* long, geez," he pouted and slumped in his seat.

"Who were you flirting with *this* time?" Kathleen rolled up her fashion magazine and jabbed him ruthlessly.

Danny slapped it away. "That girl with the purple hair in the back corner. She's from New York," he said, as though being from New York meant something to him. He gave his sisters a crooked smile and they glared back. "Hey, she's really nice, okay?"

"What's her name?" asked Catherine, still frowning.

"It's . . . Danielle," he replied.

"Right," the girls said in unison, turning their gaze back forward.

Danny shrugged.

The three siblings were on their way to Dublin for a summer in Ireland. It was a college graduation trip. Catherine was glad she could spend her summer on her beloved Emerald Isle, rather than roaming the large empty rooms of her family's estate. Her love first began when traveling with her grandparents as a child to connect with distant Irish relatives, and explore her heritage. As an adult, she hoped she would at least have some time to herself for the duration of the trip to unwind while she worked on completing the next step after graduation: getting a job. Catherine's thoughts were interrupted just then when Danny bumped her arm as he craned to look over his shoulder down the aisle. She loved her older brother and twin sister, but she found them rather irritating at times. Catherine was not looking forward to doing everything together. It had already begun to seem like a headache to her.

When the plane landed, the siblings made their way out of the airport to wait for their bus, luggage placed in front of them on the ground. It was hot, and Catherine's natural red hair glowed in the blazing sun, a rarity in Ireland.

Catherine looked around at the many busy people about them. While Kathleen complained of the heat causing her hair to stick to her neck, she just put her hair in a disheveled bun. Out of the corner of her eye, Catherine thought she saw a man with curly brown hair staring their way. When she twisted around to look at him, he was gone. Just then, a few buses pulled up and there was a rush of people and bags. The man was quickly forgotten as she hurried along.

The bus ride to their hostel only lasted a short time, and they checked in easily. Catherine and Danny had set up hostels instead of hotels for a "more authentic" experience. However,

Kathleen wanted to be pampered instead. She didn't want to share anything with anybody, especially strangers. Both hoped the lodging would be good for Kathleen's development. Only Catherine knew her sister would simply vow to never do it again. Still, Kathleen didn't complain until later in the day when she had to use the hostel's public restroom.

"I shouldn't have to share a bathroom!" Kathleen scowled. "It's fine for you," she flicked her hand towards Catherine, "since you chose this place instead of a hotel, but not me."

Danny sighed as Catherine threatened to punch her.

Kathleen tossed her hair back and sat on her bed. "What is there to do here?"

Danny laughed. "What do you mean? It's Ireland, there's tons to see!"

"Well of course, but I mean at this *hostel*..." she reiterated with disgust.

"You saw the list of activities," Catherine said.

"They have a BBQ!" Danny could hardly wait to sink his teeth into a burger.

"Right, well you know I've decided to go off meat," Kathleen wrinkled her nose.

Catherine didn't respond. It was just another one of Kathleen's phases. Danny looked at himself in the mirror, brushing his light brown hair with his hands to make it look just right before walking towards the door.

"Well, I'm going to go get something to eat, be back later," he said, shutting the door behind him.

When Catherine finished unpacking she sat down and looked through her phone to check their plans for the next few days. "Uncle Mickey wants us to visit as soon as we can," she said.

"Where does he live?" Kathleen asked.

"I don't remember, but it's in my address book. I'll figure out if we need to take a bus or a train."

"Can we wait until tomorrow? I don't want to go out for the rest of the day," Kathleen said as she peered through the windows at the sudden downpour of rain.

"It's Ireland, Kathleen; you'll have to get used to the weather."

Kathleen sighed and nodded irritably as she looked through her bags. Pulling out her compact mirror, she pouted at the already damaged ends of her long hair. She had recently dyed it black.

Catherine glanced over. "I told you not to dye it."

"Well, I'm not quite as set on our natural look," Kathleen huffed.

Catherine frowned, then clicked through to Uncle Mickey's address. It looked like it would be an early start in the morning.

Later that evening, Catherine settled in for the night, leaving her siblings to themselves. Huddling in her bed under the covers, she listened to the sound of the rain. She was happy to be in Ireland again. She always felt like it was another home to her. Knowing the excited butterflies in her stomach would eventually dissipate, she reveled in the feeling for a while before allowing the pattering raindrops to lull her to sleep.

* * *

When the alarm on Catherine's phone went off the next morning, the three stumbled out of the hostel with grunts and grumbles. It was an hour and a half bus ride and they used it to sleep off their jet lag. Catherine occasionally opened her eyes to see the green passing by her window.

Finally arriving in the town of Baltinglass, the siblings made their way through the cattle mart and explored a bit of the town centre. Danny and Kathleen had fun shopping but Catherine preferred exploring the ruins of Baltinglass Abbey, where the arches loomed above her. Kathleen found ruins creepy and she hung onto Catherine's arm. Danny dragged his feet until they got to the gravestones. After a few hours, it was finally time to go see their uncle.

The three walked along the road leading to his house. Catherine found the sound of their steps comforting as the gravel crunched under her shoes. A small white bungalow came into view, and Catherine picked up her pace. Reaching the edge of the well-kept green lawn, she heard a dog barking from inside, and a lock click as her uncle opened the front door. His eyes lit up as he pulled them into hugs and his Wicklow Terrier lapped at their feet.

"Oh it's great to see you three," he said happily, ushering them inside. "I only just saw your graduation pictures yesterday. We're mighty proud of you here, aren't we Brighton?" he said to his dog as he led them to the living room.

Kathleen smiled, but Catherine knew she secretly wanted to run back outside and away from the shaggy gray animal now sniffing her knees. Though the small thing was harmless, Kathleen's fears had always been irrational. Catherine reached down and picked up Brighton. Kathleen mouthed a silent *Thank you* as she settled into a nearby armchair.

"Ah, Brighton really takes to you, Caty," remarked Uncle Mickey.

Catherine cringed at the nickname. She had never liked it, even in childhood.

Mickey was quite the cook, the siblings found, and they were grateful for the delicious Irish stew made up of lamb, potatoes, carrots, onions and parsley. They savored the blend of different flavors drawn out to perfection.

After dinner was over, and they had caught up on all the family news, Mickey turned to his usual talk of folklore. Catherine had always been fascinated by his tales. Now it was apparent that his interest spread to every room of his small home, with ancient tapestries hanging on one wall and relic weapons on another. He was retired now after consulting with museums and schools around the country, and in the States. Catherine too, enjoyed ancient studies, archeology, and the like. It was what she had just finished studying at school. Since his retirement some years before, Uncle Mickey had continued to solve what small archeological mysteries he could, however steeped in superstition they were.

"I'm going to tell you something, Caty," he gestured for her to come closer. He had just finished recounting a lecture on ancient druids of Ireland. It must have sparked a memory in him, for Catherine could see his eyes light up as she inched closer. "'I've come across many people in my time, and I think you've got something special, Caty," he said with a smile.

"What do you mean?" Catherine asked, confused. She gave him a hesitant smile.

He looked over to make sure Kathleen and Danny weren't listening. Kathleen was busy on her phone, and Danny had gone to the bathroom. When he felt assured he wasn't being overheard he continued. "I think you're a special girl, of course, but I think you have that tinge of magic some seek. Aligned in your stars," he said matter of fact.

Catherine laughed and waved off the idea. Uncle Mickey's kind face turned serious.

"This is no joke, Caty. I've always felt you're connected more than the others to this land. And on more than one instance I've been led to think of you during my work."

Catherine shook her head, taken aback. "But that doesn't make sense to me."

"I think you feel it too. Don't ignore it, it may be your undoing. It could even bring harm to others," he said sternly.

Catherine listened, without realizing how keenly. Just then, Danny returned from the bathroom. Uncle Mickey quickly sat up and asked Danny about his plans in business, leaving

Catherine to her thoughts. The evening crept in and it was soon time to leave, much to Catherine's unexpected relief. Brighton barked rapid goodbyes, and Uncle Mickey hugged them profusely until they were literally out the door. He would have followed them to catch the bus, but the three insisted they could manage fine.

Uncle Mickey had left Catherine unsettled. His superstitions were certainly entertaining, but they were always just that, superstitions. Still, he seemed to truly believe. It seemed harder to shrug him off this time. By the time the three siblings arrived back at the hostel just an hour short of midnight, they were all spent. Catherine laid her head down and went straight to sleep. Her dreams were fraught with folklore, ruins, and druids, yet she woke up with no thought of them or her uncle's rantings.

* * *

The next day was filled with the regular tourist attractions of Dublin, starting early in the morning. They went to Dublin Castle, St. Stephen's Green, and Oscar Wilde's home. They enjoyed seeing the many musicians and artists who roamed the streets. Even the sunny weather held out without interruption. Lastly, Catherine convinced Danny to take a tour of Trinity College to finish out the afternoon as Kathleen went back to the hostel for a nap.

In the later evening, after a meal of rice and chicken they cooked together in the hostel's community kitchen, they went out for some night life. At Temple Bar, the three siblings decided to have a drink and people watch. Catherine enjoyed her first and last Guinness for the remainder of their stay.

Of course the pub was full of tourists now, being the peak season. There was hardly an Irish person in sight. Such it was for them wherever they went in Dublin. Many foreigners also lived and worked there, to save money. One couple from Hungary shared that they were there for a few years to save up enough to move to a new country and raise a family. A man from Spain and a woman from Germany were renting a house together, but only for a time. Soon after drinks and conversation were over, the threesome continued on their walk.

They ambled down O'Connell Street as the Spire of Dublin loomed high above them. It was chilly now as the wind whipped around, and the sky was overcast. Catherine and Kathleen brushed their hair from their faces as Danny wrapped his jacket tighter around him.

Afar in the shadows the figure of a man lurked, his green eyes watching them. The girls and their brother didn't see him. They continued on their way without fear or concern for anything but getting back to the hostel.

* * *

The next day, Catherine went to fetch laundry detergent from reception downstairs. One of the men behind the counter said she had a visitor waiting outside. "A visitor?" she asked, confused.

"Yes, the Garda standing there," he pointed discreetly towards the entrance where there was a shadow of a man in uniform through one of the windows. "He said he needed to speak with you right away."

"Did he say why? How long has he been waiting?"

He shook his head, "No. He just arrived, I was about to come to your room to see if you were in," he answered.

Catherine furrowed her brow."Thank you," she said to the receptionist without looking back, forgetting the detergent completely.

Walking up to the door she felt a certain tingle on her arms as she often felt when something ominous was looming in the air. Taking a deep breath, she approached the man in uniform who turned to her with a stern face. She could see why the hostel asked him to wait outside. He made an alarming first impression.

"Are you Catherine Green?" he asked in a heavy accent.

"Yes?" she answered a bit timidly.

"Are you Michael Shannon's niece?" he asked flatly.

"I'm his great niece, one of them . . . what is it?"

"I'm afraid he's passed away, Miss," he paused, "And we believe his death was not due to natural causes . . ."

Catherine shook her head slowly.

The Garda cleared his throat, "I believe he was murdered, Miss. I'm sorry to be the one to deliver the news."

Catherine was shocked, the blood draining from her face. She felt like she was going to be sick. "But-I don't understand . . . How did this happen? We were just there the day before yesterday . . ."

"We know, the locals mentioned he had relatives visiting. I'm afraid I can't release any of the details right now, for investigative purposes." He reached out a hand out of courtesy, but Catherine didn't notice and stayed perfectly still. "I'm sorry again, Miss. If you have any information that you think may be helpful—someone threatening him, if he owed money, anything at all—please do contact us," he nodded, his mouth curved grimly as he left.

Catherine walked back to the room and explained what had happened to her siblings. Kathleen started to cry and held onto Danny as his mouth gaped open. He managed to comfort Kathleen with his arms wrapped around her shivering shoulders. Catherine felt like crying, but didn't let the tears stream freely until some hours had passed when she was alone in the room for a while.

The rest of the week flew by in a blur. All they could think about was their last visit with their uncle, and what must have happened thereafter. There was a small funeral service, attended by friends, colleagues and former students, all expressing their condolences to Catherine, Danny, and Kathleen, since no closer family member was able to come.

After the service was over, and they were back at the hostel, Catherine felt the whole trip was now tainted. She didn't know if she could have fun again. Somehow it would be wrong. Danny and Kathleen seemed to have the same outlook, and they laid low for a while. After a few days Danny seemed to perk back up when a group of girls from Paris were in for the weekend and he received a smile from one of them that sent him on the chase. Kathleen agreed to see more tourist sites but on more than one occasion huffed that she would have rather gone to Italy.

Catherine found herself stuck. She wasn't close to Uncle Mickey, but couldn't seem to shake her gloomy mood. She decided to sit in the lobby and watch some football to get her mind off things. She settled in a seat at one of the big table benches amidst a rowdy crowd but didn't join in on the cheering.

"You're not a football fan?" a girl's voice piped up next to her.

Catherine, slightly startled, looked over and saw a girl of twenty-two with curly long blonde hair.

"I'm not really a sports fan," she replied kindly.

"Sorry, I didn't mean to bother you. My name's Bella," the girl said with a smile that brought out the sparkle in her brown eyes.

"Catherine," she smiled back.

"Lovely to meet you. Listen, do you have a paracetamol?"

"A what?"

"You don't have paracetamol where you're from? Where *are* you from?"

"The States. I don't have anything called that, sorry," Catherine answered confusedly.

"Yea, you seemed it to me. My headache's getting worse with all this shouting, maybe reception will have some . . ." Bella looked over to the front desk.

"Oh! I've never heard of that word. We usually use a brand name, or say aspirin," Catherine laughed.

Bella chuckled slightly, rubbing her temples.

"I have ibuprofen actually if you want that?" Catherine offered.

"Yea, I'll take anything at this point. Thanks mate," Bella said gratefully.

Catherine went to retrieve the pills from her room.

"Thank you, ah! You're sweet as pie!" she said taking two pills from Catherine's palm and chucking them in her mouth followed by water in a cup from the kitchen.

"Are you Australian?" Catherine asked when she was done.

Bella nodded.

They continued to talk for a time, and when an hour passed Catherine noticed she felt happier. The two went to get something to eat. Upon returning Catherine told her she was thankful to have met her. It had cheered her up dramatically.

"I'm glad to hear it. You seemed a bit down when I first saw you sitting there," Bella said patting Catherine on the shoulder.

"Why did you come talk to me?"

"You were the only one not shouting at the game."

* * *

One afternoon, Catherine was sitting in the lounge room of the hostel eating lunch with her new friend Bella. Since their first meeting, she had learned that Bella was in Dublin as an Au Pair. She often stopped into the hostel to mingle with other foreigners on the weekend. As she told Catherine a funny story from the pub the night before, a man with dark hair and very green eyes came through the doors. Bella's eyebrows raised when she saw him. "Look at that. Cute guy, Cathy," she elbowed her to look up from her magazine.

Catherine hated it when Bella called her Cathy. She rubbed her now sore ribs in irritation. Before she could look, a large group of rowdy men came bursting through the lounge and the man disappeared. Danny showed up just then. "Where have you been?" she asked.

"Just went for a small hike this morning."

"How was it?"

"Really great, but not exciting enough," he answered as he sat down. "I'm going to my extreme sports assault course next week. You should come with me!"

Catherine quickly shook her head. "No, thanks."

Danny laughed. "Hey, don't you have to get ready for your interview?" he asked, then looked across at their stunned friend "Hi Bella," Danny smiled.

"Oh, he's gone!" Bella said exasperated. "Hey Dan," smiling back.

Catherine finished her drink before answering. "Already went. It was this morning . . ."

"Oh, was it?" he said, dumbfounded. Shrugging he continued, "So?"

"I think it was good," she said between bites of her salad.

Kathleen returned then with some ice cream. "They were out of strawberry, Catherine. Here ya go," she handed Bella her vanilla cone as she slid into a chair to feed her own chocolate craving.

"How can you be out of strawberry?" Catherine mumbled to herself, frowning.

"What's this now? Interviews?" Bella asked.

"A few internships are available here, so I've been interviewing. I know it's a long shot though," Catherine answered.

"You might move here?"

"For the length of the internship, yes. It would only be for six months, but it's a start," Catherine sighed.

"You're the best new face out there. Don't worry about it," Bella encouraged. Danny and Kathleen nodded.

Catherine felt a little nervous of course, but hoped she had a chance. Besides the States, Ireland was the only other country on her list and it was her first choice.

"Thank you. It won't be a waste even if I don't get them. It's good experience."

"What does your family think?"

"They don't mind," Danny said, "as long as we get a job."

"My parents hate that I live far away, but I want to travel for a while, maybe even stay," Bella sighed.

"Our parents encourage distance actually. I think they only had children because all their friends did," Catherine mused.

"That's terrible," Bella said sympathetically, tilting her head to the side.

"No, it's okay, they're good parents considering how demanding their careers are. Just not very affectionate. They only meant to have Danny. Kathleen and I were a surprise."

Kathleen simply nodded while enjoying her ice cream in silence.

"Having twins would be quite a surprise," Bella laughed.

"Until recently we had our grandparents at least," Danny added, "that was enough."

Catherine's phone rang, and she left the table to answer, returning only a few minutes after.

"Who was that?" Danny asked taking a napkin to wipe his mouth.

"It was the internship from this morning," she replied.

"That was fast," he said.

"Out with it then!" Bella demanded.

"They offered it to me," Catherine smiled.

"That's great! Why aren't you more excited?" Kathleen asked with sparkling eyes.

"Oh I am, it's just the terms are different than I expected."

"Like how?" Danny asked.

"They want me for the six-month internship, but they also want to keep me on permanently when it's over."

Danny blinked a few times, understanding fully. "So you're moving here forever?"

CHAPTER ONE

Catherine was walking home from work when it started to pour. Reaching the door to her small place, she rushed in shaking off the drops over her hardwood floor. Having just cleaned it that morning, she frowned as she continued to dry herself and placed her jacket on one of the hooks by the door.

"Kathleen?" Catherine yelled.

"Yeah?" her sister called back.

"Will you please order something for dinner?" she yelled again. "I'm in no mood to cook tonight," she muttered under her breath.

"Sure thing!"

It had been two years since their trip to Ireland. Accepting the job had proved to be a marvelous opportunity for Catherine. The museum found her to be an invaluable addition. Catherine enjoyed her work, even on a day like today when everything seemed to pile up. She was thankful that Kathleen was living with her now. Her sister had moved in only a few short months ago. Sometimes it had been lonely without her, though Kathleen was still occasionally selfish and materialistic. Catherine never imagined Kathleen would come back to her rainy new home. But Kathleen was getting divorced from her rich, absent husband. Catherine never understood why Kathleen had taken that path, but she was thankful to see her sister living a healthier life again. The marriage had only lasted a year. Kathleen didn't appear to be in any hurry to move out, but was back to dating again. Only casually this time.

Kathleen answered the door to pay when the Japanese food arrived, turning the delivery guy down when he asked for her number. Kathleen laughed quietly to herself after the door was shut and she carried the food to the kitchen. Catherine came in the kitchen a few moments later already dressed in lounge clothes, dabbing her hair with a towel.

"What's with you?" Catherine asked, seeing her sister's funny face.

Kathleen shrugged.

Half way through their quiet meal Kathleen spoke. "Wanna go see a movie tonight?"

"Not really . . ."

"Oh come on! We could go to the pub after to meet up with some friends?" Kathleen begged.

"My friends, or yours?" Catherine looked up.

"Mine preferably."

"In that case, especially no," Catherine said, bringing the last bite of her Yaki Udon to her mouth. After savoring the noodles, she sighed with satisfaction.

"Okay, okay, yours *and* mine! I'll compromise!" Kathleen dropped her napkin and crouched down from her perch on a tall stool to pick it up, her red hair falling over her face. She had decided a while ago that her sister was right to keep their natural hair color, and grew it back fully natural and lengthy.

"You? Compromise? Amazing . . ."

"Please!"

"Please? I'm shocked at how much you've changed in the time you've been here Kathleen. Fine, I'll go. Just no Abby this time. I can't stand her."

"Deal."

A few hours later the two young women were at the cinema, sitting as comfortably as possible in their seats.

"Those my glasses?" Catherine said noticing her sister lay a pair of glasses atop her nose.

"Yeah, I need them, I lost mine," Kathleen replied. Seeing Catherine's glare, she quickly added "Oh don't look at me like that, you don't need them for movies, just for reading."

"You're borrowing a lot of my things recently. First my jacket, now my glasses . . ."

"Shhh, it's starting." Kathleen whispered.

After the romantic comedy flick, they went to the pub to meet up with a few of their friends. Mostly they had separate acquaintances, but they were both happy to see Bella when she came in.

"So Cathy, what are we drinking tonight?" Bella smiled brightly.

"I'm having water."

"Only that?" Bella chided playfully.

"Hmm, lemon too," Catherine chuckled, as Bella stuck her tongue out at her.

Still wearing her sister's glasses, Kathleen cinched Catherine's blue jacket tighter with the belt while standing with a small group of friends on the other side of the pub. Catherine made a mental note to get her glasses back before Kathleen broke them and turned to the bartender to get a few drinks.

"I'll take two Guinness, and a water with lemon please," she asked.

"That'll be all for ya?" asked the curly-haired bartender, flashing a winning smile.

Catherine couldn't help but laugh a little, "Yes, that will be all for me. Thanks."

Just then a man arrived and was walking up to Kathleen. He

was mysterious looking, and appeared a few years older than the twins, Catherine guessed twenty-seven. He wore plain fitting gray pants and a black T-shirt under a long black trench coat that looked more like a cloak. Though mysteriously dressed, his face was strongly chiseled, the hair on his head was a curly dark brown. He held a vague expression that leaned more towards sinister at the moment, and his green eyes held you in their gaze sharply like a wild animal.

Catherine grabbed the drinks. She felt unconcerned; guys always came up to Kathleen. It was amazing. Though the two women were twins, men didn't approach her as often. It was like the sleazy ones could tell that Kathleen was flighty. She sat down to wait the guy out and briefly looked around the pub. It was rather large, though quiet at the moment. She admired the old styled buildings. It made her feel like even though times change, some nice things remained the same.

Following Catherine's gaze Bella looked the man over as well. "Ooo, he's cute!" she said quietly.

Catherine nodded.

Bella's brows furrowed. "Though, I think I've spotted him before . . ."

The friends with Kathleen saw the man coming and became quiet rather quickly. She turned around suddenly, startled by his presence.

"Oh!" she gasped. "You scared me . . ."

The man didn't say anything in response, he just looked right through her, focused on something else in his own mind. He took one of her hands roughly and tried to forcefully pull her to the door. "You need to go."

Kathleen let out a muffled yelp. "Ouch! You're *hurting* me!"

Several of her friends stood up to stop this but Catherine beat them to it. She shoved the taller man back, releasing Kathleen from his grasp. Catherine glared at him, flames in her eyes.

"What do you think you're doing?" she shouted angrily.

He ignored her and repeated to Kathleen, "You need to go . . . Catherine you mu-"

"Catherine? I'm not Catherine!" Kathleen interrupted while rubbing her hand carefully.

The man grew puzzled.

"*I'm* Catherine," she said, still livid.

"You . . ." he looked down at her finally.

"Need to go? You said that already. That's what *you* need to do, or apologize to my sister right now!"

"I thought . . . I'm sorry," was all he said. Catherine thought his Irish accent sounded strange.

Kathleen simply nodded in return. Patting Catherine's shoulder, she sat with their friends who had calmed and followed suit.

Catherine raised an eyebrow, continuing to glare at the strange man. "What's this about?" she asked, her tone annoyed.

"Just get out of here, out of Ireland," he said.

"What?" she jutted her chin out. "Why?"

He stood there with a serious expression for a few seconds. "Because if you don't, you'll unleash them."

"*What?!*" she repeated.

Suddenly he turned and strode out the door.

Catherine stood there dumbfounded. Kathleen got up from her seat, gripping Catherine's shoulder. Catherine looked to see her glasses folded up in the palm of Kathleen's hand.

"Here. Take them back. I'll give you the jacket when we get home," Kathleen said with a frown.

"Okay . . ."

"I never want to be mistaken for you again," she said, then sat back down.

Catherine smiled to herself. At least one good thing had come out of this strange experience.

Bella carried over the drinks then. "That was simply crazy!" she said.

The food that had been ordered by the group arrived after that, and Catherine was almost able to enjoy herself with their friends. But she had not forgotten what the strange and rude man had said. What did he mean? Was he simply nuts? She was mostly concerned that he might be loitering outside the pub ready to pounce when she and her sister left.

Kathleen had certainly forgotten it after the first drink, now laughing with her friends. Catherine began to wonder if Kathleen's proclamation tonight would stick. She did worry for her sister sometimes.

If this man was stalking her, then Kathleen was, as tonight's events showed, also the target. Catherine decided she'd have Kathleen report the incident to the Gardai in the morning. In the meantime, she tried to think who the man could be. Was he connected with someone at work? Did she pass him regularly on the street? She couldn't be sure. Though something about him did seem familiar, and oddly alluring. But she didn't think she'd spoken to him before. These thoughts continued to buzz the rest of the night, so that by the end of it she was quite ready to leave and hurry home.

* * *

Catherine awoke from her warm bed two days later to a busy day. Kathleen burst into her bedroom just then.

"Don't forget to pick up Danny," she said, too loudly for Catherine's taste.

"Of course, Kathleen," Catherine answered.

Danny had called the day before and asked if he could stay with them for a while. He had lost his job, and just wanted to "get away from it all." Catherine agreed on the condition that he start thinking about getting his act together while he was there with her. She was tired of being the one they relied on for everything. She figured she could make up a space in her small living room, since Kathleen stayed in the extra room.

When Catherine first woke up she had a strange feeling that stuck with her, a feeling she couldn't shake off. She recognized it, and knew it would last all day. It wasn't a bad feeling, or even a good one. Just a strange feeling that something was waiting to happen. She would try to understand it, but couldn't quite figure it out. She kept thinking about this strange feeling on the way to pick up her brother from the airport.

"So how are you?" Danny asked when they were in the car driving away.

"Busy. How are *you*?"

"I'm good," he shrugged.

Catherine tilted her head, "Really? What are you doing here then?"

"Can't I come see my sister?"

"Danny, why'd you leave your job? I thought you had a good thing going at that company. You stayed with them since business school."

"I know," Danny shifted in his seat. "I felt . . . trapped. I don't like corporate life, it's just not me," he sighed.

"I'm sorry . . ."

"It's all right. I thought . . . maybe I would figure out what I want here. I'm always happy here."

Catherine gave a small smile. "Well, you can stay with me until you figure it out."

They drove on, and Catherine was so distracted running errands that she almost forgot her keys. She'd set them down for a second to look through her purse to find her "lost" sunglasses that were atop her head the whole time.

"You seem frazzled," Danny said, leaning on the side of the car parked in her driveway. He eyed Catherine as she bent to lift groceries from the back seat. He had been patient with the several errands, but he was worn out after a long flight.

"Thanks," she said sarcastically without looking up from the list she had stopped to check over.

"I'm not trying to be rude . . . Maybe I can help with something?" he shrugged.

Looking up at her brother with his lopsided smile and amber colored sunglasses, she smiled. "Thanks," she said again, without the sarcasm. "I'm just having an off day. It's not such a big list really."

"Are you sure? Seriously, I can figure out whatever you throw at me," he said confidently, as he shrugged his backpack on his shoulders, the only "luggage" he had brought.

"Well . . . okay sure, can you run and pick up some stamps for me at the post office?" She handed him some money. "That way I can just stay home and do some research for work before I start dinner," she finished with a wave of her hand.

"On it," he winked.

Catherine yelled back her thanks as she hurried away. She just couldn't shake this feeling. She was becoming more anxious with each passing hour.

When she turned the corner, she stopped dead in her tracks, nearly scuffing her leather boots. The man who had assaulted her sister was standing right in front of her door. He turned to her. Catherine didn't know what to do. She wasn't frightened, though she thought perhaps she should be. Though he could be dangerous, he didn't look it.

"Hello!" he called.

Catherine simply waved her hand as a reflex. She walked closer. He seemed frustrated.

"I told you to leave!" he said, agitated.

"Who are *YOU* to tell *me* anything?!" she replied pointedly in a harsh tone.

He seemed taken aback, and his voice grew softer, "I'm sorry again. It's important that you leave. I told you . . . *they* will come and you will not be safe. No one in Ireland will be safe." His concern grew with each word.

"Who are *they*?" she asked raising an eyebrow.

He seemed stand offish, "I can't say."

"Well then, I can't help you . . ."

He was unmoving.

Catherine gave out a sigh, loudly exasperated. "Well, who are *you* then?"

"My name is Bowen," his voice grew deep when he said his name.

"Bowen . . . How do you know me? Have we met before?" she asked.

"It doesn't matter," he replied curtly.

"Right," Catherine stood her ground and looked him dead in the face, "Look yo-Bowen, you've been stalking me! How do you know my name, and where I live for that matter?"

Catherine could tell he was conflicted. Her arms were getting tired from the heavy grocery bags, but she continued to stand patiently waiting.

As though he'd made a decision, his stance became rigid and he said nothing.

"Fine," she said. Bowen looked at her surprised. "I don't have time for this . . ." she muttered to herself, and stepped to pass him.

Bowen took a step in front of her. "You *must* leave. If you don't go on your own, I will have to force you. I can't risk it any longer!" he said angrily.

"Well then, what are you talking about? If you'll only tell me!" Her feet were planted, ready to swing at him if he made another move.

"I hate this . . ." he mumbled under his breath.

Catherine felt her cheeks flush with anger.

"My brother will be here shortly. And you are already on Garda records, Mr. Unknown, should something happen to me. They have your description. I won't just leave my life here because some *nut* tells me to, without a reason of any kind. So it's up to *you* how this plays out . . . you tell me, or shall we duke it out right here and now?" She dropped her bags on the ground emphatically.

"I'm not going to fight you, Catherine."

"Oh? You certainly came off pushy before," she said.

"You won't believe the truth," he replied solemnly.

"Try me," she said putting her hands on her hips, waiting.

"You haven't believed anything I say so far . . ." he mumbled.

Catherine heard footsteps and turned to see Danny come around the corner. He was holding the stamps in his hand with the receipt. She turned back to Bowen, but he was gone. She turned around frantically trying to glimpse him in the distance. But he had disappeared.

Danny smiled his lopsided grin. "What's wrong?" he asked, seeing the groceries on the ground.

"Ugghhh!" was all Catherine could get out.

"Okay . . ." he replied and held up the stamps with the receipt to his sister, "Here, I didn't want to crunch them in my pockets or bag, so they've been in my dirty airport hands."

"Thank you Danny," she sighed.

"Sorry, what was I supposed to do? Would you rather I'd bent them?"

"What?"

"The stamps . . ."

"Oh, no you did fine, it's not that," she said, bending to pick up the bags.

"Ah, then, what's your problem?" Danny asked, quickly grabbing some fruit that had rolled out of one.

"Someone was just here. That guy I told you about from the other night," she said.

"That guy who bothered you and Kathleen at the pub?"

"Yeah."

"Oh my God Catherine, *that* was the guy? He was big, you can't take him!"

Catherine looked up at her brother with a surprised expression, "I can take him just fine, don't you worry!"

"Listen, just be careful," he sounded concerned.

Catherine rolled her eyes as she patted her brother's arm before unlocking the door to go in. Though she was staunchly feminist, she was glad Danny was visiting during this drama. Catherine didn't need this right now. There was already too much going on in her life.

Kathleen was in the sitting room with her pink laptop on her lap. She was watching a favorite mystery drama on the Internet. She looked up at her siblings when they entered through the door. After she waved her hand in greeting, she looked back down quickly.

"Nice," Danny said, relieved to drop his backpack on the floor. He had packed it to the fullest.

"What?" Kathleen looked up again.

"You haven't seen me in months, and that's how you greet me? With a wave of your hand?" The irritation in his tone was mostly aimed at Kathleen, but some over the pain in his shoulders while he tried to massage the kinks out, wincing.

"I'm just in the middle of this intense scene! Jenny is about to figure out who the spy is!"

Danny shook his head, "Oh, that . . ." then he walked over to look down at the screen, and within a few minutes was locked into the drama just as deeply as Kathleen.

After Catherine put the groceries away, she was too preoccupied with everything to concentrate on her planned work research. She leaned on the counter in thought, wondering where Bowen had disappeared to, and just when he would reappear again to cause trouble. Walking into her room she threw herself on her bed. She stared at the ceiling in a daze. Relishing this moment of peace, she thought of nothing, absolutely nothing. After some time had passed her mind began to wander again, but aimlessly this time, and she fell into a deep sleep filled with strange shapes and occurrences. Her dreams led to their graduation trip to Ireland, and one of the days they ventured out of Dublin to some rural spots surrounded by trees, hills and lakes. She remembered feeling watched in one area, but in this dream Bowen appeared in view to startle the scene.

Knock Knock.

Catherine couldn't tell where the knocking was coming from. She looked around the still figure of Bowen before her, and behind her as well. Bowen's hand reached out for her.

KNOCK KNOCK.

Catherine fumbled awake.

"Catherine?" came Kathleen's voice.

"What is it?" her voice was only slightly groggy.

Kathleen opened the door, "The internet went out. Can you call the provider company?"

Catherine sighed for a moment while holding her head. Then she smiled. "I was thinking we'd just go out for the rest of the day, like we did during our last trip here," Catherine replied.

"Why?"

"Just to get out of the house. Let's go revisit a few places."

"Danny, did the reset button work?" Kathleen turned and yelled behind her, completely ignoring Catherine's suggestion.

When Kathleen was no longer overcome by the show's cliffhanger, she reluctantly consented to going somewhere, as long as it wasn't a tourist spot.

"That's not revisiting places though . . ." sighed Catherine.

They soon agreed on finding a nice spot outside the city. Both girls decided a walk, as long as it was nice weather, would be pleasant. Leaving Danny, who didn't want to go, the twins set off in Catherine's compact car. Once the drive went far enough away from the city, it was easy to find a quiet, hilly place in the country. As they cruised the rural road, Catherine kept an eye out for the best place to stop, but suddenly recognized the eerie tingling sensation on her arms. Worried it was a warning about something on the road, she chose to stop right then and parked off to the side. The sensation remained, as it usually did, for some time, so she ignored it. They stretched their legs before beginning their walk to enjoy the scenery. At first, they stayed on the road for a while and took in the lengthy land off to one side speckled with hills in the distance. The sun was high, and the grass was green. They could see layers of flowers that gave a different hue of color wavering above the green.

"It's been a long time since we've walked together, just the two of us, to talk," Kathleen said looking ahead.

Catherine thought about it for a moment, "Yes it has," she agreed.

Kathleen paused to breathe in deeply. "Ah! It really is so beautiful here, it even *smells* beautiful," she remarked.

"Mhm," Catherine agreed, chuckling quietly.

As they continued, their steps fell in sync after a while. Catherine kept watching her sister and thought she seemed peaceful for the first time in many years.

"You know, I'm very proud of you," Kathleen said, breaking the momentary silence.

"What for?" she raised her eyebrows.

"For accomplishing your dream with work and moving here," she smiled.

Catherine smiled back, "Thank you, that means a lot."

They continued to talk about anything and everything, just like they did as children. Kathleen's infectious laugh reminded Catherine of how much she enjoyed spending time with her sister, how she once was. When the laughter died down to a calming roar, they slowed their pace and decided to sit for a moment on the gravel. The dirt felt hot under their hands as they lowered themselves down.

"Kathleen, why aren't you like this more often?" Catherine asked as she fiddled with some grass.

"Like how?"

"Like you, the real you. Why do you hide it away? I mean, it's almost like you want nice people to dislike you," Catherine said, then quickly realized she might have gone too far. "I'm sorry! I just mean—"

"I know what you mean," Kathleen sighed, fidgeting over a split nail on her index finger. "Catherine, you've always known what drives you, what you wanted. I never found anything like that for myself. I felt lost," she said.

"I see . . ." Catherine was stunned by her honesty.

"So I changed," Kathleen continued, "because I had nothing meaningful in my life. Nothing to strive for. I became shallow, and consumed with unimportant things. I became mentally, and emotionally lazy. Unfortunately, my standards in myself, as well as in men became lazy too. I thought he cared about me . . ." she cleared her throat. "I'm still me, the me you know, I just buried it. It's all an act. I'm a fake, Catherine!"

Catherine could see she was holding back tears.

Softly, Kathleen continued, "It's just easier to act the way I do, rather than admit I'm going nowhere. I—I feel I have no purpose. I should have found it by now, right?" she asked. "I know how you and Danny must have thought of me all this time, of how I act. Selfish, and rude. I know I'm a pain! But being meaningful, I can't. Especially now with the divorce. I know I did this to myself. It's just too much to handle. What do I do, Catherine? I don't know anymore!" Kathleen's tears flowed freely now.

Catherine was feeling teary herself at this sudden confession from her sister, and she reached over to hug her. "I don't know, Kathleen. But I'll help you in any way I can! We'll figure it out together now that you're here with me. Keep letting your real self out, and maybe the act will fade away," she said holding her tightly. She pulled back to look at her, "No one figures everything out right away. You'll find your purpose!"

Kathleen sniffled and leaned back on Catherine's shoulder, giving her a sweet smile. After a time, they both felt better and continued on their walk.

* * *

About an hour later, Catherine walked alone down a small hill as she mused about the scenery. She usually felt calm surrounded by nature. But not today, not right now. Catherine's senses were off. She felt uneasy, and she didn't know why. The not knowing was probably the worst of it. So as she passed bushes with her feet kicking up dust, and as the heels of those feet felt the harsh rocky ground beneath them, swinging her arms trying to appear cheerful, Catherine began to whistle. But she soon felt silly and instead resigned to stop for a break to take in the sky and the outstretched land on her left.

Stepping over to take in the view she sighed, and looked back the way she came. Kathleen had said she wanted to sit alone for a while because her feet hurt from walking. *I'll go back soon* she thought to herself. *But not too soon. That way Kathleen won't feel I'm being over-protective as always.*

Catherine looked up at the sky and saw an empty blue mass. Not a cloud. The sun was bright, which made her squint. But she loved every minute of it. She closed her eyes to feel the sun warm her face. *Just a few moments* she thought. While soaking in the sun, Catherine thought that it amazed her how opposite she was from her sister. Thinking of their childhood made her smile. Where had all those nice times gone? Kathleen was the same person somewhere in there after all. This outdoor venture had been the first showing in many years. Catherine missed that side of her sister, and wanted to see it more often. A deep breath of the fresh air mingled with dust from the road filled Catherine's lungs, and as she exhaled she firmly decided to have another talk with her twin sister about her feelings on the matter. She opened her eyes and turned away, trying to blink the spots from the light of the sun out of her eyes. *Perhaps that was longer than a few moments* she thought.

Walking along, Catherine all of the sudden felt very strange. It was an unsettling feeling which made her skin crawl and caused her body to shiver. Then came a hot sensation in her core that calmed her. There was an invisible and deeply rooted pull inside her to change direction. As she followed the eerie feeling, it lessened the further she went. Suddenly, as she turned a corner to her right, Catherine stubbed her toe. Around the bend there was a pile of giant rocks in a wooded area. Gritting her teeth to avoid cursing, she leaned against the offending rock as it jutted out in a spot above her shoulder. Moving a step further she could see it was connected to the rocky hill. She saw a bubbling creek and hobbled over to it to inspect the water. It seemed clear enough so she took off her shoe and quickly stuck her foot into the numbing stream to bring relief to her inflamed toes.

Catherine watched as blood mingled with the bubbles and quickly spread. The impact had apparently cut part of her ankle as well. It wasn't a bad cut, though she would have to clean it better when she got home. She was taking one of her socks to soak in the cold water to dab with, when the sock flew out of her hand. Catherine struggled to hobble over to retrieve it from behind an old standing stone that came to her elbow in height. She was excited to notice the stone had very worn illegible markings carved into it, methodically arranged. After briefly studying it to no avail, she then used it to help her lean over as she picked up her sock and returned to the creek to complete her task. Plopping herself down full force on the ground to leave her aching foot in the water to soak comfortably, she thought she heard a noise. Suddenly, someone appeared to her left some feet away towering over her. She started.

"No need to be alarmed," Bowen said, his long arms crossed in front of him.

Catherine let out a yelp, and looked away irritated as she hit the top of her thigh in frustration. "Geez! You didn't have to sneak up on me!" She took a breath. "You can't just say 'No need to be alarmed' and expect me not to be, just so you know."

"I see . . ." he looked past Catherine, lingering for a moment, then returned his gaze to her judging hazel eyes.

"What are you doing here? You shouldn't be following me."

"I'm not trying to threaten you. I'm warning you. What *you're* doing is incredibly dangerous-"

"Incredibly dangerous? Hiking with my sister, and stubbing my toe?" Catherine interrupted.

"Why are you being this way? I'm trying to save you, to save everyone!" Bowen said as he slapped his hands down against his sides in defeat and frustration.

Silence surrounded them as Catherine took out her foot to look it over.

"Is your foot all right?"

Catherine side glanced up at Bowen, but didn't answer.

Bowen sighed and walked closer before sitting down. "What can I do to make you see that what I'm saying is true?"

"That what I'm doing is dangerous?" Catherine said.

"I'm not talking about your stubbed toe. I mean you being in Ireland, and walking *here* . . . it's uncanny," Bowen said gesturing around him.

"Why, what's wrong with here specifically?"

"If I tell you then you'll promise to go?"

"Of course not," Catherine replied.

"Why on earth not?!" Bowen shouted.

"Because I can't make a blind promise to someone I don't trust. Sorry." Catherine said flatly.

Catherine noticed Bowen's hair was curling down his neck from the heat of the day. His green eyes blazed at her. She felt oddly aware that she was attracted to him, and wondered if he felt it too. Catherine scoffed at the idea, knowing every time she'd seen the man he was telling her to leave. Yet the stalking was sending mixed signals, along with that look he gave her. She laughed under her breath. *I know how to pick 'em.*

"It's insulting you think this is funny . . ." Bowen huffed.

"I don't! Honestly . . ." Catherine held up her hands in surrender.

Bowen stared at the ground.

"Look, I'm sorry that you hate me. But it's really not my problem. Maybe you should see somebody about that, and just stay away from me if I'm making you so angry that you want me to leave Ireland."

Bowen's eyes widened then narrowed. "It's to save everyone . . ." he mumbled.

"What?"

"It's the only way . . . to save everyone from them," he looked at her, and added " . . . I don't hate you."

Catherine's eyes locked with his. In that look, in that moment, she could see he believed what he was saying. And for some reason so did she. "Save everyone from who?"

Bowen was about to speak when a new thought crossed his face. He suddenly looked troubled.

"What's wrong?" Catherine asked.

"You said you were walking with your sister. Where is she?"

"She stopped to rest, back a-ways. Why?"

"We must go to her. Now," he said.

"We?" Catherine mumbled as she was pulled up by Bowen's strong arms. She pulled her shoe on carefully.

Just as the two of them walked around the rock in the bend, Kathleen appeared and almost ran right into Catherine. "Oh! There you are!" Kathleen said. "I didn't know how far you'd gone. I'm terrified of getting lost, you know!"

Kathleen glanced at Bowen, surprised by his looming presence. Catherine thought it odd that she was not more alarmed but the thought passed as Bowen helped her up the hill. As they walked, Catherine couldn't help but notice Bowen's strong hands and arms wrapped around her elbow and occasionally her waist. She felt a deep flush in her cheeks.

Yet Bowen seemed to never be looking at Catherine. Whenever she glanced through her hair, or took a quick side glance, he was looking ahead or surveying their surroundings. She felt a stab at her ego, realizing it was all in her own head.

Bowen helped Catherine into her seat in the car as Kathleen swiped the keys from her outstretched hand. She leaned slightly on his shoulder to bend more easily to sit down, and Bowen stiffened as he felt Catherine's head against his chin. He had noticed her the first moment he saw her, and every moment since.

When he first found her it was a strange sense that led him. He had to follow it. She was captivating, and he was breathless. He kept watch from then on. He noticed the different ways her eyes flashed with each mood. The flame when she was furious, or the way they lit up when she was happy or had an idea. He had come to notice a lot about Catherine over the time he had been watching her. When he touched her he could think of nothing else. She consumed him. He'd finally realized what this could do before he went to her at the pub. It was the reason he had to act quickly now to protect her, and everyone else in Ireland, if not the planet. He didn't want to tell her everything, knowing it would disrupt her whole life. But it was no longer safe to keep her in the dark. Once Catherine was seated he simply nodded to the two young women before turning to go.

Catherine hesitated, "Uh-Wait," she held open the car door, "do you need a ride somewhere?"

Bowen looked over his shoulder and said "No, thank you." He wondered why she was being courteous all of the sudden.

"Will we see you again soon then?"

"Definitely," he said, suddenly warmed. He shook his head. *No, she must go,* he thought forcefully.

Catherine nodded and shut the car door. Kathleen started the engine and they took off with a slow start up the road. Bowen felt uneasy. He didn't understand Catherine even after all his observing. Her moods changed so suddenly. It unsettled him. He shrugged as the car drove away. He had something more worrisome to check on now.

Bowen walked for some time through the trees to another side of the high reaching rocky hill. He walked up to a hollow overgrown with great varieties of plant life. In the rock there was a deep slit that was wide enough to fit an arm through. Bowen stood next to it for a while, still as the rock itself. He had a blank expression on his face.

"Must you keep standing there like a statue?" a deep voice rumbled from inside the opening.

Bowen didn't say anything, seeming immovable.

After a while, the deep voice growled loudly "How DARE

you!" with a rustling sound of tiny rocks falling from his end deep inside the stone.

The corner of Bowen's mouth twitched downward, startled somewhat by the sudden falling rock. He looked at the rock in front of him with disdain. He laid his hand near the small opening, and leaned forward slightly.

"I don't deserve a response from you?" the deep voice was now menacing, "You've come to stand by my door only twice before, pleading, always pleading for me to stop!"

A sound of something hard clashing with stone came from within. When Bowen heard it he looked forlornly at the ground as he struggled to listen further.

The voice laughed then, chilling Bowen's spine. In a mocking tone the voice said, "'You're ill, please stop this!'" a low guttural growl "Well I'll not stop Bowen, I'll never ever stop, not until my dying breath. And you can't do anything about it," he chuckled.

Bowen waited, he knew there was more. There was always more.

"When I'm free there won't be anywhere for you to run from me, I-" he paused "wait, something must have changed, it's been too long since I saw you. There must be a *reason* you're here *now* . . ."

Silence deafened Bowen's ears, and he imagined the worst.

"Oh," breathed the deep voice.

Bowen froze.

"You've found *her*? It's *finally* happened! Soon I'll be free!" maniacal laughter ensued.

Bowen's heart sank. He shouldn't have come, even if only to check that nothing had changed.

"What is it, dear Bowen? You don't laugh as well as speak? How DARE you not speak to me! I'll make you suffer for this on top of everything else! And after that I'll kill you and spit on your body in front of everyone! Speak to me. Bowen, NOW!"

Bowen's hand slid off the rock as he turned to walk away. He hesitated at first, but kept going. Even at a distance he could still hear the mad screaming echoing behind him.

CHAPTER TWO

INSIDE A LARGE cavern where very little light shone through, there was a madman. He rustled around in turmoil, holding onto a bitter anger because it was the only thing he believed kept him going. Since he had already torn his clothes in previous fits of madness, he instead hit his hands against the walls of the cavern near the opening where Bowen had just been. So many times before had he torn at himself and tried to break his bones and die against the caverns.

"No . . ." he said to himself in a moment of clarity, "it's no use continuing . . ." then he sat down using his bloody hands to hold his head up while he wept. He absentmindedly wiped the blood on his thighs.

He sobbed, softly whimpering. "Oh my darling, how—" he stopped mid-sentence and his eyes widened as he looked at his hand slowly. Then he whirled himself up to hold his hand into the light leaking through the cracked stone.

"Blood," he remarked quietly, then shouted, "Blood!"

Others in the cavern heard his cry. Accustomed to his fits, they usually ignored him. But his words drew them in and they thawed into living beings once more, aware of their surroundings. The bleeding man ran some distance to the original opening of the cave. It had been blocked last he checked. When he arrived, the space was reopened. He simply stood there taking in the scene, his eyes beaming with sparkling fire. He felt a sense of adventure. At last he would get Bowen, and be at peace. Others who had followed him to the opening stood behind him, reveling in amazement. Their eyes squinted at the sudden burst of light, turning away from the sun as they laughed with long awaited relief.

In an ancient Gaelic language long dead, "Freedom," was uttered in hushed and awed tones.

* * *

A few days passed, and Catherine's foot healed decently. She didn't limp anymore, though it was tender with bruising. She sat calmly at the edge of her bed staring out her bedroom door watching the dancing lights from the window on the stair banister. Catherine wondered when she would see Bowen again, wanting to know more about what he said. Was she really endangering herself, her family, even everyone in Ireland? Just by being here? And from what?

The front door slammed and Kathleen stomped up the stairs, "I met a guy!" she said happily.

"A guy?" Catherine's eyes were wide with surprise.

"Yes, I was on my way to meet Bella at her new apartment."

"They're called flats here you know . . . What happened?"

Plopping herself down on the other side of Catherine's bed she grinned. "I dropped my phone accidentally, and when I bent down he ran right into me! We both fell; oh it was perfect!" Kathleen said dreamily. Catherine laughed. "We helped each other up and went for coffee. He is amazing! And I never say that about anything or anybody, Catherine," Kathleen leaned forward and touched her hand for reassurance.

"That's great, Kathleen! Did you forget about Bella?"

"Oh no, I texted her. We talked about lots of things. Catherine,

I think I'm in love, I really think so, it was one of those at-first-sight things."

"You're talking too fast, calm dow—"

"He seemed really interested in me, too. We have a lot in common. I wish I'd taken a picture of him to show you." Kathleen brushed off Catherine's hand and ran out of the room.

Catherine shook her head and smiled. She got up and went to her dresser to change, looking through her jewelry to find a pair of antique pearl dangling earrings. But she could only find one of them. Then she remembered Kathleen had helped her take them out the day they saw Bowen on the walk. "Kathleen!" she yelled out the door.

"I'm on the phone!"

Catherine stood still, irritated. The earrings belonged to her grandmother. She couldn't bear to lose one.

Kathleen appeared in the doorway with the phone at her side. "Yes?"

"When you took my earrings out did you put both right here?" Catherine said pointing to her jewelry box.

"No, you only had one in," Kathleen said.

"What?! I was missing one of grandmother's earrings and you didn't say anything?"

"I was preoccupied getting bandages for your bleeding foot!"

"That was THREE days ago Kathleen! It's probably gone forever!"

"I saw you had both of them when we went for the walk. Maybe you lost it when you hurt yourself? I didn't notice until we were home."

Catherine growled under her breath, "I can't believe this . . ."

Kathleen walked back out of the room with the phone to her ear again.

Catherine fell back on the bed. She'd received them for

graduation. They had been a gift from her deceased grandfather to her grandmother before they were married. Sad that she had lost such a treasure, she laid there longer than intended and drifted off. A few hours later she woke to Danny's face as he yelled her name.

"What, oh my God, what?" she whined.

"The car is gone, and I need to get to work! I can't be late my first day," he complained.

"You have a job?" Catherine rolled on her side.

"Yeah, I told you I did. I'll be in the sorting room at the post office," he gestured in the building's direction out the window.

"Then why don't you just walk?"

Danny sighed, "I can't, I'm training somewhere else!" he pulled the pillow from underneath her, "THE CAR!"

Realization finally struck. "The car is gone?" Catherine pushed herself up rubbing her face.

"Look for yourself . . ." Danny waved toward the window facing the empty driveway.

Catherine reached and grabbed her phone.

"What are you doing?" he asked exasperated.

"I'm going to call the Gardai, Danny, what else would you have me do? Go hunt the thief down myself?"

"Maybe . . ." Danny said sarcastically, a little hurt.

Catherine looked at her phone unmoving.

Danny was impatient, "Well?"

She got up and put her phone in her pocket, a text message flashing off the screen. "Kathleen has the car. She went to look for my earring."

"That's a relief. But I'm still gonna be late for work . . . I have to tell her to bring back the car!"

"You can't, she said her phone was dying, and she forgot her charger. And stop yelling at me!" She threw a warning glare at him.

Danny ran a hand through his hair as he tried to control his frustration.

"I'm really more concerned about Kathleen. She shouldn't be out there alone, she doesn't know the area well enough for that, she could get lost. And now being unreachable, this is so stupid . . ."

"What? Nah, she won't get lost, she'll be fine," said Danny.

"She said so herself. Plus, it'll be getting dark before too long. I don't like this," Catherine put on a jacket hanging from her desk chair, took her wallet from her purse and put it in the jacket's inside zipper pocket.

"Where are you going?"

"To go get her, of course," Catherine said.

"Without a car?"

"I'll borrow Bella's," she said, as she left for Bella's place. Catherine didn't have a good feeling about this, and couldn't think clearly, having been roused awake in alarm.

While driving she thought maybe she should have brought Danny with her, but shrugged it off as she tried to remember which spot Kathleen might think the earring would be. Catherine hoped she guessed right and would look where she ran her foot into the rock. That was the most logical spot. But Kathleen was not often logical.

At the hill she parked and walked down to the spot, more carefully this time. Kathleen was nowhere to be seen. As Catherine searched, she noticed some foot-prints in the mud close by. There were other markings in the ground but Catherine couldn't read them. There were a few others that all seemed different from each other. Catherine's heart went into her throat and that bad feeling increased rapidly. Kathleen was missing, and wherever she was there were several other people involved also. Possibly very bad people. Catherine tried to shrug it off. Maybe it was some friends she ran into who were hiking, or maybe Kathleen brought her friends with her. Catherine took some deep breaths to calm herself, and began following the prints.

It was quiet. Catherine didn't notice how quiet last time. Kathleen was missing. Her twin sister, the only other girl in the world who knew her completely. She gulped as she thought of her sister possibly not being alive anymore, then shook her head to vanquish the thought. Having a twin was a connection so unique from any other relationship, at least for Catherine. She felt something was wrong, deep down, in that twin place, she could just tell. And this uneasy feeling wouldn't go away. Catherine thought again of Kathleen being materialistic, and superficial, and how much that annoyed her. But of course she knew that wasn't the real Kathleen. Her Kathleen. *Where is my sister?*

Catherine had walked a good distance away in the other direction from the rock and past the bubbling creek that cooled her wounds the other day. She feared continuing as darkness fell. Catherine again regretted not bringing Danny, zipping up her jacket and pushing on. *Kathleen,* she thought. She stopped where she stood suddenly. She saw the edge of the wooded area ahead, and felt a pinch of relief. But the panic filtered in. Would she be able to find her way back? Was Kathleen out there? She was about to take a step when all of the sudden she heard voices nearby. She froze and listened. They were male voices she was sure, but she couldn't understand what they were saying. She didn't know why, but instinctively, as quick as a cat, she hid herself behind some bushes. It was just in time, for the men walked by as she did. Catherine's breath was quick, but she covered her nose and mouth with her jacket to silence it.

She could tell now there were two men as they walked closer. Their features were visibly clear. Both wore what looked like simply wrapped cloth around their torsos that hung loosely, then openly at their ankles. The cloth was dark and looked very grungy and ragged hanging off them. One of them had a belt fastened around his middle that looked to be made of fine rope entwined with some sort of metal loops. The other had a basic sash, which, though speckled with holes, was tied at the bottom atop his hips. Their faces seemed gruff, and their wet hair soaked their clothes around the neckline. At knee level she followed their movements mostly by eying their feet, which were either laced in sandals or covered in a crude looking boot. One of them was snapping twigs in his hands as they walked. The men had a look about them that made you think their bones were heavy inside them, for they hunched over strangely. They looked strong, and sturdy. Catherine wondered why the strange men were here, and hoped desperately she could escape without them noticing her. Her legs were beginning to throb. Very slowly, she managed to stretch them without a sound. She knew she needed to be ready to run at any minute, and could not afford to have her legs give out beneath her.

Suddenly, as she saw the men disappear out of sight, she heard screaming in the distance. Her heart leapt in her chest. She quickly strode to the edge of the woods some feet away. Catherine's eyes widened at what she saw. The scream was apparently coming from a single man standing out on an empty, slightly overgrown field. Like a madman, he was waving his arms around wildly as he strode from left to right.

The two men who had passed Catherine joined a group made up mostly of men who looked equally ragged. The wild man was headed away from them as he paced. The expressions of the people were all different, but all very concerned as they stood and watched. They wore garments that looked raggedy, but they were worn and draped around them like once dignified robes, for their mannerisms suggested they were once very fine fabric and fully covering. It was windy and Catherine struggled to keep her hair and the bushes out of her face and eyes long enough to see clearly. There were a few other smaller wild crews sporadically placed on the large field before her, huddled together as if they didn't know what to do in wide open spaces.

In the far distance, the sun was about to set over the hills, about to disappear in its last light. Catherine nearly popped up from her crouched position when she saw Kathleen sitting on the ground ahead with her arms being held tightly behind her. She looked unharmed other than that, so Catherine suppressed her tears. She watched, and waited. It was a wide open field. She couldn't get her sister out of there now. Catherine regretted again, bitterly this time, that she did not bring Danny with her.

"Why did you bring me this woman?" the wild man said in a growling voice directed at four of his men, who were now surrounding Kathleen, "I want *Bowen* damn you!"

"She saw us. We didn't want her to tell anyone," said one man, his brown hair whipping in the wind. It had picked up, and everyone but Conall now felt the crisp air scrape at their faces. Conall was too heated to notice, his madness rising and falling at random.

His wildness calmed momentarily, but his eyes still looked enraged. He walked towards Kathleen. Kathleen looked up at him angrily, dried tears and dirt staining her cheeks. He leaned down and pulled her fallen hair away from her face in one swoop of his hand. Catherine clenched her fists as she watched.

Kathleen grit her teeth and glared back at him. "Hmm . . ." he said in a guttural voice, "and why were you watching these men?" Kathleen said nothing. "Speak!" he screamed, and Kathleen started but held her ground.

A tall man in the group stepped forward. "Our language, no doubt, is not the same, Conall. She cannot know what it is you say," he put his palms out to reassure Conall he meant no challenge to his authority.

Catherine was still watching helplessly from the tree line. She had no idea what language these men were speaking, but they were definitely not from around here. She had to think quickly about how to get Kathleen out of there. She hadn't time to go run for help. She pulled out her phone to tell Danny where she was in one text, but before she could explain what to do, she was discovered. Pulled up roughly by her arms and dragged while she struggled to free herself, she dropped her phone where she had been hiding in the process.

Catherine was thrown down by her sister who pulled herself free in that instant from one of the men holding her arms with their painful grasp. She reached for her embrace.

"Catherine! Thank God! I didn't think I would ever see you again! These men grabbed me when I was looking for the earring. I think they thought I was spying on them. I didn't even notice them, but they won't listen to me. I can't understand a word they're saying," she said frantically.

"It's okay, I told Danny where we were. We just have to hope he gets here soon with help," Catherine explained quickly and held Kathleen in her arms.

Everyone was staring at the two women with blank expressions. Except for Conall, who was watching intently with deep interest.

"Why, they're twins!" he said excitedly, looking them over.

Catherine somehow knew what he said, for she saw realization flash across his face, and a shiver ran through her. He locked eyes with hers and stood still for a moment. The tall man walked out and spoke to Conall quietly.

"I don't care if you think it's a bad omen or not!" Conall

shouted savagely as he waved his hand at the man, "I'll do as I please!" and ended it with a slap across his face without holding back. The man flinched in pain, but backed away lowering his head in submission.

Kathleen was burying her face in Catherine's neck. Catherine held her tight, but looked away from Conall when she saw movement a ways off. Catherine's eyes widened. "Bowen," she breathed out.

Conall heard, and understood instantly. "Bowen?!" he shouted. He grew livid with rage, his neck and mad eyes whirling around.

Bowen had been trying to approach stealthily. Now he stood still, a mixed look of frustration and pity fixed on the mad man staring at him some distance away.

In a cool slithery voice Conall said, "Oh Bowen! After all this time, to see you standing looking just as you did before, at last, I am happy. I told you I would be free, I knew it would happen!" he walked a few steps away from Catherine and gestured towards them. "One of them is your woman, am I right?"

Bowen said nothing.

"I'll not be ignored, Bowen!"

Bowen shook his head, exasperated.

Conall threw himself toward the twins and ripped them from each other. He grabbed Catherine's face and looked at her closely while screaming at Bowen, "It's *this* one, the more defiant one!" He put his other arm around her shoulder pulling her body closer. Disgusted, Catherine held her breath and clamped her mouth shut as his spittle dampened her face. She turned her body sideways and pushed with her arms using all her strength. But Conall was stronger.

Bowen ran towards them but was blocked by the wild crowd. They held him steadfast. He yelled and flung out an outstretched hand through the wall of people, grasping at air. Panic and frustration flooded through him.

Conall grinned evilly at Catherine, "Thank you for releasing me," he whispered, their noses just inches apart.

Catherine's eyes were tearing up. She couldn't fathom what he wanted from her.

"I have her, Bowen!" Conall screamed, "And because she is so important to you, I will make you suffer by making her suffer!" He turned to face Bowen, "It's only fair . . ." he gave him a lingering smile.

"Conall, don't do this!" Bowen fiercely pleaded.

Suddenly Catherine was released and pushed to the side. Conall ran inhumanly fast at Kathleen. She screamed, though it was quickly stifled as he picked her up by the neck and started choking her. A smile spread widely across his face. Catherine steadied herself, then looked up in horror. She threw herself at him but Conall was like a heavy bronze statue, entirely unmoving. She felt weak and helpless. Time was almost out! Catherine began to panic.

Kathleen was crying as she gasped for air. She tried to pry at Conall's hands and arms. She tried to kick and push, but Conall held his grip firmly and looked over at Bowen with a smirk. He relished Bowen's pained and tortured face as he helplessly watched. He looked down at Catherine like an evil cat over a trapped mouse, and upon seeing her sorrow, he became frenzied with excitement. Looking back at Kathleen, he brought her nearer to him and with a brisk flick of his wrist snapped her neck, letting her body drop. In one horrid instant, Kathleen was gone. Her body lay limp on the ground as lingering tears wet the dirt beneath her.

When Catherine heard the cracking of cartilage and bones, everything stopped. Shocked into silence and stillness, she felt her sister ripped away from within her. Now there was nothing.

Catherine dropped to her knees, grabbing her head with both hands, her nails digging into her scalp, releasing a bloodcurdling scream while slamming her eyes shut.

Conall motioned for his followers to let go of Bowen. He ran to Kathleen's body and felt her pulse. She was gone.

Conall stood over him. "This is only the beginning of your suffering Bowen," he spit out his name in disgust, as though it were a creeping crawling thing. Then Conall looked over at the tall man who had tried to warn him about the omen and said, "Don't worry, I'll kill the other twin soon enough."

The man simply nodded humbly in acknowledgment.

Bowen looked sorrowful and his arms rested, palms upward, on his thighs. He raised his eyes from the empty vessel that once held the soul and spirit of Kathleen. They met Conall's. Conall seemed unsettled by this but didn't react.

"How could you keep doing this to innocent people, Conall? I was right that day when I told them you had gone mad. You can't control it now, can you? Are you completely gone now?" Bowen said, his gaze searching Conall's face, as though desperately trying to see through a fog in the distance. He hoped to see a glimpse of a man he once knew. Not the distorted person standing before him.

"I told you I'd make you speak to me again, Bowen. You made me do this! It has always been your doing. Her blood is on your hands, not mine. Just like the blood of . . ." he stopped short and shivered madly. His eyes were filled with panic and pain. One of his followers, though she had originally been from a different druid order, came up to Conall and put her hands on his head. Conall still shook but was drawn to her face. "Thank you, my sister," he whispered. He seemed weakened then and laid his head in his own hands weeping. The woman moved her arms around him for comfort as they turned away. She peered back at Bowen and narrowed her eyes in hatred.

Bowen watched them walk away toward the hills. Their figures didn't take long to disappear in the darkening twilight. Darkness seemed to be rapidly pouring itself over the land. Bowen dreaded what was to come, not just from Conall but from the next few moments. He turned to see Catherine, a blank stare across her face. She didn't flinch when Bowen was in front of her closely, trying to see into her eyes through the dark. Her hands and fingers felt like bones covered with soft ice when he touched them. He pulled his hand back suddenly in surprise. Her face looked ghostly in the night. "Catherine?"

Silence.

Bowen became afraid, "Catherine?!" he shouted as he stood her up with him and gently shook her. He held her close to him and rubbed his hands up and down her back to try to warm her. His face buried down in her neck and he could feel she was breathing a steady breath, though all of her exposed flesh was cold and clammy from her sweat mixed with the cold. Bowen pushed her back to look at her face again, his hands rubbing her cheeks.

"Please . . ." he said quietly, "show me you're still there."

Catherine blinked and slowly her eyes cleared. She saw Bowen before her. "Bowen . . ."

"Yes, it's me!" he hugged her close, turning her away from the cold lifeless body on the ground.

"I saw you, you saved us! Kathleen will be so relieved. What happened? Where did everyone go?"

Bowen said nothing but kept holding her tightly. Catherine grew nervous. She flinched involuntarily. "Bowen," she said slowly "where's Kathleen?"

Bowen squeezed tighter, "I'm sorry, just keep breathing, Catherine," he said, his voice muffled in the neck of her jacket.

Catherine's breath hitched. "Let go of me! Where the hell is my sister, Bowen?!" she shouted angrily.

Bowen pulled away and turned his head. He didn't want to see what was coming. He didn't want to see Catherine destroyed again. Catherine glared at him for a moment, then looked around and realized for the first time how dark it was. She knew suddenly that something terrible had happened. She felt an emptiness she had never felt before. She was no longer her whole self.

After she turned around, Catherine stood still. She stared down at her sister for a few moments before slowly scooping her up in her arms and sitting down in one fluid motion. Holding Kathleen close, she looked at her face and caressed her cheeks.

"Kathleen?" she whispered once, and then again louder. Each time she grew increasingly hysterical.

"Kathleen, please! KATHLEEN!" she screeched painfully, burying her face on Kathleen's chest and sobbing as she rocked back and forth.

Bowen stood a few steps away. Her wretched state clawed at his heart. After some time, he noticed it was getting unbearably colder. The night had crept in entirely. Catherine had fallen silent and still. She stared out ahead.

Bowen held back his own sadness and crouched down to grab Catherine's shoulder, "We need to go get help, Catherine. We can't stay here any longer," he said gently.

Catherine stopped moving and said rigidly, "No . . ."

"Catherine?"

"I'm not leaving her here alone!" she yelled and looked straight up at Bowen. Though it was dark, the light of the starry sky let Bowen see her torn face and tears streaming down her cheeks to fall off her chin. It wracked his spirit.

Catherine suddenly ripped Bowen's hand off her shoulder and threw herself at him viciously.

"Catherine, stop! Stop!" Bowen grabbed at her flailing arms and fists.

Catherine grew weak and let her head fall on Bowen's chest, her balled fists on either side. Bowen relaxed his grip and put his arms around her shaking body.

"Catherine," he said with severity in his voice, "listen to me, this is not the place to do this. I will get you home, and everything will be better. But you must do as I say. Let me help you."

When no answer came, he grabbed Catherine so they were face to face. "Catherine, I genuinely care about you," he said very seriously. Catherine could see the concern in his eyes, and snapped herself to a state coherent enough to follow directions.

"I-I don't want her to be left here alone . . ." She looked down forlornly.

Bowen looked at Kathleen's dead body for a moment thoughtfully. "Okay," he said and letting go of Catherine he leaned down and scooped the body up in his arms. "Let's go."

Catherine lingered over the spot Kathleen had been, where she had held her closely to her chest. She closed her eyes remembering what it felt like to feel Kathleen's face warm on her neck. She balled her fists again and clenched them to her collarbone. She remembered what it was like just a short time ago to feel Kathleen's arms hugging her back.

"Catherine, come with me now," Bowen's voice called to her from a short distance away, heading towards the direction of home.

* * *

Danny led Catherine to her room and sat her down on the bed. Catherine didn't move, staring ahead with a horrified blankness.

"I'm not going to . . . I can't deal with this . . ." Danny stammered, but Catherine said nothing.

Danny looked at his sister's stricken face and realized she was like an empty shell. He understood. His own heart was aching in his chest, and his stomach felt sick. He wanted badly to go to sleep and never wake up again. He wanted to talk to Catherine about it. To tell her how he felt. To ask her what she saw, and how their sister was taken from them. He was angry, but he was more sad than angry right now. Danny didn't want to cause more pain to Catherine. She already looked like she would never be the same again.

"Catherine, I'll check on you in a little while. Try to sleep," he said moving his hand through the top of her hair gently. Just like Kathleen's hair. That fact both helped him, and hurt him.

When Danny left the room Catherine remained exactly as she was. Her face was sunken, and dark circles traced her puffy eyes. She seemed to have aged a full decade in that one night. At first she was as still as stone, but slowly she started to fidget with her now warm hands. Nervously she picked at a small hole in the fabric of her long sleeved shirt. A thousand thoughts ran through her mind. Danny's last words. Suddenly some morning light streamed into her room. The entire night had finally passed. Sleep, Danny said . . . she could never sleep again. Or so she felt. Never the same. It would be nothing but tortured and fitful hours of struggle for sleep for her now. No, it would be easier to stay awake and die from exhaustion.

* * *

Bowen sat on a large padded chair in the living room downstairs, his chin resting on his hand. He thought about Conall, about the night trying to stabilize Catherine long enough to get her home to a safe place. He slowly blinked away the memory of how empty she looked when he told Danny what happened. What would he do now that Conall was released? How could he keep him away from Catherine, and stop his plans? He didn't know.

Danny appeared then, leaning in the archway and eyeing him suspiciously. Bowen closed his eyes.

"She needs to know what's behind all of this. Frankly so do I," he told Bowen flatly.

Bowen nodded before returning Danny's gaze, "You're right, of course." He waited knowingly.

Danny walked over and sat across from Bowen, his eyes narrowing. "Bowen, is it?"

"Yes."

"I'm going to tell you what I think, okay?" Danny asked, and Bowen nodded his assent.

"I'm thinking you should go tell my sister what she needs to know so she can eventually find closure. I'm also thinking that when that's over you need to leave and never come back. I don't want to see you, and I don't want my sister to see you. I don't know who you are, and really I just don't care. But you have no business being in our lives, so you need to leave as quickly as you arrived," he said in an even tone.

Bowen listened intently. He was used to people hating him by now. "I do not blame you for hating me, Danny," he said "and I understand if you hold me accountable for Kathleen's death."

Danny blinked slowly a few times and sat back on the couch.

"I'm sorry I couldn't stop him from killing her. I am so terribly sorry you lost her," Bowen finished.

Danny's eyes were red from stress and tears. He clenched his fists, took a deep breath, and stood over Bowen for a brief moment. He looked conflicted, then steadied himself.

"I may forgive you. We'll see if Catherine will," was all he said before leaving the room.

* * *

Catherine didn't sleep. Just as she knew she couldn't. She had laid down to rest, and wept interchangeably throughout the day and next night, but still no sleep came. Danny knocked on the door and came in to try to convince her to eat a few times, but to no avail. One time in and out of drowsiness she thought Bowen was in the room sitting across from her, but it was too dark and she was too weak to be sure. Danny helped her force down some water eventually, which helped her burning throat as the cycle continued.

Catherine lost track of time. She would have to return to work eventually, but she couldn't imagine ever returning to normal life. Catherine felt like her whole identity was gone. Could she ever reclaim a future for herself without her twin sister? Days like this droned on. She finally slept on the fourth day, but fitfully, woken multiple times by horrific nightmares that resulted in her being drenched in sweat and tears while her throat ached from the screams escaping it. Each time Danny would check on her, or she would wake up being held by Danny as he tried to calm her down. Often she would be screaming and wouldn't wake from it. Catherine felt trapped, she saw no end to the torture.

One night she stayed perfectly still in her bed with the light on for hours. The moon was out and stars winked at her through her window. She fell in and out of sleep. She thought of Kathleen and that horrible day. And then Catherine popped up in her bed, her eyes finding the closed door of her bedroom in front of her. *My God* she thought. Catherine remembered finally. In her dreams it had all happened right in front of her. As she slept she felt trapped in her frozen body, forced to watch the scene play out. Tears streamed down her cheeks freely. She didn't cringe. She silently cried, still as a corpse. After a while she realized she wasn't just crying over missing her sister, or at witnessing her sister's death. She was crying because she felt angry. So many times Catherine had jumped in to protect Kathleen. But she couldn't save her this time. With all her strength she had tried.

She now felt weak, and had been made a victim. She was angry with herself for not being strong when Kathleen needed her to be.

Catherine had never hated before. She knew immediately what it was she felt. Her anger and sorrow welled up deeper and deeper. It festered inside of her until it became a consuming poisonous hate. She directed it not just at one person though, but many. One being the most hated, Kathleen's murderer, Conall.

Hours went by like seconds to Catherine now. No longer wallowing in sorrow, she had found a new way of dealing with the pain. She spent hours hating, and it gave her false strength. She no longer felt the pang of sadness except at random spurts of uncontrollable grief, or during her fitful nightmare-filled nights. The hatred allowed her to not just feel strong, but to let her push away all other feeling, to ignore what she could not do anything about or handle. And Catherine knew this. She knew the extent this could go. She knew what was happening, every step of the way. She felt she could never recover her former self, even a glimpse. But she felt if she let go of the only stable ground she had, she would crumble. So she was at an impasse. What else could she do? How could she save herself from this blackened night, full of endless pain and suffering? She didn't know, but she would hold onto that hatred for dear life until she did.

Catherine's thoughts were interrupted by sudden movement. She looked over and saw Bowen bumping into the bed as he entered the room. "What are you doing here?" she asked, her neck outstretched from her laying position as she looked up.

"I've given you time. But we don't have any more time to spare I'm afraid," he said with a serious expression.

Catherine turned away.

"Catherine?"

"This is your fault," she mumbled.

"What?" he asked.

"That all of this happened. You caused this chain of events!" she said turning rapidly back towards him and throwing the blankets off her.

Bowen looked bewildered. "I tried to save her, Catherine. You saw me try!" He started to come closer but when Catherine flinched back uncomfortably at this, he simply sat on the edge of the bed. Catherine stared into his eyes. Her own eyes felt dry and swollen from what seemed like years of crying. Her hands shook so much she gripped her pillow sharply to stop them. Catherine realized she must appear a mess. But her anger melted away into momentary peace, and in the liquid green of his stare, she forgot how awful she looked and felt.

"I'm sorry, I am so deeply sorry for what happened to you," Bowen said, concern growing on his face as he watched her.

Catherine believed him. Bowen saw her forgiveness start in her eyes. "Catherine . . . what I said before, when we were leaving that place," Bowen paused to take a longer breath "I meant it. I really did."

"That . . . you care about me?" her voice was small.

"Yes," he said. Catherine nodded slightly. " . . . which means I hope you can trust me. I will do anything to protect you. As long as I'm with you, I won't let anyone harm you."

Catherine felt a rush of feelings go through her, but she buried them quickly. She wasn't sure what he meant precisely.

"Bowen . . ." she started "tell me about Conall."

Bowen stood up and went to a window. Then he turned and sat closer to her on the bed, clasping his hands together. "What I'm going to tell you will not sound believable," he said with a sigh.

"It's already unbelievable for me, but . . ." Catherine shook her head. "I understand."

Bowen ran one of his hands through his hair. His gorgeous

hair, Catherine thought before reproaching herself to pay attention. "What is your knowledge of the original Druids? The ancient real Druids?" he asked.

Catherine blinked a few times at the question. "I don't know much, just that the actual Druids were a society, and not just of supposed magical people," she said, confused.

"Hmm . . ." Bowen said, he tapped his index finger on his leg.

Catherine raised her eyebrow. Her hair fell from one side as she shifted in the bed, and searched his face for answers.

Bowen breathed in and out deeply once before speaking again. "I'm over two thousand years old Catherine. I'm an ancient Druid who lived here in Ireland all those years ago," he said calmly, before watching Catherine closely.

Catherine felt as though maybe she had gone insane, that seeing her sister's death was too much for her. Maybe she had lost her mind earlier than that and Kathleen could actually be safe and back in the States still. She immediately shook the thought out of her mind. She nodded. And with her eyes wide and slightly frightened she simply replied, "Continue . . . please," as she cleared her throat and looked down to avoid his gaze.

Bowen sighed again in a reluctant manner, but he knew that she must know the truth.

"I was a doctor, I healed people with our methods of the time. I had no living relatives. They had all died from illness, and as I grew up I wanted to prevent that from happening to as many people as I could. Conall . . . I knew him, and his wife. They were a young couple when I first met them. He was so happy then." Bowen seemed reminiscent as he said that. Catherine looked over at him. "His wife died one day, and he was never happy again. As time went on he became mad. Mad with rage and unimaginable sorrow. He became so vengeful and evil that my people had to put a stop to him. Nothing we did cured him. He brainwashed many of our warriors and caused an uprising against the priesthood. He said the priests were worshiping false gods and using our beliefs to control us all for power. Rapidly his followers became as evil as he, and they hurt innocent people in their wild path." Bowen's face looked strained. He paused for a moment to swallow. Bowen rubbed his face, then clasped his hands again to continue.

"One of the women of our order was a master with magic. I didn't believe in such things, but regardless, she was the high priest's daughter. She put a curse on Conall and his followers to trap them in caves hidden within the hills and rocks 'as long as their evil thoughts remained' she said. And the only other way they could be freed is if the curse was broken by a prophesied woman. And that woman is you, Catherine. Until that day you freed them unintentionally, they, and myself as well have lived in an ageless state. A state where we cannot be injured, and cannot die. That's all changed now. This is why I wanted you to leave Ireland, to prevent this from even accidentally happening. Now they are free, and they will hurt everyone they can. They will hunt for me and they will kill you to get to me. You can't stay here any longer."

Catherine sat still, thinking. He was staring at her, and it made her blush. Bowen decided to add a little more. "After I saw the high priest's daughter cast the curse in front of me, I—well I can't remember after that. I just know I woke up sometime later far from home with the sun shining above me, and I was alone with grass grown thickly around my body. My clothes were worn but my flesh and all of my body was the same. It could have been years later. I don't know what happened."

Bowen took Catherine's hand, "When you broke the curse, it was like I could breathe again. I'm hungry, I get exhausted, and thirst. I'm aging normally again. It is as though I held my breath for a long time without it being a bother to me, or even noticing really, and suddenly now my breath is back, bringing all my senses and life along with it. It's so strange, Catherine."

Bowen noticed Catherine's hand was soft and warm in his. And Catherine noticed how his large manly hand closed over her small one completely. His touch sent another rush through her, and she felt the excitement of noticing every part of it. Each finger, each slight unconscious caress on her skin. It was just a gesture of sincerity that only *could* be interpreted as something more. But which was it? Her breath was quicker, but she didn't allow him to see that.

"I must figure out a way to get them back into the caves to avoid further bloodshed," he said pulling his hand away.

"If they are no longer ageless, can't you just kill them?" she asked quickly as she worked to control her breathing.

"I can't do that, I'm a healer. I can't just kill anyone, unless in defense."

"Even if they are evil and will hurt others, Bowen?"

"I can't kill them unless I have no other choice," he replied.

"In that time didn't everyone know how to fight to survive?" Catherine was puzzled by Bowen's unwillingness.

"Most yes. I do know how to fight Catherine, I'm not unable. Nor am I a coward if that's what you're thinking." He looked at her, slightly irritated.

"I wasn't trying to imply that but . . . It really is just because you're a doctor?"

"You seem to think because I can fight I'm sure to win it. The group of Conall's followers we saw that day, well, it wasn't all of them. There are hundreds," Bowen stated.

"What! Hundreds?" Catherine's voice cracked slightly.

Bowen's lips curved into a slight smile, "If it had only been a few dozen people rising against us before, a curse wouldn't have been needed. There are hundreds, perhaps thousands, I can't be sure exactly how many. They were scattered separately in the depths of the earth and rocks of Ireland. I spent a good portion of time looking for where exactly. Like Conall, most were trapped in caves where they couldn't be bothered by stray people. And they couldn't see them either, or much of the outside world. The curse was explained to me as being not only to protect others from these people, but as a form of punishment for their actions."

"So Conall can't speak English because he's been trapped, but you can because you've been roaming Ireland for two thousand years?"

"Yes, essentially. I adapted to my surroundings. People couldn't know who I was. Especially in the modern age. For the most part, I hid, never to meet anyone new for decades at a time. I couldn't trust anyone, or take that risk." He paused to think before continuing. "Catherine, as you may have noticed when you met him, Conall is strong . . . unnaturally strong. One day he suddenly became this way, no one knew how. He and his followers were almost unbeatable in my time."

Catherine had noticed how strong Conall was. She nodded in response, and silently pondered this amazing story, which to her misfortune was no work of fiction. So many questions were forming, and she was eager for answers. One came to mind that she was particularly curious about.

"Bowen?" she asked, breaking the several minutes of silence.

"Yes?"

"Why was I the woman she said could break the curse?"

Just at that moment Danny walked up to the open doorway. Catherine looked up as relief flashed across Bowen's face. He quickly composed himself. "Hey, we should go do a missing person report down at the Garda station before too much longer, Catherine," Danny said.

"Right," she agreed, and looked at Bowen, "because we can't explain that she's dead . . ."

"No one else should know about this, Catherine."

"I know. I really have no choice now . . ." her voice trailed off as she remembered Bowen making a burial fire and burning Kathleen's body in front of her before they could return home. Catherine had collapsed and watched as the blazing fire reached up to the stars. She thought of how powerful fire was, how very little could fight against it. It destroys, creates and erases, but also cleanses. Her thoughts turned morbid as she thought about the ashes of her sister's bones in detail, and how her own would look if she were cremated one day. Danny snapped her back to reality with a meaningful grunt, much to her relief.

"Yes, Danny, we'll contact the Gardai to file the missing person report, or whatever it's called here."

The doorbell rang suddenly, and Danny went to answer.

"Are you sure you're ready to leave this room?" Bowen asked her.

Catherine wasn't ready to heal if that's what Bowen meant, but she was sure she could step across that threshold. All because it meant getting a step closer to avenging her sister. "Yes."

Bowen eyed her curiously, he knew there was something more, but didn't say anything. He couldn't be sure exactly, for Catherine kept retreating, a closed book. Bowen left the room to let her dress. His brow furrowed. Suppressing grief to deal with it, retreating inward from others, it was only a matter of time before she would explode. He was brought out of his thoughts when he heard Danny talking with someone at the door. He waited for Catherine.

She soon came out dressed in earth tone colored yoga pants and a T-shirt. Bowen lagged behind a bit as Catherine walked into the next room ahead of him. She saw the front door open with a man's tanned hand placing a card in Danny's. She heard Danny apologize and thank him before shutting the door.

"Who was that?" Catherine asked.

"A guy to check on Kathleen," he said sadly.

Catherine felt a lightning bolt of alarm flash inside her chest. She felt sick knowing she would have to keep up a lie for the rest of her life in order to save everyone else's life. She wondered if she could handle it all without breaking. Catherine wished suddenly she were the pile of dust being blown away out in the distant fields and woods instead.

"He said she was supposed to meet with him a while ago for coffee, for a date," Danny finished after a moment.

"Oh . . . yeah, that's right, she was," Catherine said quietly to herself.

"He left me his card with a note on it for her," he said, tossing it on the counter.

"You didn't tell him she was— you didn't tell him?" Catherine gulped away her desire to cry.

"No, I couldn't deal with it; he caught me off guard Catherine," he answered. "I'll remember to say she's missing though if it comes up."

Catherine just nodded. Turning to the fridge for something cold to drink she was stopped in her tracks when she saw the magnet pictures. The pictures she had of Kathleen on her phone or in her room she had moved or hidden away. The corners of her mouth perked up slightly when she saw the familiar picture of Kathleen's silly expressions as a child, her favorite. Catherine remembered putting it up when she moved in. She hadn't thought about her sister dying, at least not for decades in the future. Many decades. Catherine realized she had always subconsciously assumed that she would die before everyone she cared about. She took down the magnets. Then, feeling the absence of her sister amongst the other pictures of the rest of the family and friends there, she cleared the front of the fridge of all pictures and threw them in a drawer. Catherine felt more comfortable now. Though when the hallway mirror on the wall caught her eye, she saw herself for the first time in a while. The mirror image which stared back was haunting. She could never feel fully comfortable with a mirror again. Would anything be normal now? Anything tolerable? She turned quickly away from her reflection.

Danny had left the room and returned in that time saying he was ready to leave. Catherine noticed the bags under her brother's eyes. He looked sullen and exhausted, but he continued as if perfectly fine and unaffected. Catherine knew he was only keeping it together for her benefit. She worried about Danny, and seeing him like this did in fact make things harder for her. She decided not to mention it.

Catherine took a deep breath. *Next step, go outside.* And she did.

* * *

Catherine asked Bowen to accompany her with Danny to *An Garda Síochána,* otherwise known as the Garda station. She was anxious before, but everything was blank now. Speaking with the officers, and getting the report went smoothly. Though the idea of having to do such a thing was upsetting for both of the siblings, they kept each other calm.

While Catherine was trying to remember what Kathleen was last wearing for the missing person report, she saw a woman in custody brought into the station. The woman looked dirty, and her clothes were mismatched with some new fabric wrapped around atop old torn ones. One of the Garda spoke to her, apparently not for the first time based on his frustrated tone, but the woman seemed unable to reply. Catherine was paying full attention now. She knew this woman must be one of the formerly cursed people. She thought she would feel enraged at the sight of one of them. But then again, after what Bowen said about there possibly being thousands of the ancient druids here now, it was very possible this woman wasn't even there when Kathleen was killed. Catherine didn't recognize her face at all.

Catherine nudged Bowen. Upon seeing the ancient woman, he drew a sharp breath.

"What is it?" she whispered.

"I've seen her before, among Conall's followers. I can't place it, but I know I encountered her before the curse," he whispered back. He looked over Catherine's head and said "Where did you find her?" to a Garda standing closest to them.

The Garda answered casually "I haven't been notified, I just arrived. All I know is she won't speak to anyone, she's not in records of any kind. We suspect she's from another country, since she doesn't seem to understand Gaelic or English."

"Thank you," Catherine said. The Garda nodded and walked away.

Bowen took a few steps forward and spoke quietly to the woman. Catherine couldn't dissect the ancient Gaelic language into comprehensive words. It ran together too quickly to even make a guess. The woman looked up at Bowen with hate in her eyes. She seemed to know him too. Her low reply was muffled but her anger was evident in the way she spat out the words. She glared and emphatically stepped back from him.

"What did she say?" Danny asked Bowen curiously. The woman shifted her eyes to Danny when he spoke, then turned away from them entirely as if she were alone in the room.

"She hates me, though that should be obvious to anyone," Bowen said.

"Well yeah . . . Did she say anything else?" Danny was very confused by the strange language.

"I can tell you her name is Síne."

CHAPTER THREE

THE THREE OF them walked by a park a ways down from the Garda station. Catherine found a wooden bench to rest on. She felt weak from the exertion of their errand. She hadn't been out of bed, let alone the house for some time. Bowen and Danny gave each other glances of concern when they saw how exhausted she was. Bowen leaned against a tree not too far from the bench. Danny sat down next to his sister with a worried look across his face.

"Catherine . . ." he put his arm around her.

"I'm okay, Danny. I'm just tired," she lied.

"You're stupid if you actually think you can fool me. Who do you think has been staying at home making sure you weren't suicidal?"

Catherine looked at her brother. He was too right for her to roll her eyes at him.

"You need to start regularly eating again, no excuses. I don't care if you don't *feel* hungry," he continued.

"Hm," Catherine wrinkled her nose and frowned, "you're a good brother, Danny," she said with a smile. The first smile Danny had seen in a while.

Danny grew more serious now, "Catherine, why is this guy

hanging around us still? I mean, who is he really? Did he ever tell you?"

Catherine turned away as she thought how to explain.

"Too many weird things going on to keep on without answers about him. It's creepy really . . ." he sighed, scratching the back of his head with his free arm.

Catherine looked down, fidgeting with a piece of string from the fabric of her pants. She knew he would believe her, but she was reluctant still. A moment passed before she looked back up at Danny and said, "Yeah, he told me who he was . . ."

After Catherine glanced over at Bowen, she turned back to her brother to tell him Bowen's true identity, the curse, and who the strange woman at the Garda station was. Danny seemed to take the news well, considering. Afterwards he was silent, then excused himself to take a walk alone. Before leaving, he passed Bowen. Danny furrowed his brow, and seemingly tried to examine his face for evidence of his very advanced age. Catherine held her head in embarrassment. Bowen stared right back at him, completing the awkward moment. Bowen's eyes followed Danny until he disappeared into the park. He sighed to himself as he came over to sit next to Catherine.

Catherine had gotten over her brief embarrassment. She leaned back on the bench and looked up at the sky like she usually did on a nice day. The sun was covered by clouds today though. There was no warmth on her face, which always brought her happiness, but rather a chilled breeze that brushed her cheeks and made her shiver. But she embraced it. The clouds appeared to be moving quickly high above. The leaves on the trees wildly blew around their grasping branches. Catherine smiled to herself and shut her eyes. She wanted to feel something familiar that she enjoyed again. A feeling she'd had when life was more real to her, more normal. She missed that time. It felt so long ago.

Bowen looked at the grass between his shoes. He wondered

how many blades, if any, were the exact same shade of green. Realizing his mind was wandering, he brought himself back to think of what to do next. He felt lost and frightened, but he knew he had to find a way to stop Conall. He took his right hand off his knee to place under his chin.

And then Bowen became distracted again, this time by the beautiful Catherine at his side. He found himself fixated on her every feature and movement. He noticed her thick eyelashes that gently brushed against the top of her cheeks, the curve of her lips as they went into a smile. He wondered what she was thinking about. Her lovely neck was outstretched as her head was held back. The red hair normally dangling well past her shoulders was in a thick braid that she laid casually over a shoulder to hide in between the folds of her jacket. Bowen's own dark brown mass of hair usually covered most of his forehead, but was blown aside in the increasing cold wind that swept around them. He cocked his head sideways on his hand.

"Bowen?" Catherine said with a smooth tone, unchanged from her position, her eyes still closed peacefully.

Bowen's eyes remained fixed on her, "Hm?"

"Do you know what we should do about the bad druids yet? Got a plan?"

Bowen chuckled to himself at her phrase, "the bad druids."

"What's so funny?" Catherine asked, curious.

"Never mind. No, *I* don't have a plan yet," he said.

Catherine caught the hint and peeked sideways over at her bench companion. He stared back intently. She snapped back, eyes shut, and ignored the flushed feeling that spread from her chest up to her face and into the roots of her hair. She continued on and said, "I'm going with you, Bowen."

"It's too dangerous," he said. "Though there is no point in you leaving Ireland to run from them. No, I must hide you somewhere close by . . ." he mumbled.

"I'm not leaving you to deal with this alone. Wherever and however you're going to stop them, I'm going to be right behind you." She rubbed her face with her palms and looked at him, "So you might as well let me handle it with you."

Bowen just smiled slightly. This made Catherine uncomfortable. He was too handsome to be how she imagined an ancient druid. For a moment she wondered what his ancient clothes had looked like. Even when he annoyed her she found him charming. This bothered her. She smiled a quick smile back, and busied herself with something, anything, in the small purse she'd brought. Though Catherine didn't see it, Bowen's smile got bigger.

Catherine and Bowen heard some footsteps rustle the grass not too far away and they twisted to see Danny returning. Síne was with him.

"I've agreed to be her surety," Danny said immediately.

"What?!" Catherine yelled, and stood up.

"If what you told me is true, then she can help," he said with confidence as he stopped behind the bench.

"But Danny, she's one of Conall's followers. Who knows her motives? She could be just as mad as he is!"

"It doesn't matter."

"Oh, it's okay if she's insane then?"

"Don't! I'll watch her. That's what a surety does." Danny was more than frustrated now.

"And precisely where did you get the money to bail her out? You're supposed to be saving, not blowing it on *anything* right now!"

"Catherine, please . . ." he said, closing his eyes and taking a breath. "The Gardai have no idea who she is or what to do with her. They'll be less suspicious if she's not hanging around them."

"What about how dangerous she could be? You're going to watch her like a hawk every waking moment?" she replied.

"I said I'd watch her . . ."

Catherine took a deep breath and controlled her voice, "Okay . . . I'll trust you. I'm sorry, I know you're just trying to help, and what I told you was a lot to take in after all."

Danny nodded. He figured if Síne did try to escape, she would lead them to Conall. Either way would be a win-win, he thought.

Catherine looked from her brother to Síne, seeing her angry gaze, then back to her brother. She threw up her arms in exasperation as she abruptly walked away. Bowen just stood in silence. When Catherine walked away he caught Síne's glare towards him before he turned to follow.

Danny shifted his weight where he stood, and glanced at the woman next to him. Síne was persistently defiant, but less so whenever Bowen wasn't around. Danny was an intelligent person, he felt this was the right choice to make. It was going to help bring about the end of the horrific nightmare that caused Kathleen's death. Danny kept holding onto that thought. He had to stop Kathleen's killer. He had to protect Catherine. Danny felt guilty about not being there for both of them. Maybe he could have stopped it. Fraught with guilt now, he buried it deep. He wouldn't dare burden Catherine with it. He could see she had enough problems to deal with.

Bowen caught up with Catherine as she paced around the park. "Catherine, it'll be okay, I'll watch out for both of you. I won't let Síne get away with anything," he said.

Catherine seemed a little calmer at this.

"I do have a plan, Catherine. Remember, since we can't kill them, we have to trap them again."

Catherine's eyes got wider, "How are we supposed to do that with that many people? We can't involve the Gardai, and we don't have an army to drag them away to jail."

"No, we don't. Nothing will hold them."

"What do you mean then?"

"Except . . . we have to cast the curse again," he said seriously as he looked down at her.

Catherine wrapped her arms around herself to stop the chill that went up her spine. She did not have a good feeling about this. "How?" she asked.

"We have to find the remnants of my people, and," Bowen paused to think, then he mumbled "Arlana may have left something for me to fix this there, in case it happened."

Catherine figured Arlana must have been the priest's daughter who cast the curse in the first place. Putting one hand in her pocket, and massaging her temple with the other, she said, "So we have to somehow find a message from 2,000 years ago in the ruins, which could be buried by the way. Also cast a powerful curse, and that's only if we can figure out how to?" Catherine couldn't help but sound skeptical.

The corners of Bowen's mouth curved into a small grin, but he was quite serious when he said "It's the only way . . ."

Catherine saw the grin, but chose to ignore it. "Fine, so what do we do first?"

"There are a couple of things we need to retrieve. The first is easiest I think."

"What is it?" she asked.

"A staff. It belonged to the high priest," Bowen answered.

"Okay, where do we find this staff then? Buried with the ruins, I suspect?"

"No, traditionally it stays with the high priest."

"What does that mean?"

"It's buried where his ashes are enshrined, which isn't where the ruins of my people are."

"Okay, enough with the cryptic speech please. Just where do we have to go to get the staff?" Catherine huffed.

"He's hidden away in the mountains, with the staff next to

him. When the people of our religious order die, it was said they should be buried in a secret and sacred place so that enemies couldn't disrupt their remains, or rob them. The mountains were both sacred and a place of secrecy."

"Do you happen to know which mountain, Bowen?"

"Traditionally yes, the same mountain was used for many generations. However, since he died after the curse was enacted I wasn't around to know for sure. It's possible they moved on to another one, but I doubt it."

"Great. How is this easiest?" Catherine sighed.

"The journey shouldn't be long, but we should go right away," Bowen stated.

"I have my job still. I can't just leave, especially after being absent for so long already," Catherine said. She wasn't sure how she was going to get out of work for who knew how many days more without losing her job. They were being understanding since they believed her sister was missing, but she would have to return on a regular basis soon.

"It will be a mistake if we wait. There isn't time." Bowen seemed agitated.

"I'll just go in now and see if I can talk to them," she replied, and turned to go.

Bowen gently grabbed Catherine's shoulder, "What about Danny?"

Catherine looked over at the distant figures of her brother and Síne. She didn't realize they had walked so far away.

"I'll call him later. I can't be around that hateful woman right now," she said meeting Bowen's eyes with her own again. And with that she left, Bowen following close behind her.

* * *

On the way out of the museum, after speaking with her manager, she was looking for Bowen when she ran into an older man who had been lurking around a corner outside the building.

"Oh, I'm sorry!" she said startled, and scrambled to pick up her phone.

The man was tall and burly, with leathery skin. His graying brown hair was tied back into a small bun at the base of his skull. His hawk-like eyes caught Catherine's when she stood straight again. It unsettled her.

"It was my fault," he replied with a nod of apology and a polite smile.

"No, I was walking too fast, excuse me," she said as she waved. The man just stood still. She felt awkward as she walked away, but that quickly passed as she called Danny and explained everything Bowen had told her. Meanwhile, she eventually found Bowen waiting for her on the sidewalk in front of the museum as she finished her argument with Danny.

"What's wrong?" Bowen asked when she reached him. Clearly he had overheard her frosty tones.

"Danny wants to come with us, and of course that means bringing Síne," she replied.

Bowen considered. "It could be safer for Danny if all three of us were watching her."

Catherine shrugged, exasperated at the idea of having to be around Síne. She hadn't agreed to being her surety, and wanted to keep as much distance as possible. It was yet another annoying thing on her back that she had to worry about.

"Your job understood?" Bowen asked.

"Yes, I have to go in tomorrow, but then we can leave."

* * *

A line of attached two-story houses all laid unlit in the dark evening, except for the house on the end. All the cars were in their regular spots for the night. The street was quiet, but eerie because of a slight fog. Some brawny men appeared through it, their faces hidden by the robe garments they wrapped around themselves. The night's shadows aided their stealthy approach near the house on the end. Suddenly, they set it ablaze. The men gathered again, and after surveying their work they turned and disappeared.

* * *

Bowen appeared outside Catherine's museum right as she left the next night. He had been waiting only a short time, knowing she would be working late. To any passerby, Bowen might seem to be lurking in the dark, stalking Catherine from a short distance behind.

Walking home, Catherine felt good about her work day as she remembered how fun it was helping on a project with an archeologist intern named Sharon. The intern was a very hard worker, and it was nice to have the extra hands for a couple of hours. Catherine mentally checked off everything that was finished since she had to close her department alone. She was looking forward to soaking in a bath. Though she had a few hours of time to herself while she worked, she managed not to think about Kathleen or Conall all day.

Bowen was a different story. She wondered what he was doing. A chill suddenly came over her, and she shivered as she bundled her jacket around herself tightly. The day had been unseasonably cold and bled into the night. The street was mostly empty, except for some walking alone like herself. The night was too quiet for her taste. Her shoes noticeably slapped against the sidewalk and echoed back to her.

"How was your day?" Bowen suddenly strode up next to her. She gasped loudly, startled.

He smirked, "I'm sorry, I didn't mean to scare you . . ."

"Sure, I'm only alone walking home at night; it wasn't scary at all!" she replied irritably.

Bowen looked down, bemused. Catherine glanced over at him a few times. She noticed that Bowen was a quick learner, especially when it came to her. He obviously tried to avoid pushing her buttons, though he failed more times than she would like. Still, she was always pleased when he showed up. Catherine had noticed he was fast and agile, and his hands were smooth. Perfect for a doctor she thought.

"My one day back was good, thanks," she said curtly. He nodded. "And yours?" she asked.

He stopped abruptly, "Catherine, you can't go home."

"What? Why not?" she pivoted toward him.

"It's on fire. Some men of Conall's destroyed it thinking you would be there at this hour."

Panic struck, Catherine dropped her purse and grabbed his arm. "No! Danny?" She felt sick thinking about it.

"He wasn't there, he wasn't in danger," Bowen reassured.

Catherine took deep breaths to calm herself. A second passed before she felt the worry return, "Did anyone else get hurt?"

Bowen shook his head, "I can't say. I left straightaway to come watch over you," he said.

Catherine thought a moment, wrinkling her brow, "But a fire doesn't make any sense, Conall wants to kill me himself, I'm sure."

"Maybe. I don't know, there is no way to be sure. Conall is unpredictable," he said.

Catherine merely nodded calmly, though wide eyed. Then it hit her, "What am I going to do? All of my things. I have insurance, but still—" she said, realizing everything left of Kathleen was gone too. She felt shaky and tried to push the thought away.

Bowen stretched his arms out and held her shivering shoulders. In his smooth deep voice he said, "I think you should take advantage of this."

"What do you mean?"

"Everyone thinks you're dead, including Conall, for a while at least. This will give us time."

She began to shake her head, "Oh, no, no I don't think I can do that . . . I mean that's too out there for me, Bowen," she said doubtfully.

"You don't have to do anything. That's the beauty of it. Don't contact anyone you know, and keep yourself hidden from familiar places or people. Outside of that don't give people too much information about yourself," he said, dropping his hands off of her.

Catherine still felt unsure, "What about my car? We need one to get around. And my family and friends will be told we're dead, this seems a little heartless . . ."

"It's necessary. It may even keep them safe. As for the car, ask your friend Bella to borrow hers again. She doesn't know anyone else you know, so she'll be able to keep it secret, at least long enough for us to hopefully succeed."

"How do you know about Bella?" she asked.

"Danny told me he was returning the car to her that day . . . when you borrowed it before," he responded carefully.

"Oh," Catherine looked back in the direction of the museum, lit up by the street lamps, "My job . . . everything. I can't come back from faking my death, Bowen," she said with sadness in her voice. Yet another thing taken from her, she thought.

"If we all survive Conall's plans then we'll worry about that when the time comes," he answered quietly.

Within the hour the two surprised Bella at her front door, where she answered dressed in lounge clothes and bunny slippers with a pint of ice cream in one hand. Her short hair was pulled back in a large clip on the top of her head. She looked at them in shock.

"Cathy?" Bella managed to say.

"Bella, I don't have time to explain, but we've been the best of friends and you're the only one I can count on. I can't give you an explanation now, but can I borrow your car again, for a time?"

Bella wanted to answer but hesitated, her eyes filled with concern as she looked from Catherine to the shadowy tall figure of Bowen outside her doorway.

"It's for everyone's safety, otherwise I would never! Please?" Catherine pleaded.

"I can do without it for a while . . ." she answered looking back at Catherine.

"Oh, thank you!" Catherine squeezed Bella into a hug.

"Yeah, no problem, Cathy. Hey . . ." she kept Catherine from pulling away so she could say softly, "are you okay?" She shifted her eyes again to Bowen.

Catherine realized what must be running through Bella's mind. "Yes, I'm okay. There's just some things going on, very strange and important things. You may even hear that I'm missing or dead, but please don't say anything about this." Catherine took the keys Bella handed her, "I promise I'll explain everything to you later!" she said with two kisses for each cheek before she turned to leave, with Bowen following close behind.

Bella was left dumbfounded at her doorstep, her pint of ice cream melting.

With Catherine at the wheel, the two drove to a small pub where Danny was known to be in the evenings. Luckily he was already outside stretched out on a bench with Síne sitting as far away as possible from him. No one else seemed to be around.

Danny immediately caught on to the urgency when he saw

Catherine's face. Pulling Síne by her arm, "Come on," he said before getting in the backseat of the compact car. "What's going on?" he asked his sister, alarmed.

"I'll explain on the way," she answered.

Bowen interrupted any possible questioning from Danny by saying "Go drive by your home."

"What? I thought you said that—"

"I know what I said, just go."

When they reached the road that turned around the corner to Catherine's home, Bowen urged her to stop the car at a distance and turned sideways in his seat. "Give me your phones," Bowen demanded from Catherine, then Danny. With both in hand, he left the car.

"What is he going to do with them?" Danny asked.

"How should I know?" Catherine said half to herself as she watched him walking away. She could smell the heavy stench of smoke filtering into the car already.

A few minutes passed and he returned. "We need to go now," he remarked nonchalantly.

Catherine began to drive. "Can we have our phones back now?"

"No, I had to get rid of them."

"What!" Danny nearly shouted.

"They needed to be burned with the rest of the house if they're going to believe you're dead . . ."

Catherine hadn't thought of that. Luckily she kept a small address book in her purse for emergencies, though she hadn't imagined it would be needed for quite this reason. Danny was infuriated as Bowen explained what had happened. Catherine could see the huge flames as they passed her destroyed home. The warm sting of tears welled in her eyes, but she quickly wiped them away. Catherine drove discreetly around the commotion of the fire and firefighters. The blaze of the fire quickly faded behind them in the rear view mirror as they sped away unnoticed. The home she had built for herself over the years was burning to the ground. It felt symbolic somehow. Catherine felt another pang of anger but forced herself to focus on the blank road laid out before her now.

* * *

By morning of the next day Catherine was exhausted. Danny was the first to fall asleep in the backseat, and one by one they nodded off. The four journeyed on, following Bowen's directions to the mountain. Eventually they came to the point where the rest of the way had to be made on foot. Catherine and Danny were not exactly looking forward to this. Though they liked hiking on occasion, they did not much like the idea of searching an unmapped mountain.

"Yes this was the mountain, it took days to get here from where I lived. We go across," Bowen said pointing at the lengthy stretch of overgrown land as they exited the car. "Then at the foot of the mountain there should be a small forest. Once we get through that we can make our way up to the caves."

Catherine was especially unhappy at this announcement. She wasn't prepared for any of this. The air was chilly, and her thin jacket wasn't made for this kind of activity. All she could do was rely on the outdoor trek to keep her warm. Before leaving Bella's car in the open, she looked through it to make sure no valuables were visible and surprisingly came upon a pair of hiking boots and a sleeping bag in the trunk. She quietly thanked Bella over and over again for the unforeseen help. Bella and Catherine's shoe size was just about a match, and Catherine hugged them generously to her chest before putting them on and catching up with the others.

"How long do you think it will take for us to get through the forest?" Catherine asked Bowen.

"Probably late tonight. We should keep walking until we get to the foot of the mountain."

"Do you think Bella's car will be all right there for a couple of days alone?" she asked.

"It doesn't look like a busy road. Any passerby will most likely think it needs a tow," Bowen responded with a shrug.

Catherine nodded.

Bowen, with legs like a Viking, walked like a machine. Catherine and Danny fell behind rather quickly. Síne was ahead as well, but stayed a noticeable distance away from Bowen.

Danny stayed close to Catherine. "Once we find this staff, Bowen can cast the curse, and we can go back home?" he asked.

Catherine glanced at Síne, and only saw Conall looking back. She managed to push down the gnawing rage within her before speaking. "No, once we find the staff there's more to do before the curse can be redone. But then yes, hopefully, we can return to our lives afterward," Catherine replied. Though she wasn't so sure if it would work out that way. She wasn't exactly optimistic.

"Hm," Danny thought a moment, "What did Bella say about all of this when you borrowed the car?"

"I didn't tell her."

"You didn't tell her?" he sounded disapproving.

"I didn't have time . . ." she paused to sidestep a couple of stones in the ground. "Plus, I didn't think it was a good idea . . . all things considered."

Danny didn't say anything. Catherine didn't care if he agreed with her actions or not. She was doing the best she could do with what she had. Bella didn't need to know all the details right then, for her safety and for theirs. They continued in silence as they walked. The sun didn't emerge once, and it began to drizzle miserably, making Catherine hate the hike even more.

Bowen occasionally looked back to check on the group, mainly Catherine. He saw her mood turn. The sleeping bag she was carrying slipped out of Catherine's grasp just then, and Danny picked it up to carry for her the rest of the way. When the two siblings were talking a moment before, Bowen noticed Síne listening in, as though trying to understand a bird's chirping. Her eyes would flash awareness when she heard Conall or Bowen's name. Bowen kept a watchful eye on her, and Síne didn't try to hide from him that she knew he was doing so.

Some hours passed by the time they reached the thicket of green woods, now dripping from earlier rain. The mud was caked onto Catherine's boots and it grew harder to walk over the forest soil. Where there was no mud, the rocks and rampant sticks stabbed at her legs. There hadn't been a trail here for quite a long time, if ever. During this time Catherine sent constant telepathic thank yous to Bella for the boots.

Under the forest canopy, it was even more difficult to see where to step. Danny offered to help, but Catherine knew his clumsiness would only make it worse. Bowen looked over his shoulder and decided to walk back.

"It's not your usual hiking conditions is it?" he asked when he reached her, and offered his arm for support.

Catherine took his arm without hesitation. Bowen was sturdy like a rock, and she had seen how he walked with careless ease ahead of her.

"No, well, I don't have as much outdoor experience as you do," she replied.

Bowen simply chuckled. "It'll be nightfall shortly, and then not too much longer before we'll reach the stopping point," he remarked.

Catherine looked up at Bowen from under her jacket hood, and even in the darkness of the forest she could tell how chiseled and handsome his features were. "Thank goodness."

The group soon reached the end of the forest, and here the drizzle stopped altogether. They made a small fire with some difficulty due to the dampness, and camped for the night. Síne was being heavily watched by Danny, and Bowen. Catherine wanted nothing to do with her, though she did eye her occasionally to make sure she wasn't anywhere in her reach.

Catherine's wakefulness drifted while watching the fire figures dance across a black stage. She laid in Bella's sleeping bag on the wet ground. Thankfully it was more rock than soil, so very little water seeped through. She let her mind wander, exhausted, and fell asleep quickly. She slept soundly only for a short time since her dreams were filled with nightmarish imaginings. Her eyes snapped open, and she woke a second later to see the fire low and some moonlight cascading down one side of the mountain causing a gloom amongst the previous pitch black that was the night around them. Her heart had been pumping harder in her chest, and she felt sweat cling to her neck and shirt. Relieved the dream world was closed to her now, she slowly sat up and saw Bowen sitting across from her behind the fire. Danny was still sleeping a few feet away, leaning against a standalone tree. Síne was somewhere in between them, sitting alone and showing them only her back. Holding her knees to her chest she rocked back and forth, gazing into the distance. Catherine found it curious, guessing it was a side effect of madness.

"You should sleep more if you can. We have a hard climb up the mountain trail very soon," Bowen said.

Catherine pulled herself completely out of the sleeping bag. "I'll be fine," she replied, knowing that she and Bowen had very different ideas of what a trail was.

"You really should try."

"I can't sleep anymore; I'll feel worse if I do. But thanks," Catherine reassured him.

Bowen nodded.

"Did you sleep?"

"Some."

"And her?" she jerked her head in Síne's direction.

He looked over at the gray balled up figure. "Some," he repeated. "You and Danny aren't used to this kind of living, you need more sleep than we ever needed in our life before."

"And now? It's the same?"

"A bit. Having not slept for centuries under the curse, it is strange to need to again."

"I see," Catherine said, trying to imagine what that would be like. She quietly got up and stretched before rolling up her bag and smoothing her hair as best she could.

"You could never not be beautiful," he said softly when he noticed her fussing over it.

Catherine stopped and looked at him in surprise. Just then, Danny stirred from sleep. "My back!" he complained, rolling on all fours in pain.

"I told you not to sleep that way," Bowen said, shaking his head. "Too soft," he muttered.

The group managed to ready themselves for the long haul, then began the journey up the mountain. Catherine left the sleeping bag behind, figuring it was best to have both hands free. Bowen led the way again, with Danny and Catherine taking up the end while they spoke.

"Are you doing okay?" Danny asked.

"Are you?" she turned to him.

"Better than you, I think," he said gently.

"Probably so," she sighed.

A few minutes passed as they dodged sharp rock and brush. Danny took Catherine's hand in his.

"Did you ever find your lost earring, the one Kathleen was looking for?"

"No," Catherine replied, surprised by both Danny's random show of affection, and at her own forgetfulness. "It doesn't matter now, the other one's burned up at the house any way . . ."

Danny squeezed her hand, then let go to steady himself as they hiked on. Within ten minutes their calf muscles were screaming from the burn of the uphill walk. They both cursed under their breath at themselves for not being in better athletic shape. Bowen and Síne seemed to sprint up the mountain and were obviously holding back for their benefit. Hours passed, and it didn't seem like much progress had been made. Out of breath and exhausted, they took frequent breaks. On one such break, Bowen announced it wouldn't be too far now.

"To the top?" Danny asked looking doubtfully at the length left up to the jagged peak.

"No, to the caves. It's buried *inside* the mountain," Bowen called back.

The wind grew harsher as they climbed higher, but Catherine welcomed it. She was sweating like an animal. Grateful for each cold slap of air against her skin, she continued on. The sky was overcast again, though the clouds did not threaten rain. From where they now stood they couldn't see their campsite because of the rocky terrain and uneven layers of the mountain. Still, the view was fantastic. Catherine could just make out the trace of road where they had parked Bella's car.

As they sat down to rest on grassy area before the last long lengthy climb. Catherine massaged her feet. Bella's hiking boots were apparently relatively new, and she was getting the grand honor of breaking them in.

"It's time," Bowen announced to them.

Catherine and Danny begrudgingly stood up, and moved around a boulder to continue a rocky path up the mountain side.

"Where are you two going?" Bowen stopped them "It's this way now," he pointed to the left to a smaller path, more overgrown with shrubbery.

"But that's leading down . . ." Danny said, puzzled.

They followed behind the two ancient Celts and found relief in the downward slope. As they rounded a bend, they stumbled onto another breathtaking view between tall leafy trees that lined the "path." Rocks that had fallen over the centuries occasionally blocked the way, and they found they had to do some fancy maneuvering to get around them without falling over the steep drop off. Catherine glanced down once, and felt dizzy at the idea.

Síne always stood apart from the rest of them, and would lean against something with a scowl when they were busy working as a team. Catherine preferred this anyway. The rest of the way became darker as the trees grew closer to the mountain wall and leaned over top of them. At one point they had to hunch over to duck through, and Catherine felt like Alice in Wonderland trying to make her way through giant flowers. Though these plants pricked her as she passed.

Finally the group made it through the wild tunnel. They now stood at what appeared to the two siblings to be a dead end. But the two Celts showed no sign of worry. Catherine stopped short and looked curiously at Bowen. He glanced down at her and smiled.

"It's through here," he said. He took her hand as they walked one step further and he turned his body sideways. Catherine followed suit, and the rock seemed by magic to open and reveal a few feet of a path that led to the gaping black mouth of a cave. The illusion of the dead end was astounding to Catherine, and she glanced back to see Danny following behind Síne with an equally amazed expression.

"We're not too far now. The staff should lay within a carving in the cave wall. And if we go deeper we will find the most recent remains of my people."

"Why did they do it that way?" Catherine asked, her inner archeologist coming out.

"To show respect to each one before burying the next," he replied.

"I see," she nodded, fascinated.

With his free hand Bowen leaned over and picked up a thick wooden stick amongst the overgrown shrubs.

"I have a light," Danny stepped forward, and as Bowen held the stick steady, he lit it ablaze with his lighter.

Bowen tightened his hold on Catherine's hand, and she did the same. They entered the darkness using the torch as a guide. To her surprise the passage felt airy and didn't have a stuffy smell. It was also surprisingly dry. As her eyes adjusted, she could see that the ensuing cave room was very large and open; no holes or underground rivers to trap them here. Still, she had seen enough movies to be wary of where she stepped, and she followed Bowen very carefully.

He led them through the chamber entrance, and Catherine could see what appeared to be marble lining. She couldn't see the tall ceiling for it went high up past the light and into blackness. Catherine felt like a small insect, but as they continued the big passage turned into a very comfortable hallway, which then turned into a small passage where they crawled on their hands and knees. This suddenly opened into a large hall, and it was here that they saw the first remnants of a culture long gone.

"Here," Bowen uttered to himself with reverence in his voice. Indeed, the shrine emitted an aura that demanded respect. As though disobedience would incite the dead to strike vengeance. He glanced back at Síne who looked appalled at the remnants of her enemy as the group passed the possessions and bodily remains of generations of holy men. Danny simply stared at the objects on the ground, and the drawings on the wall as they passed. Catherine was in awe, knowing that she was the first set of human eyes to see all of this for perhaps thousands of years.

Suddenly Catherine thought she heard a noise. She snapped her head back. It sounded like it came from behind Danny.

"Did you kick something?" she asked in a hoarse whisper, stopping Bowen with a tug of her arm.

Danny shook his head, too unnerved to speak.

The top of Catherine's arms tingled, and that familiar bad feeling swelled within her. Bowen swung her arm gently to bring her out of thought. She could see his smile in the light reflecting off his face. He turned back around and began to walk again with Catherine in tow. She took a deep breath and followed, though the tingle remained, nudging her along the way.

They passed many generations of men. Catherine had to remember that people did not live very long centuries ago. Bowen could feel her fidget, and squeezed her hand as he said quietly, "Soon." Finally, the passage stopped short. Bowen looked around and found several staffs, each resting within their own space carved into the wall. One staff, in particular, captured his gaze, and he reached for it in awe. Catherine couldn't see it clearly in the light, but he handed it to her before taking her free hand in his as they turned to face the way they came. She could feel how cool and smooth it felt between the bony ridges. From its weight, she could tell that the priest who owned this was very tall, just like Bowen. It reached high above her head and stabbed at her sides and arms until she learned to hold it better.

"It didn't go too much further after your priest. Do you think they moved on to another part of the mountain?" Catherine asked Bowen, her voice slightly above a whisper.

"No, I think it ended there. Sometime between after I was gone and a century or two later when my people faded away. Any surviving descendants forgot our culture, and melded with others. That's why so little is known now." Bowen's quiet voice trembled slightly.

Catherine looked back briefly, wondering how deep the

mountain's passages went. Imagining all the secret tunnels made her more curious than alarmed. She suddenly understood the sport of caving, though Catherine was thankful she didn't have to wriggle through any more low passages, or if they were deeper, run into potential floods.

Danny waited for Bowen and the others to pass him so the group could go back out in the order they came. Bowen went with the torch, and Catherine passed Danny with Síne after. Reaching the cave entrance again, they found their eyes painfully blinded by the overcast sky. Bowen and Síne recovered quickly, but the siblings were in pain for quite some time. Until then, they had no idea just how sunny it actually was on a cloudy day.

Disposing of the torch, and letting go of Catherine's hand, Bowen stepped away from the group. Catherine sat down on a stone to relieve her blistered feet. She examined the ancient staff in her hands. In the light she could see it clearly. It appeared to be made of ceramic pieces fastened together, which explained the rough sharp points that stabbed her and the smoothness in between. The bottom looked worn with use, but the areas where hands had grasped it looked smoother still, leading up to the top, where a small knob seemed notched to hold many a jewel or stone. Catherine tried to imagine a white robed priest holding the staff, standing tall and noble. She enjoyed running the tips of her fingers on the smooth surface as she followed along with her eyes. The blackness of it overwhelmed the entire object. It was truly a work of art.

As Catherine examined the relic, she suddenly heard an airy whistle followed by a cracking noise. She looked up at Danny and felt herself sinking back, then falling. The stone she sat on was giving way. She heard Danny yell for her as she fell, and in a quick second managed to reflexively grab hold of several small trees and sharp bushes which cut her mercilessly but slowed her fall. The staff had caught at an angle against a tree and she grabbed at either side until she was hanging against the cliff. Dirt fell on her from the small landslide she created on her way down. She had tumbled a very short distance, but her blood pumped hard in her ears.

"Catherine?!" Danny screamed from above.

Catherine couldn't move, other than dangle. Every time her body swung she felt a horrible pang, and thought that moment would be her last. She couldn't say a word, she could barely breathe, so she hung helplessly. Focusing her weight and hands on the staff, she struggled to keep hold. Her upper body was not her strong point, her arms were already exhausted, and she wondered how much longer she could last. Unable to look up or down she stared stupidly at the ground.

"I'm coming down to get you!" Danny shouted. He had never been afraid of heights. As a boy, he would throw himself from trees, and cause great stress to all who had been forced to watch. Since boyhood, he had matured to skydiving and other thrill-seeking skills. Rock climbing was nothing to him.

Though Catherine was terrified for him since it was clearly a very unstable area, she knew he was her only hope. She was no acrobat, and she was paralyzed by fear. She considered her imminent death, and wished Danny would leave her to it and not risk himself. A light in the back of her mind reminded her she would see Kathleen again, and that this torture would end. But then she remembered she had to live to help Bowen. She couldn't leave him to fix her mistake. The mistake he had tried to prevent. Catherine slowly came back to the here and now, trying to keep her grip on the staff whose smoothness she had quickly grown to resent. She tried to hold still, and keep her hands inward so as not to accidentally slip off. Held tightly to the sharp protruding edges, her hands began to feel like they were being cut in slow motion.

Unable to see her brother from her dangling position, she

listened desperately for anything and finally heard movement along with gravel and dirt tumbling down around her. Squinting her eyes, she held her breath and waited. Within less than five minutes, Danny slid to a stopping point by hitting the tree she relied on for survival. Catherine's breath escaped loudly as her eyes flew open. "I'm here!" he said, as he made grunting noises trying to steady himself.

Still unable to look up, Catherine wondered what he planned on next.

"Listen to me, Catherine, when I say so you need to let go."

Catherine slowly shook her head. He was talking crazy. There was no way she was just going to let go.

"Only one hand. I'll be there to grab it," he said firmly.

That was certainly less crazy, though she had doubts as to her ability to do as he asked. Catherine quickly wondered how Danny was going to pull this off. She knew they didn't have any rope with them. She worried once again for his safety.

"I'm going to say 'now' in a sec, and that's when I need you to let go of the staff with one hand, okay?" He sounded unsettled by her silence. Though he clearly understood she was in some state of shock, he worried that she might completely freeze up.

Catherine waited for Danny to give the word, and she tried to prepare herself for the sudden death that might follow. *Wait!* she thought in a panic. He didn't say *which*! *Which hand!* she mentally screamed, and cursed herself inwardly that she couldn't break her silence. She thought madly. Which would he reach for? He knew she was right handed, but maybe he wasn't able to get to her right hand? She couldn't possibly be sure either way from where his voice came above her, for the tree was thin where it didn't block sound, and the gravel came from both sides when it fell. She would have to take the chance and hope he would know. Catherine waited.

"Now!" Danny shouted. In two seconds Catherine let her right hand fall off the staff, causing her to swing so her head could look up. No longer frozen, she stretched to reach as far as she could.

Catherine gasped in horror, seeing now that he wasn't reaching for her right hand! This was the end of her life, and she only hoped it would end quick. She had already doubted it would be painless in her situation. Her body didn't have a chance to fall though, for Danny grabbed the staff as it swung upward, and Catherine held to it with steadfast strength. As her body limply hung, relying entirely on the staff, she used her free hand to grab above her other hand for a more stable chance.

"Climb up! You've got to move!" Danny was clearly struggling with the weight.

Somehow, with much effort, Catherine now managed to move up the staff until she reached Danny's hand, and he grabbed on with a slap. Danny was steadying himself on a groove in the stone and leveraging with the tree, so his whole upper body could be used to save his sister. Catherine was pulled up to him, and he moved her arms to hold his middle from behind. She still held the staff uncomfortably between her arm as it rubbed painfully through her clothes. Like a skilled animal, Danny climbed carefully up the rock, with Catherine perched on his strong back. Within a short time, they found themselves scrambling over the edge, to lay breathlessly on the ground.

When they had both caught their breath, Danny looked over with mixed anger and gratitude. "What the hell happened?"

Catherine finally found her voice, though it came out small and weak. "I'm surprised that didn't break . . ." she mumbled, referring to the ancient staff. Then turning her head, "I don't know, I heard something crack from above me, like a twig," she gulped some air as she stared back at the sky above, "and then I felt the rock give way . . . it happened so fast, I couldn't do anything."

Danny's anger faded after a moment, but he furrowed his brow. Catherine watched him stand and walk towards the tree and stone where she had fallen. She felt her hands sting and brought them up to examine the damage. They were incredibly sore, and appeared cracked and bleeding in places. She pulled herself up to a seated position and winced in pain when she attempted to push off the ground. Both her wrists were apparently also very strained. When she finally did find the strength to stand, though her legs were wobbly, she managed to look around for Bowen, and grew concerned with each passing moment she didn't find him. She was surprised he hadn't heard the screaming, and also upset he hadn't come to their aid. He shouldn't be far enough away to not have heard some of the commotion.

"The noise," Danny said from over by the tree, looking up closely.

"Yeah?" she asked, returning from her brief search.

"Was there a shooting noise before it?"

"You mean like a gun? No," she said confused.

"No, like an arrow," and Danny pulled a sharp crossbow bolt out of the now damaged bark of the tree.

Catherine came nearer and they looked at each other before pulling a small piece of paper wrapped around and fastened to the bolt. There was a handwritten message, which at first was difficult to read since its thick black ink had bled into the paper in several spots.

"I have your friend. If you want him alive, I want the relic. You have until tomorrow afternoon," the note said. As they rolled the paper to its end, they saw a strange set of directions where the kidnapper apparently wanted them to go.

The siblings looked up at each other in alarm. "Bowen!" Catherine said.

"Who could it be?" Danny asked, shaking his head in disbelief.

"Someone was following us! I knew I heard something strange before . . ." she remarked, infuriated with herself for ignoring her instincts.

"What are we going to do?" Danny asked, rereading the message.

"We have to go. What choice do we have?"

Danny looked worried but nodded.

Taking the message and bolt from Danny, Catherine turned towards the way out as she placed them in her jacket pocket. "Let's get moving back down the mountain." She was determined to save Bowen, whatever it took.

"Wait! Oh no!" Danny shouted.

Catherine jumped, "What is it?"

"Where is Síne?"

The two siblings looked around in sudden realization. Síne had used her chance to escape. Catherine sighed as frustration gathered on Danny's face. With the Gardai thinking the two siblings had died in the fire, they would have assumed the same for Síne since Danny was her surety. Therefore, Danny wasn't going to be in trouble with them unless he went back home. Catherine couldn't worry about that right now. She had to focus on Bowen and their current predicament.

"Well, what am I gonna do now?" he said.

"We can't do anything until we save Bowen! We have no idea which direction Síne went anyway . . ."

Danny marched off ahead of her without saying anything. Before following, Catherine picked up the ancient staff from the ground where she had left it. Her cracked and partially cut palms would ache but she accepted it without complaint, and they left together to trace their way back down the mountain.

CHAPTER FOUR

DANNY CONTINUED TO fume as the hours passed. By the time they reached the bottom of the mountain, night had fallen. It was evidently faster for them to travel down than up. Catherine couldn't tell if that was because both of them were deep in thought, or if it truly was less strenuous. The rocks still hurt under her blistered feet, but she was getting used to it. Holding onto the staff helped her too. She felt like a regular relic hunter strolling along with it in her hands.

Catherine smiled to herself as Uncle Mickey suddenly came to mind. She wondered how he would react to recent events. "You're having adventures now!" she could hear him excitedly say. Though she was not so enthused about her situation, Catherine knew he would have relished the chance to see the ancient druid relics and remains that were now hidden again in the caves. The thought of her uncle saddened her. She hadn't thought of him for a while. She hoped she had inherited his sense of direction, since she had no idea whether she was reading Bowen's kidnapper's directions correctly. How they were going to pull this off, she couldn't say. But she kept walking forward, confident she would know what to do when the time came.

The two decided to press on through the night, stopping only to look at the directions by the small flame of Danny's handy lighter. They were led to circle the mountain's side far into the much larger and thicker woods hidden there. Before they entered though, Catherine looked back at the steep slope of the mountain and trembled at the memory of falling. She could see its looming silhouette against the dark blue sky. Now, they trudged in the darkness trying to avoid trees, and kept in a straight line together as best they could.

"We're going to get lost in here . . ." she mumbled.

"Let's stop until the sun comes up," Danny suggested.

Though Catherine couldn't imagine such thick woods ever being touched by sunbeams, she quickly agreed. Resting their backs against the same tree, they watched and waited. An hour, maybe two, passed. Catherine found herself nodding off, and eventually fell asleep altogether. She saw a blanket of quiet softness behind her eyes, the pleasant sleep she was seeking even in her crouched position. It didn't last long though, and she awoke with stiff legs, her head leaning on Danny's broad shoulder. He nudged her a few times to confirm she was awake. Tiny streams of light were shining through the forest, providing enough light that they could see for a distance further than an inch from their faces. Dawn danced across the plants in front of her, and she watched its performance for a few moments, allowing the remaining calm and silence to drift away from her as she slowly awoke to life again.

"We should go," Danny said, standing up as Catherine raised her head.

"Hold on," she said, trying to slowly stretch up, her legs aching from the crouch.

Danny walked off to relieve himself, while Catherine finished her stretch and took out the ransom note for reexamination. From what she could tell, they shouldn't be too far now. Somewhere in the middle of nowhere was apparently where this madman had marked the spot. Catherine didn't like that the location seemed very plainly to give the kidnapper an advantage. He could easily kill them both without getting close, once they walked into his very likely trap.

Danny returned, and they continued walking for a time while Catherine thought of what to do when they arrived. Just before she was going to share her concerns with her brother, she thought she smelled something that made her nose twitch.

"What's that smell?" she asked, stopping to take in a good whiff.

"There's no reason to be rude, I'd shower if I could," Danny replied irritably.

Catherine waved her hand in the air with a serious expression, "No, not that . . ." her brows furrowed while her tired mind tried to place the smell. Danny took some steps away, sniffing carefully and looking around as he went. But Catherine stood perfectly still. Whatever the smell was, it was on the tip of her nose, prancing in front of her eyes. Then it clicked.

"It's smoke," she said suddenly. She could recognize that smell anywhere. It was a nostalgic smell from childhood, and reminded her of the last night she saw Uncle Mickey. His little home was filled with the smell of his cozy wood burning stove.

Danny looked back at his sister, "I don't see any smoke, I'm sure it isn't a forest fire. It's too damp . . ."

"No, no, it's chimney smoke. It can't be too far. Come on, let's find it!" Catherine said grabbing her brother's arm with an excited squeeze before rushing off ahead, following her nose.

The day was steadily getting brighter as they hurried on, following the crisp scent of firewood. The smell was almost lost to them a few times, noticeably fading away as they went the wrong way, but each time they found it again and managed to follow its reaching grasp. The invisible guide finally led them to its place of origin. Catherine and Danny could now see the smoke ascending from what would have passed as one of the many trees from far off, but instead was clearly a man-made structure carved into a peaceful tree. It was surrounded by the camouflage of natural plant growth.

The two hid themselves when they realized they had found what they were looking for. The last thing they wanted was to be spotted. Catherine was sure this was where their enemy was lurking, or at least where he made preparations. Her heart raced at the thought that Bowen may actually be waiting for his rescue inside.

"Do you see a door?" asked Danny quietly.

Looking at the tree structure, Catherine couldn't see any visible entrance. Craning her neck, she could see a few holes, mostly at the top of the trunk. She wondered if any were made into windows, from which Bowen could be looking out right now.

"No, but there's got to be one somewhere . . ."

Danny adjusted his stance, "I'm gonna go around the other side to see if there's anything." Before she could stop him he was gone. Catherine, uncertain what to do, settled into her position and waited.

Suddenly a strange noise echoed around the kidnapper's tree, and she instinctively crouched lower while peering over the shrubbery. A metal screeching rang out as a piece of the wooded structure directly ahead opened. It appeared that metal plating had been formed in a crude metal door frame in the tree. Out stepped an older man, his facial features at first hidden in shadow by a dark brown snap brim fedora which looked a bit weather worn. Underneath, long graying hair hung limply down to his shoulders. He was wrapped in some sort of handmade grass cloth that puffed out from his body and scraped against the ground as he walked. It hit his faded tall black boots, which completed the unusual ensemble, and they clunked the metal of the door before silencing on the dirt.

The man stretched himself backward to maneuver his grassy cloak, revealing his face to the light. Catherine's eyes widened, as she repressed the urge to gasp. It was the old man she had run into at the museum! A dozen questions flooded her mind. Who was this creepy man, and why was he following her? The familiar stranger finished his fiddling around and then reached to shut his secret door. He walked away from his apparent lair at an appallingly slow pace, which after some distance made him look like walking moss until he disappeared into the scenery altogether.

Catherine breathed in relief as she stared out, trying to take in all she saw. Danny startled her as he showed up just then. "I didn't find anything, but did you see that grass man? He must be our guy." He pointed in the direction of the stalker.

Catherine wasted no time. "Danny, that man followed us somehow. I collided with him outside the museum the day before we left! He's obviously dangerous, we must hurry!" she gripped and shook his arm.

Danny was surprised but said nothing, and they both quietly sped to the side of the tree structure. Hoping not to alert the clearly trained hunter now lurking in the woods, they stood next to the invisible door. Catherine scanned the wood climbing up to the tall top.

"This is where the door was," she said, her hands feeling carefully, searching along the real and manufactured bark.

Now that she was up close, she could feel and see the difference. Danny was close beside her as they tried to find a latch or secret button of some kind that would open the door. As the minutes passed, Catherine grew increasingly more alarmed. Though she knew the hunter was on his way to break his word to them by clearly not exchanging Bowen at the meeting place his note indicated, she worried about eyes watching them, or his return at any moment.

Bending down now, Catherine felt along where the ground met the bark. Just when she was about to give up hope, and risk yelling Bowen's name, her thumb found a small springy button. Danny caught the thick door as it sprung open.

Holding onto the staff, Catherine pulled the door open and hurried inside. It was dark at first, but she kept moving and her eyes adjusted quickly. Along the wall were many different hunting weapons. Rope, and other hunting gear was carelessly thrown on the ground, or lay across furniture. She saw that the warm fire was coming from a wood-burning stove in the corner of the living area, obviously the cause of the chimney smoke they had followed there. A tea set was sitting on a low table nearby, clearly just used and left unfinished as if the user had lost track of time. There was a mess of clothes, and trash spread all over on one side of the room, and Catherine silently condemned the hunter, imagining what his slovenly appearance must look like up close. She then spotted a flight of stairs and quickly climbed up, searching the few rooms at the top. They all appeared to be empty.

Already feeling on edge at the thought of the hunter returning at any second, she was devastated not to find Bowen. Wild thoughts rushed through her mind and her hands shook. What if he was already dead? That sinking feeling hadn't left, and now at the vivid thought of his demise, the pit of her stomach felt like it was too full of burning liquid pain ready to rip her to pieces. Finally terrified beyond control, Catherine gave in to her inner urge and shouted his name. No answer. She tried again, repeating his name several times, with a prayer hanging on each syllable she uttered. Danny followed suit while he examined each room a second and third time, weaving in and out of them.

Just when she was going to give up everything, and fall apart completely, Catherine heard something. Danny continued to yell. She hunched over slightly, straining her ears to catch the sound again.

"Shh!" she hissed at her brother, and Danny's voice finished echoing off the walls.

Silence lingered as she waited desperately, until suddenly the two heard a faint reply. Like owls, both their heads swiveled in what they thought was the direction of the cry, and they ran towards it. They found themselves in one of the rooms they had already checked. Sure the sound came from this room, they stood still and waited again.

"Catherine?" the voice said faintly.

Catherine bolted. It was coming from the corner of the room. "How?" she said under her breath, her eyes searching wildly. She pressed her ear against the wall and listened.

"Bowen?" Danny said towards it.

"Danny, help."

The two siblings saw a small knob right above the baseboard of the room. They looked at each other briefly. Then Danny pulled at it, creating a crack in the wall. What looked like fresh white walls now crumbled at the crack's seam before them to reveal a door obviously painted over. Catherine helped her brother pull the heavy door open completely. As light flooded within, Bowen looked up at them, gasping for air.

Catherine forgot herself and reached desperately for him. "Bowen! Oh thank—"

"There's no time," Bowen said, interrupting Catherine sharply.

"What?" Danny said practically dragging Bowen out of the hole in the wall.

"He knows you're here."

"No, we watched him leave," Catherine whispered.

"He's watching this place; he can see every room. I saw his phone with the camera, before he buried me in that hole," Bowen said.

"So the hunter isn't far . . ." Catherine gripped the top of her head.

"We have to run!" Bowen struggled to stand on his cramped legs. He had been smashed from all sides for hours and hours.

"Can you?"

"Yes, in a moment, but you shouldn't wait for me."

Danny looked shocked. "We just risked everything to get you back. We're not leaving you now!"

Catherine looked Bowen over as they waited. Even now he looked impossibly powerful. "How did he get you?" she asked.

Bowen inhaled deeply, then exhaled while he rubbed the back of his legs. "All I remember is hearing something behind me, then everything went black. I woke with a terrible head pain, and it was dark outside. I remember I was outside still because I saw trees and stars moving above me," he stood up straight then.

"Why didn't you run away?" Danny asked, as he looked quickly behind him.

"I couldn't move most of my body, he must have drugged me," Bowen answered. "The next thing I remember was this room as he pushed me into the wall hole. Before he shut the wall, I saw his phone. When my strength returned I couldn't reopen it, and the air started to thin."

"We must go. Can you move now?" Catherine asked.

"Yes!" Bowen's voice sounded hoarse as he took a few steps. They raced for the door.

"Do you know who he is?" Danny asked.

"No," Bowen replied.

As they neared, the door slammed open. They halted. A withered man stood in the threshold. The hunter was back. Catherine's breath was caught somewhere inside her, and she felt trapped. She squeezed the ancient staff, prepared to defend herself.

The old man coughed to clear his throat. "Aye, I knew you'd find him," he voiced gruffly, looking straight at Catherine. He kept still otherwise but looked her up and down briefly. She could see his eyes gave a kind of twinkle of recognition as he focused on the staff in her hand.

In one of his hands Catherine saw he had a lit cigar. He brought it up to his mouth, and his eyes squinted ever so slightly.

"Your hair," little puffs of smoke came out from between his lips. "You have the same shade of red as him," he grumbled, the cigar bouncing slightly with the movement.

Catherine's brow furrowed. The man waved his hand as if to apologize for not clarifying. "Mick," he said.

"Mick?" she mouthed silently.

"If only . . ." he trailed off, smoke billowing out of his mouth and scaling up like a chimney. "I think if you hadn't shown up that day he would've gone through with it," he said.

Then it dawned on her. "Uncle Mickey? How did you know my uncle?"

"He occasionally acquired relics that I wanted. If I threatened him he usually would give me anything I asked for." He paused to blow out more smoky air. "However, when I wanted special information regarding a particularly high priced item, he wasn't sure about giving it up. I seemed to be close to getting it out of him, just a little more pressure . . ." his voice sounded pained. "When you and your family arrived I even threatened you, but that had the opposite effect I expected, and he refused. And well, you know what happened, don't you," he explained, tugging on the cigar with a few fingers.

Danny looked furious as it came together, and Catherine stood wide eyed as sadness and anger rolled up from her stomach and into her chest.

"He wasn't making me much more money anyway," the man finished.

"*You* killed him," Catherine said, as if saying it out loud was going to confirm it.

"You're so alike, it's amazing," he mumbled, then coughed deeply in his throat once before saying louder "amazing as what you've got in your hand there." He pointed to the ancient staff clenched tightly in Catherine's grasp.

"Give it to me now, and I'll let you leave without further harm."

Catherine clenched her fist. Her arm and other muscles were still sore, but all her strength came back in a surge of adrenaline.

"Now," the hunter held his gaze on Catherine. "Come on then," his fingers wiggled from his outstretched hand.

Bowen and Danny were still. Bowen looked at Catherine, trying to gauge her next move. Danny was about to snap. Suddenly everything happened at once. Danny rushed at the old man in a fit of rage, the shape of his hands formed into claws, his voice screeching. And Catherine, ignoring her damaged hands, took the staff up over her head and swung with all her might. Bowen, reacting quickly to the sibling's outbursts, lunged at Catherine to push her away from harm. As she tipped with him into a chaotic fall, the staff hit the wall and shattered into thousands of pieces.

Catherine and Bowen quickly looked up from where they fell to see the staff destroyed on the ground before them. Danny was still fighting the hunter, who fought back desperately. His crossbow was knocked off his back as Danny attacked skillfully with his fist, leaving him to rely on his not-as-trained body strength. Arms flailed as he struggled to get Danny off of him long enough to find something to fight back with. He managed to do that once, which he viewed as his only chance, and took it. Wrapping a hand on a decorative pot just inside the doorway along a shelf, he smashed it on Danny's head. Danny released him as he fell to the ground.

Catherine and Bowen stood together in one motion, their eyes locked on Danny, and went to him. They all tumbled through the door frame into the sun outside.

"Danny!" Catherine exclaimed wild with worry, and she pawed at the back of his neck and head where he had been struck.

"Are you all right?" Bowen asked with a steady voice, though he looked concerned.

Danny winced at the pain, kneeling on the ground where he had caught himself. He couldn't answer in the midst of his blinding pain. Meanwhile, realizing the hunter was still a problem, Catherine rapidly looked up to fend him off. But to her surprise, he was gone. Nowhere to be seen, the old man had fled the scene with his crossbow. She assumed he was dismayed at the destruction of his prize, and left to nurse his wounds. This was her hope anyway, so she kept a lookout in case.

"I think so," Danny finally replied.

Bowen looked him over and stated he might have a concussion, but besides little scrapes and bruises he should be okay. Danny waved a hand in thanks as he massaged the base of his skull seeking relief. Catherine's breathing became normal again as she looked down at her brother, then over at Bowen. She felt relief now that the three of them were together again.

While Danny and Bowen were gathering themselves, Catherine noticed some glass and clay shards from the staff had caught in her clothes and hair. She shook them out as carefully as possible.

"We need to leave!" Bowen said suddenly, peering alertly through the woods.

The siblings agreed quickly and moved in unison. After maintaining a quick pace for some time, the three soon found themselves walking through the woods as if they were simply out for an afternoon stroll. None of them voiced it, but they were wondering what to do from there.

A sudden bite of cold in the air made the hair on their arms prickle, but somehow Catherine felt a warm sensation in her hands. She held them up, noticing finally that they were covered in blood. The tussle must have reopened her wounds from the fall. She and Bowen examined them together.

"What happened?!" Bowen reached for them carefully.

"It happened after he took you," she answered calmly.

"These are gashes. How did you do this?"

"I fell off the cliff by the cave entrance," she said, flinching as his fingers neared the cuts.

"These need to be cleaned," he said, "they've been torn open further." He let out an annoyed sigh. Bowen ripped two small pieces of his shirt and gently laid them across Catherine's unsightly cuts.

"This will have to do," he said as he tied them off.

"Thank you," she said. Catherine could see his sad face as he looked down at her hands, his touch very tender. "What's wrong?"

He shook his head slightly, "I'm sorry I wasn't there to help you, and that all of this happened."

Catherine shrugged and tipped her head to the side to catch his eye, "It's okay, none of that was your fault."

He smiled. Then craning his head around in all directions, examining the surrounding plant life, he came to the conclusion that he couldn't use anything there for disinfectant or antibiotics. He looked back down at Catherine's damaged hands. The blood around the wounds was clotting now, the strips of cloth combined with pressure by tying it off was helping. Though slowly, allowing for blood to continue escaping, which still concerned him. His brow furrowed. "It will have to wait to be cleaned until we get back to the supplies in the car I'm afraid."

"We're really bringing out the doctor in you today, aren't we?" Danny laughed as he walked back a few paces towards them.

"What are we going to do now, Bowen?" Catherine asked.

Danny crossed his arms, "I thought we were going back to the car from here . . ."

Bowen nodded. "We can still reset the curse," he answered her.

"But the staff is completely destroyed?" she said puzzled.

"There is another way. I don't know it though. We'll have to find it."

"Where? That sort of information must have fallen with the ruins," Danny asked.

"Exactly," Bowen stated, "I need to search my home, in the ruins."

"And where would that be?" Catherine asked, her eyebrows raised.

"It shouldn't be too difficult to find," he said, though he looked unsure.

"That's reassuring," Danny rolled his eyes, then threw up his hands. "Look you guys, I've got to find Síne, I can't go with you on this escape, slash journey, slash goose hunt."

"Alone? Are you kidding me?" Catherine said, appalled at the idea.

"It's my responsibility, and you don't have time to look for her with me *and* go do this," he replied.

Catherine couldn't believe that he would want to do such a thing. She didn't want her brother to go off alone and possibly get killed. Síne could be anywhere by now, and he had nothing to keep him alive on his search.

She opened her mouth to retort, but Bowen stepped in between them. "Stop!" his voice boomed. "I think we should worry about that when we get back to the car," he said, also irritated at Danny's persistence. "Let's get there first." He turned to walk and the others followed suit.

Silently, Bowen planned to stay awake later and watch Danny, in case he tried to slip away. Feeling everything was some way or another his fault made him more convinced that he had to keep Catherine's brother safe.

The sun was setting now, and the three finally reached the spot under the mountain where they had camped days before. Upon stopping, Bowen turned to Catherine first. "Wait here, I'll go see if I can find something small to eat nearby." He looked down at her drained face, then said, "Danny, can you find some—" he looked behind her then stopped short. Catherine at first feared the hunter was back, and whipped around to grab her brother. But Danny had disappeared.

"Danny's gone . . ." she said slowly.

Bowen balled a fist, the last of the sunlight over the trees flickering in his eyes, and cursed under his breath.

Terrified of losing her brother, Catherine's hands began to shake again. She was slowly unraveling at the seams and turned away from Bowen to grab hold of anything. When nothing was there she fell to her knees and tore at the grass. What was she going to do? She knew she couldn't go after Danny. She wouldn't know where to start, even if she had the time. But time was running out. Finally she resigned to stick to the original plan. It was her only hope to save everyone, including her foolish brother. Catherine blamed everything on Conall. As much as she tried to forget, her need to kill him wouldn't go away. She must do whatever it took, even if the road got bumpier along the way.

Catherine's eyes teared up and she pulled her knees up to her chest. Danny had gone off alone, and with a concussion no less. She prayed silently that he would be okay.

Bowen left her to sit quietly for a time to get her bearings. When he himself had cooled down a bit, he drew closer. "Can you keep going?" he asked, holding both his hands out. She reached up as he pulled her to her feet.

"Bowen, I'm worried about him," she said sadly.

"I know, I am too. But he left us. There isn't anything we can do right now that won't put you in danger too."

Catherine blinked the tears from her eyes. Then she looked at the chiseled face imploring her, and simply nodded in agreement. He gently kept one of her hands in his, and helped her move away. The two left the old campsite and continued on their way, retracing their steps back to the parked car.

* * *

It was twilight, and the small group of followers who had been trapped within the caves of Ireland for centuries with Conall still stuck together. At first, they kept to the shadows and thickly wooded areas. After some time passed, they edged into the open fields near towns. However, when Conall sent them out to steal food, or useful tools, they couldn't bring themselves to stay away long. This proved inefficient since they wouldn't get enough from one trip, and they couldn't split up individually, only in small groups.

When the followers would leave, anxiety spread through their bones with every step they took. They had forgotten the feeling of grass under their feet, and the warmth or cold of fresh air. Everything made them uncomfortable, and they felt stuck, even longing to return to the caves. The priesthood they had fought was no more. But they followed Conall still. His ravings and threats made them cower before him, showering him with promises of loyalty for fear he would otherwise kill them. No one spoke against Conall, no one dared. They couldn't trust each other not to betray them. The many groups of ancient druid rebels were tired, some of life, some of the cause, and some of Conall. Each group wanted different things from when it all began. Only the ones locked in the stone cells with Conall felt completely loyal. Still the fear remained ever present.

The rebel groups combined now to make two separate armies, one from the south and one from the north. They were going to meet soon to join forces and devour everything. No one would see them coming. Conall cherished this thought, and the thought of dragging Bowen through it all, to watch him despair. The thought made him giddy as he gnawed on a meat-covered bone, licking the grease from his lips as he watched his followers fanning out from the fire to the deep woods.

"Conall," a short gruff man appeared next to him.

Conall was happy, and leaned an elbow on one boney knee as he looked up. "What?" he said with a toothy grin.

"We didn't find Bowen, or the woman," the man said nervously.

Conall's eyes narrowed. "You . . ."

After killing the twin to Bowen's woman, and leaving them to journey back to the land of their ancient home and site of war, Conall left the gruff man with a few other loyal fighters to keep watch over Bowen. He didn't want to have to scour the land for Bowen when it came time to complete his ultimate revenge.

Conall swallowed the chewed meat he had pushed to one side of his mouth. "You didn't follow them?"

"We did—"

"Then how did you lose them!" Conall shouted.

"They had plans, as you assumed, but when we burned their home they left before we could learn where they were going," the man bowed his head in submission.

"You simply must be an idiot," Conall quietly stated. Then he stood up and threw his food into the fire. "They obviously went to find the staff." He scratched his arm at the phantom feeling of an insect.

"We'll go now—"

"No, you fool, by this time they should have already arrived."

he turned back to hover over the gruff man who was now wringing his hands. "I'll deal with this myself," Conall said.

The man wasn't sure if he was dismissed. Conall, irritated by his lingering, pushed his face away with a large greased hand. The man let out a muffled cry of pain, but didn't fight back. Conall released him with one last shove which sent him bouncing off a trunk to fall unconscious to the ground.

His appetite returning, Conall went back to eat the last piece of meat. A follower he hadn't seen since before the seclusion in the caves had unfortunately taken the last of the carcass meat for himself. The man realized his mistake and reached out to give it to Conall.

Conall stood in front of him with a frown smeared across his face. He was reminded how everything had been taken away from him, and his body swelled with rage. Conall snatched the bone while simultaneously kicking the man off his feet. His head turned sideways flat in the dirt. Conall then stomped his heel into the man's jaw. The victim flailed and screamed as his counterparts went about unfazed. Conall ground his heel down harder. He did not handle people taking his things well.

* * *

Catherine's eyes opened to see the roof of Bella's car. The car was moving and she turned her head to see Bowen driving. She blinked a few times, and rubbed the sleep from her eyes before pushing herself up with her hands to a sitting position and took in the passing landscape. The sun streamed brilliantly. Catherine vaguely remembered the long, all night trek back to the car. By dawn they had finally reached it. She practically fell into the back of the car, and drifted into a deep sleep until now.

"Where are we?" she asked hoarsely, then coughed to clear her throat, blushing.

"Far away from the mountain," Bowen answered with a

smirk, "I wanted to put some distance between us since we don't know if the hunter will come back."

"Why would he come back? The staff's pieces are scattered all over his floor."

Bowen shrugged, "I just wanted to be cautious."

"Have you been driving the whole time?"

"Yes."

Catherine stayed quiet for a while as she watched the edges of the land shift against the sky. She enjoyed being the passenger for just this reason. When current problems crawled back into her thoughts, she sighed and turned to Bowen. "So where are we going?"

"I don't know the current name, but the general region of my home. I know a few villages popped up, I just don't know which the ruins are in."

"In all these years you never went back?" she asked.

"I couldn't go near it, while under the curse."

Catherine was confused. "You *couldn't*?"

"It's hard to explain. There was a kind of barrier, invisible, stopping me if I came too close. So as time passed, and the land changed with it . . . I can't be sure of the precise location."

"Hmm. How do you plan to find out?"

Bowen frowned a bit. "We'll have to investigate."

"Ah, some digging," she said to herself, then louder "We're not going to have to dig, are we?" Catherine sat up straighter, worried.

Bowen laughed as he saw her expression in the rear view mirror, "No, we don't exactly have the ability to do that."

"What's your plan if everything is buried?"

"Nothing. There is no clear path now, just a chance. But I can't give up, I have to try." He grit his teeth.

Some time passed, and the scenery outside turned into a rural dirt road winding through thick woods, with occasional bungalows and the like in between. The sky was clouded over, making the drive a gloomy one all of the sudden. Catherine missed the sun now, and turned to watch the road ahead. Bowen looked at her in the mirror. They needed to talk. He pulled the car over and turned in his seat.

"I'm sorry about Danny," he said.

"It's not your fault," she said, then wrinkled her face. "Stop apologizing for things you can't control. It's my idiot brother's fault for going after her."

Bowen bobbed his head a bit in agreement, but didn't say anything more. "Oh!" he said, then got out of the car. Catherine wondered what he was doing. He walked around to the back and shuffled through the storage.

"What are you looking for?"

"I'm sure there's one in here . . ." he mumbled.

"One what?" she said to herself.

"Aha!" Bowen exclaimed in triumph, and hurried to Catherine's side, opening her door to reveal a first aid kit.

"Give me your hands," he ordered kindly, and she did so.

Wiping the dirt and grime off the cuts was excruciating, though Catherine never minded the sting of disinfectants. Soon she was all bandaged thanks to the skilled hands of the ancient doctor.

"I actually was the one who bought this for Bella," she pointed at the first aid kit. "It was a gift for when she went hiking, in case of emergency. Ironic that I'm the only one to use it," she added. She had noticed that he had to break the sealed wrapping to open it.

"Yes, well, I'm glad it was here," he said, and stood up with a look of accomplishment across his face.

Catherine smiled up at him, "Thank you."

"It's in me to help anyone hurt if I can," he said. His words reminded Catherine of the Hippocratic Oath. She felt safe in his care, though not only because of his convictions as a doctor. Bowen leaned down suddenly, their faces intimately close.

He gave her an unwavering look, and Catherine found herself pulled in by the strong gaze, unable to look away. "But it's also in me to help you," his voice was deep and soothing. Though she felt relaxed with him, she also felt self-conscious. She fidgeted slightly, unsure what to say. "No need to thank me," he said seriously.

Catherine was confused and struggled to hide it. Bowen could see every movement of her face, but he didn't seem to mind. The corner of his mouth twitched and then he pulled himself back. She missed inhaling his warm breath. Catherine stared, dazed, straight ahead. She felt oddly calm and watched while green leaves tossed around their branches as a breeze swept through, tossing her red hair into her eyes. As she pushed it away, she caught sight of something in the woods. Suddenly, she stiffened like a board.

Bowen had sensed something wasn't right, and was already alarmed. He stayed still, trying to gauge the danger.

"Bear," Catherine could barely mouth.

The first aid kit fell out of his hands as Bowen threw himself towards her. Pulling the car door shut behind him as he flung Catherine's legs up to push her inside the car, the door slammed just as the bear was upon them. Catherine's stomach lurched, for the millionth time, and she began to panic. Before them was an incredible creature of nature, with powerful claws that easily reached four inches long. It towered above them on its hind legs. The brown bear was terrifying as it gave its animal cry, and Catherine could see a familiar rage in the dark and frightening eyes.

There was no time to lose. The bear could destroy the car and them inside it at any moment. The bear lunged again, and Catherine screamed as Bowen scrambled to climb over the seats to the driver's seat, but in the process knocked hard against the door and window. The bear seemed to be toying with them. It growled and looked directly at Catherine a few times before surveying its enemies. The animal rocked the car a few more times, while Bowen struggled. But finally Bowen started the car and tried to drive it.

"Go!" Catherine shouted.

"I'm trying!" he said, "It won't go!"

They both watched the bear, hoping it wouldn't break through. Finally, the bear pulled itself off, and Bowen instantly sped away. Looking back, Catherine could see the bear roar wildly as it turned away and ran off back through the trees.

Catherine found her voice. "I thought bears were extinct in Ireland?!"

"They are."

After nervously biting on the tips of her fingers, she pulled her hand away from her face. "Then . . . how?"

Bowen didn't reply, he just drove. A brown bear suddenly back and roaming free in Ireland, and at that size? He wondered how and where it could have come from, and why it was attacking them.

CHAPTER FIVE

WITH EVERYTHING THAT had happened, it seemed like ages since Kathleen's death. Still, Catherine held her close in her thoughts, hidden away from the people around her. Keeping busy, all the while getting closer to trapping Conall allowed her to feel at least the illusion of peace.

The group, now couple, had been on their journey for days. Catherine had thought it a doomed quest, but trusted that following Bowen would somehow make everything work out for the best. During her most down moments all she really wanted was to kill Conall. When she was blinded by this need, she didn't care what happened to the rest of his followers. She would fantasize about different ways to do it. She'd find herself hoping for the chance to kill him before they cast the curse, but her hopes were quickly dashed by the memory of his strength. It didn't matter what happened to her; she just needed to find a way to beat him. She suspected Bowen knew what she wanted. Catherine disliked this part of herself. She hated that it was consuming her, like a blackness creeping over her with each passing day. But if she tried to let go she would begin to unravel. So she held on tighter, staying the path darkly lain out for her.

Bowen led the way. They had tarried in a few places as

Catherine used cash from her steadily emptying wallet to find and pay for them. Bella always had some stashed in the glove compartment for gas, but that too was decreasing as they drove from one small village to the next.

It was the morning in a small, mostly empty pub, and Bowen was sitting alone at a table for two. The room they stayed in the night before was located upstairs, and Catherine had slept in. Bowen was an early riser, and whenever he wasn't watching over her as she slept, he would survey the area as best he could from outside. Here he enjoyed sitting where drinks and quiet were provided in the early hours. He watched the news playing on a small television with the volume setting on low, and it left him thinking.

The news reported about a recent upswing in crime. These crimes were committed during broad daylight by "strangely clothed people." But clearly, the druids had ceased shortly after they started. The public concluded that the unsolved crimes were simply disgruntled youth or gang-related. Bowen assumed the inactivity meant they must have all united. Conall had changed their tactics. Crimes continued on, some by the normal populace, but there were also strange stories of animals or food gone missing. Some vanished before the eyes of their owner. Amongst small towns, people would gossip, and suddenly superstitions would come out of the woodwork.

Bowen was also confused by the vanishing items. At first, he wondered what they were making because it was clear they were, in fact, making something. Then he figured it was for weapons. But something still wasn't settling in his mind. He couldn't understand how they were doing all of this. He knew these people were fighters and people of many trades. Bowen flinched in his seat. Magic.

Conall must have learned before the curse, enough to build on throughout the centuries. Or else some of his followers had been involved in the druid order outside of the priesthood that dabbled in those studies. Bowen himself had learned only what was needed to draw on herbs with his healing. However, he never used it, or studied further than he needed to do his work. If Conall knew any magic, or had it at his disposal on any level, this was worrisome to Bowen. But that *must* be it; it was the only thing that explained the items vanishing in plain sight.

Bowen recalled the times he had gone to the rock to check on Conall. During Conall's fits, sometimes Bowen felt the rock shake impossibly and small pieces crumble from up high. He always thought it was his imagination, his fear of Conall's escape getting to him, and he would shake it off. But maybe his inhuman strength was real. Conall had killed Kathleen with such physical ease, as if she was a twig. No man with normal strength should have such power. It hadn't occurred to Bowen since his focus had been on Catherine.

Catherine entered just then. She looked her usual fresh self in the morning, cheeks slightly pink from the scrubbing of her face for the start of the day. Her hair was pulled back into a loose bun. Bowen thought it looked nice. He grinned to himself, remembering that he always thought she looked nice. Catherine saw his grin, and blushed as she went to get some breakfast. But Bowen's face quickly became like stone, hard and still. He still needed to mull over the bear incident.

While Catherine ate and sipped her tea, she worried about Danny. One of the worst things was knowing he couldn't get in touch with her. However, she found comfort in the fact that he knew how to contact Bella. Catherine held onto that, hoping she would hear from her brother soon. Afterward, excusing herself from the table, she used a public phone to call her friend to check in.

Bella sounded concerned but relieved to hear Catherine's

voice on the other line. She understood Catherine couldn't tell her much, but she still had questions. "Are you okay?"

Catherine joggled her head back and forth, "I'm surviving . . ."

"Is my car okay?" Bella couldn't help but ask.

Catherine smiled into the phone, "Yes, it's—" she stopped with a wince at the memory of the bear. "Well . . . there was a bear, but I think it's just a few dents."

"A bear?!" Bella paused then said slowly, "There aren't any bears in Ireland."

"I know, it doesn't make sense, but I'm telling you the truth."

Bella sighed with disbelief.

"I'll fix the car when all of this is over, okay?" Silence.

"Bella?" Catherine asked when she didn't hear a response, worried she was too angry to answer.

"Oh, sorry! I was nodding. Of course. Just . . ."

"Yes?"

"Be careful."

"The car will be fine."

"No, I mean *you*," corrected Bella.

"I promise I'll be as careful as I can be," Catherine replied. She knew Bella wouldn't feel reassured by that, but it was the best she could do right now.

The call ended and she returned to Bowen.

Before sitting down this time, she noticed one or two people eyeing her torn clothes. This morning after a quick shower, she had realized the state her clothes were in. Other than a few holes, her jacket had held up. But the rest of her clothes needed desperate attention. Catherine didn't want to give passersby reasons to remember her.

"Is something wrong?" Bowen asked.

Catherine sighed, "I need to buy new clothes."

Bowen looked her over curiously, "Do we have enough money for some?"

"I think I can find something cheap," she replied.

They left shortly after, and Catherine felt victorious when she spotted a second-hand shop close by. She hurried in and purchased clothes to change into right after. Catherine was happy to be dressed in clean clothes again. Since the wind was extra chilly today, she splurged a little more to get a better jacket. Because she did, the shop owner threw in a free scarf. It was warm and soft as she looped it around her neck. Royal blue always looked nice on her.

When Catherine returned to the car, the two continued on their quest to find the ruins of Bowen's ancient druid home. A villager in one of the small towns they visited pointed them up the road. When they came to the place, it looked the same as any other small town they had passed through. They stopped at a small eatery that served pastries and coffee, to sit and survey the passersby.

Catherine and Bowen found a table next to a large window that looked out on the village centre. Bowen pulled out her chair for her, and she nodded her thanks as she sat.

"Where did you learn these manners?" she said suddenly.

"I was not locked up in those caves, as you know. Do you think I was primitive before meeting you?" he scoffed.

"No, that's not what I meant at all. It's just—it's becoming old-fashioned to do things like open a door for a woman," she blushed.

Bowen shrugged and picked up a menu, "When chivalrous manners were a bigger part of society I thought it the right way to do things. It is one of the many downsides of the modern world now that it's fading . . ." he sighed. "We wouldn't even be in this situation if it were not for the modern world."

Catherine felt confused, "What are you talking about?"

"Before, when I told you to leave Ireland, to avoid all of this. The curse would never have been broken," he replied.

"What does that have to do with the modern world?"

"It's a modern thing—a woman defying a man," he said, gripping the menu.

Catherine replied in a harsh whisper, "So you're saying because you're a man I should have automatically just listened to you, even though you're a stranger?"

"No, but I am saying in our situation it would have been better if you *had* listened to me!" He sat back in his chair and wavered, then continued softly, "However, I should have handled it differently. I was incredibly nervous," he said, his green eyes burrowing towards her.

Catherine's temper cooled, and she just nodded in reply. They ordered shortly after that. Bowen finished first, so he took to peering out their window to examine the square.

He stood. "Please stay here," he smiled, charming as ever. That smile, mixed with the gorgeous brown curls and sparkling green eyes made Catherine agree without an explanation. She inwardly reproached herself immediately afterward.

He left Catherine to enjoy her cup of coffee as he went to observe what he could. Their quest called for a certain amount of discretion. She watched him leave through the window, and observed him for as long as he was visible.

As he disappeared around a corner, she imagined what it would be like to kiss him. She felt her face grow hot, and quickly covered her cheeks. Catherine wondered why she was attracted to him besides his looks. He was smart, charming, certainly strong and kind. All good things she liked in a man. But they argued more than she liked, though it was usually over her staying safe from harm. And she had to admit these clashes were part of the attraction. Perhaps because he was showing his strength, but he was also gentle. They had chemistry, that much was obvious. She wondered if it was obvious to everyone, or just her.

She shook her head, then turned her thoughts to the ruins. How would they find the message? What if there wasn't a message to find? She doubted there was anyone who would know, and they could hardly go around asking everyone in sight. It would make for very awkward conversation. Still she was excited to possibly find people who may have knowledge passed down over the centuries. From her studies at college and the museum that meant knowledge passed down from druids of the medieval times, not the original druids of two thousand years past. She found it a fascinating situation however terrifying the cause.

Circling her forefinger on the rim of her coffee cup, she thought of a conversation she had with Bowen. He didn't seem to want anything to do with magic, yet he was a druid. A healer in the druid community, but a druid still. From what she knew they studied for twenty years at least to become a druid of magic. Memorizing knowledge, no writings that they knew of. She wondered if Bowen would be open to telling her about it if she asked. Was he angry that his life was taken from him? Catherine couldn't tell.

Taking the last sip of her coffee, Catherine looked over to see a disheveled old woman eyeing her from a nearby table. Her hair was white and the waves were placed haphazardly around her head and hanging off her shoulders. She took in the woman's appearance with a mildly surprised expression. Her clothes looked like they had been pulled out of a suitcase that was packed weeks before and left untouched until that day. Glancing up again, the old woman's blue eyes startled Catherine with their intense color. Catherine politely nodded with a slight smile and went back to her coffee, pretending there was still some in her cup. She glanced back casually after a few moments to check, and was upset to find that the old woman hadn't stopped staring. Uncomfortable and forgetting she agreed to stay put, Catherine left some money on the table and walked out. She had a bad feeling in her gut and wanted to find Bowen as soon as possible. She couldn't see him anywhere. She walked through the village centre, intending to go to the end of the road ahead and turn back around.

A wind rushed through and caught Catherine in the face with her scarf. Moving strands of her hair off her cheeks, she noticed some residue from a snack she'd eaten at the coffee shop hadn't been wiped off entirely. Rummaging around in her jacket pockets without looking, she was in luck to find a napkin she'd stuffed there. She pulled it out and accidentally dropped it.

"Ah!" she said as she turned half around, looking down, then stooping to pick it up.

As she straightened up she stopped to see the same old woman from the shop standing a ways behind her. The old woman didn't say anything, nor did her expression change. She just stared at Catherine as she had before. As if she wanted something. Catherine stood straight up and looked around her. There were a lot of people mulling about for a small town, even if it was the village centre. Still not seeing Bowen anywhere in sight frightened her, and heightened her fears. Sensing a possible trap, she trusted her instincts and turned to walk away at a quicker pace. Looking back, she saw the old lady was still following. Was the whole town following her too? She couldn't tell. Towards the end of the string of buildings, many connected by layered stones, Catherine took off running. She quickly passed by the rest of the small shops.

After a few minutes, she was clear of the town road and away from the hustle and bustle. The road became rugged, and woodsy brush surrounded it. On one side it was quite thickly wooded, and she could barely see through the trees from the road. It looked rather dark in between the sagging stems and brush. To her other side there were a few trees and brush sprinkled on the edge of a large green field. The sun wasn't high in the sky yet. It was still early morning.

Catherine noticed no one had followed her from town. She was alone. It didn't occur to her to go back yet. Instead she continued strolling at a slow pace. As a child she remembered exploring like this during her family visits to Ireland with her grandparents. She could revel in her imagination for hours. Kathleen went exploring with her sometimes, just for the company. Catherine always thought it was only because they were twins that Kathleen felt the need to do this sort of thing. She meant to ask her one day. Now she would never know.

She pushed Kathleen out of her head and examined her surroundings. Realizing she had gone quite far, and knowing Bowen would wonder where she'd gone, she was just turning around to enjoy the walk back when something rustled in the trees ahead. Her body stiffened tightly. The sound was coming from the thick wood. The skin on top of her arms prickled. That familiar bad feeling was in the pit of her stomach, and fear crept up her back. She regretted leaving the cafe, and not heeding Bowen's words more seriously. The rustle was now between her and the road that led back to town, to Bowen.

Once again, Catherine wished she had a phone, and that Bowen had one as well. She stayed silent as thoughts whirled around in her mind. She thought if she made a run for it, whoever, or whatever would see her and chase her down. She kept her feet planted, steady on the ground and waited.

The rustling sound finally broke through the mighty wooded wall, revealing a man stumbling slightly, then he stopped in the middle of the road. Catherine remained still as she beheld the figure. He was a large Viking-like man. He was wild looking, and his unruly hair was very noticeable. Probably as a result of the chaotic brush he just fought to reveal himself. His body was clad with what appeared to be bits of armor and old worn out cloth like Conall and his followers wore from the centuries of decaying in caves and tunnels.

Seeing the giant man look at her with hunger in his eyes, Catherine could see that he was alone and happy to be so. It was clear she could not pass him safely. She felt her rising fear take hold as she stood. Her right foot made a small movement to step back, and he suddenly made for her like the wild animal she first imagined he was. She twisted in a running turn and fled. Managing to keep him far enough behind her at first, she felt exhausted rather quickly. Catherine realized she had forgotten that her endurance was next to nothing. Perhaps her time was actually up this time around.

When she was not overrun, Catherine quickly realized her pursuer was no longer behind her. She glanced behind her to be sure. No one. She paused for a momentary breather. She could see the last remnants of the town ever so far away. Fighting her temptation to run back towards it, she flew off in a sprint again. This time she went up the slightly elevated ground and crossed over to the wide open land. She didn't want to be on the road. Wherever the barbaric-looking man was, she knew he would look for her there first. She ran, panting wildly.

Catherine looked around her every so often in panic. She wished Bowen was with her. Gasping to catch her breath, her lungs burned inside her body, and her heavy breath scraped against her throat. Her thirst was overwhelming, but she stayed focused. She stopped suddenly and realized, examining the view, that she was lost. She had no idea how or even if she could circle around to get herself back to town safely, regardless of the man chasing her. There wasn't anywhere to hide either. So Catherine dropped to the ground and crawled. She crawled for what felt like too long. A sudden noise made her flinch and freeze where she was. She listened. Nothing now. Catherine still didn't move.

Suddenly the large man moved past at a speed like a wild beast from hell, quickly finding her groveling there. She popped up quick as a rabbit running from a farmer. This time she turned to face her attacker. Staring him down, she prepared to do whatever it took to survive as her adrenaline kicked in.

He took a step forward. She took a step back. He laughed haughtily at this. They repeated this sequence once more. Then before Catherine knew it, he was charging her. She dodged the first attack. The second, she grabbed his arm and flipped him over using his large weight against him. She turned to run back the way he had come, blindly hoping it would lead her to town. But he had recovered from her defensive move too rapidly. As she was running, the large shadow of the man appeared and enveloped her again. He scooped her up with one colossal arm and swung her over his half armored body. She kicked and screamed at first, but no matter how hard she fought she couldn't break free.

Catherine hung from him uncomfortably as he walked with long legs and feet clearing a path wherever they went. The walk was tiresome in this position, but she didn't try anything again for fear of being beaten or merely squeezed to unconsciousness. She tried to pay attention to where she was being taken, but it didn't stick in her mind very well. Everything looked the same to her. The sky was getting darker from oncoming rain clouds, and she became more worried each passing minute that Bowen wouldn't know what happened to her. At the very least, she was thankful she wasn't hurt in any way during the attack by this wild Celt from two thousand years ago. Also thankful he didn't kill her, at least not yet. There was still hope for rescue or escape.

They entered through the edge of woods and throughout were scattered men and women. From their clothes alone, Catherine recognized them as the ancient followers. Most didn't notice her, and she hoped her captor's plans for her weren't devastating.

But her hope faded to the background when she was brought before Conall. She was practically dropped from the Viking's shoulders on rough dirt scattered with small branches and the like.

Conall said nothing at first, only offering a crazed smile by way of greeting. She knew if he wanted to kill her, she would suffer, and that frightened her more than death itself. Her mind was filled with too wild an imagination. She shivered involuntarily, and looked down. Catherine's breath stopped as she watched his dirty and callused feet walking closer, one in front of the other. Her body cringed at his filthy appearance. Conall stood in front of her glaring down with eyes full of madness. He lifted her up off her feet, gripping her arms and clawing at the cloth of her jacket.

"You've come to see me!" he said happily, though she still could not decipher his strange language. Setting her back down on her feet, he pushed her against a tree. She cried out as the sharp bark opened a painful gash across her back. She fell back gasping, the air gone from her lungs.

She looked at him in surprise, then with horror. He was just too strong. Catherine let herself sink to the ground. She reached around behind her back hoping for a rock but found only dirt. Firmly held within, she rested her hand on the ground, waiting for the right moment, she hoped a chance would come. She noticed the back of her head felt damp. With her other hand, she reached back and felt the blood trickling down.

Conall was strutting in front of Catherine now, his hands behind his back, neck outstretched as he looked upward. He wore a puzzled expression.

"I knew I would see you again . . . and how is Bowen?" he said, practically giddy, his smile wide and frightening.

Catherine understood Bowen's name, "Leave him alone!" she cried out.

Conall chuckled to himself and looked forlornly away. "He's mine," he said surprisingly calm, but clearly unstable. He twitched and looked back at her suddenly, "But I wonder why you care?" He watched her face closely.

Conall could see Catherine's eyes ablaze with hate and anger. He tried to intimidate her, but she locked her jaw tight and stared straight back. After a moment or two he smiled only slightly and backed away folding his arms across his broad chest.

"Hmm . . ." Conall's throat hummed deeply, growing fainter as he moved away. Catherine relaxed her hand and let the rough dirt fall.

Conall looked to one of his men and gave him a signal for them to watch her. Catherine recognized him. He was one of the two men who had passed her at the edge of the woods when she was trying to rescue Kathleen. She didn't make eye contact with him, but kept her eyes on Conall until he disappeared from view. Conall left her alone for a while, much to Catherine's relief. She didn't move from her spot, except to take painful breaths and watch the guard in the gloom. There was minor light from the small fire nearby. The shadows played with Catherine's imagination as she watched the reflected lights scatter in the darkening night.

Many hours passed. The blood on her head wound seemed to have clotted rather quickly. She wasn't drenched with it. Still, the gash stung terribly. She tried to think of the most immediate issue. Escape. She could still see other druids in the distance, and hear them behind her. They all wore grim or scornful expressions, and she wondered briefly why they would ever follow Conall, who was clearly a madman. A common purpose only goes so far.

Soon Catherine began to feel ill, and she hunched against the bloodstained tree. An onset of vertigo came shortly after, probably brought on by being jostled so hard, or perhaps a concussion. Her vision was blurry and everything spun around her. Her eyes hurt, along with the pounding in her head. The pain in her back still ached, but it paled in comparison. After a while, Catherine lost all track of time. She couldn't know if she had been there for hours, or all night. For a time, she thought she had fallen asleep, so it could have been another day entirely when she woke to see it still dark. The fire had been rekindled sometime in her unconscious state, making it brighter. Catherine's vertigo was still there, but she could control her urge to throw up, and the pounding in her head wasn't so bad now. Though, considering she had a head injury, she was thankful she did in fact wake up.

Catherine's lungs ached as she took a deep breath, and when she went to hold her chest to brace herself, a finger caught on her torn clothes. They were damaged from the coarse bark of the tree, and the Viking's sharp armor. Her scarf was missing as well. She noticed the holes were only in the front and back of her clothes. She gave a quiet chuckle when she thought they still weren't as torn as her last adventure's clothes that now lay in a trash heap somewhere. Catherine didn't like the recent pattern she was following of completely destroying her clothes.

Suddenly, loud and chaotic hollering ensued somewhere far from where she sat against the tree. Catherine looked over at the watching guard, a different one than before. The first man's face had been of mere dislike as he watched her, but now this guard held a concerned expression. She looked away from him to see if she could make out what was happening. A tall dark shadowy figure appeared in front of the fire. She jumped slightly and looked up.

"Catherine, you're alive!" Bowen's voice echoed sweetly in Catherine's ears. Though her heart swelled with happiness to know he was near, and she was thankful for his help, her heart also sank at the thought that he too was in danger.

The guard saw him too, and rushed forward, thrusting from his side then swinging a crude sword. Bowen grabbed the man's arm and twisted it over so he could knock the wind out of him with his knee jabbing hard in his belly. The guard collapsed, and Bowen punched him quickly before he could make much noise. He fell silent on the ground, breathing with difficulty in his unconsciousness.

"Bowen! You shouldn't have come here," she whispered.

"I couldn't leave you, Catherine!"

"You know he wants to kill you, this is too dangerous. I could have already been dead!"

"Yes, I was sure he would kill you on sight, but either way I had to know," he squatted next to her as he looked around to see if anyone else had noticed him.

" . . . Bowen," Catherine mumbled. She started to stand, but wobbled like she was on the deck of a ship in a wild storm on the high seas. Grabbing hold of the tree behind her with one hand she lowered herself back to the ground carefully.

Bowen's strong arm grabbed her waist and eased her down until she was stable. Catherine saw his face in the fire light. He seemed worried but also amused. "Are you really angry with me for trying to rescue you from a madman?"

"I'm angry because you could have been killed. You still can be!"

"If we run this way they shouldn't catch us, especially in the dark," he said quickly, pointing behind Catherine's steadying post.

"I can't, the vertigo. I can barely stand." Her head felt on the verge of bursting.

He looked her over, "Come on, I'll carry you!"

Before Catherine could think to put her arms around his

neck, a great laugh rose from behind them. That laugh had been burned into her memory and left a chill every time she heard it. Conall couldn't be seen, but they both knew he was near.

Suddenly, Catherine felt empty air where Bowen once stood, and a blast of cold air stung her face as if someone had run past at unthinkable speed. Bowen was pulled and thrown several feet away, with Conall standing over him. From where Catherine was it looked like Bowen's body was contorted in a way that his neck must be broken. Catherine heard a horrid scream escape her dry throat. Tears welled up in her eyes. Letting go of the tree she had been clutching for support, she moved her hands up to her face and saw that they were shaking. At first her mind and heart revisited the image of Kathleen lying dead, but soon all she could think over and over was *Bowen*.

She watched Conall yell over his limp figure, and hoped that meant maybe Bowen was still alive. When Bowen had first been thrown, his arm around Catherine's waist had been ripped sharply from her at such a speed that his arm wrenched from its socket, and was scraped badly as it hit a passing branch. His head hit the ground so hard that it knocked him out.

Catherine's screams now roused him, but he couldn't move. His body felt weak because of the position he had fallen in. Pain surged through him. Conall, his face illuminated by the fire, stared down at him. "Conall," his voice was raspy and quiet as he tried to speak.

"Your woman is still in Ireland, a risky choice. There must be a reason. Ah, what are you planning, Bowen?" he paused, but no answer came. "Hmm . . . no matter, I will find out another way. I knew you would come after her. You thought I would kill her immediately, didn't you? Because you *know* you *deserve* that. With every action you prove to me your guilt!"

"Conall, please listen to me," Bowen spoke in their ancient

language, and managed to twist enough to lay on his side. He suppressed a cry from the searing pain in his arm.

Conall wouldn't listen. "For years you told me you didn't do it. You acted like it was an accident. But I knew! I knew the truth, Bowen! You can't hide from me . . ." his voice screeched as his rage grew.

Bowen felt his strength returning, though the pain still tortured him. He let it go out of his mind as he tried to signal to Catherine in some way to run. Looking over, however, she seemed too fragile. He could see such relief in that deathly pale face that just a second before had been filled with sorrow. He was sure when she lost Kathleen that she couldn't possibly look more distraught, but he realized he was wrong now. Bowen had only seen that face on one other person before, the man standing between them now.

Bowen looked quickly back at him, hoping he didn't notice his gaze change, "It's true that I am to blame for some of this. I understand why you can't forgive me Conall, I do, but—"

"DON'T!" Conall yelled angrily, "You admit it! You admit it!"

Bowen fell silent as he watched the madness unravel in horrid awe. Catherine did the same as her body grew rigid, her heart blackened by her hatred for the man who had caused her so much suffering.

Conall hunched over and began to shiver at an alarming rate. His body shifted slightly and began to contort, adding to the already unnatural movements. He seemed to almost grow in stature, but before much change occurred, Conall looked as if he changed his mind and everything halted briefly. Bowen's eyes grew as he watched, and it suddenly clicked.

"It was you!" Bowen exclaimed.

Conall smirked. "You didn't know?"

Catherine was puzzled by Bowen's sudden outburst.

"You truly are a madman to dabble in such magic!" Bowen shouted at Conall. "By manipulating what was not yours to manipulate, you've brought evil to your body. You've made yourself inhuman!" Bowen felt sick to his core.

"Ah Bowen, inhuman strength is what I wanted, what is wrong with that?"

"That you ask, tells me there is no point in answering you . . ." Bowen felt defeated. He dejectedly looked to Catherine, who had puzzled at the animal-like cry escaping Conall. Then it clicked in her mind as well.

"He was the bear!" she shouted, then quickly looked to Bowen for affirmation.

Bowen nodded sadly.

"I didn't do it for your approval, did I? I did it so I could destroy everything, and slowly. No matter how strong I became, you would always be stronger. I knew I had to change, to transform. So I found a way." Conall looked pleased with himself.

"How? Who of our order would teach you?"

"I stole the knowledge. I forced answers during some of the raids, before that detestable Arlana came along," Conall squirmed when he said her name as if she was standing there in front of him, like a hideous wound in his leg that he couldn't bear look at.

"Wha-you can't retain the change long can you?" Bowen said, beginning to understand.

Conall scowled, "I couldn't get the complete manipulation, no. The hateful woman ended everything before I could." Then he smiled slightly. "I've been perfecting it slowly on my own all these centuries," he finished proudly.

Bowen was astounded. Catherine had replayed the bear attack, trying to see Conall in the monstrous animal that towered unbelievably high that day. She couldn't believe it, but knew it was true. She shook her head.

Conall became hysterical and lost all sense completely. In a flash, he was in front of Catherine. He stood her body up in one motion with his strong arm, his hand grabbing the curved bare spot between her neck and shoulder, his fingers digging hard into her collarbone. Catherine gasped in pain, but then was caught against a short stone wall as he threw her down behind them, causing her to quickly suck in a gulp of air. She felt a terrible sharp pain in her ribs which hurt with each breath. Her blood was warm as it trickled down her spine. The gash on her back had reopened. Bowen ran towards Conall, trying to rush him. He was forced to stop short when Conall pressed a jagged stone knife to Catherine's throat. Conall was swift with the knife but careful not to cut her at first.

"You tell her!"

"Wait! Conall, please!"

"Everything! Tell her NOW!" Conall screamed.

Catherine felt faint from the pressure of the cold, sharp stone against her neck. The surface of her skin was cut at Conall's last emotional outburst, and a single stream of blood soaked her tangled hair.

"I didn't tell you everything Catherine," Bowen said quickly in English, though in a thicker accent than usual. He was flustered. He didn't want to say something that would push Conall completely over the edge, so he had to tread carefully. Conall relaxed his hand. Catherine's neck stung but the knife wasn't as heavy on her throat. Blood dampened the front of her clothes. The warmth rapidly cooled against her chest. She found it difficult at first to register what Bowen was saying, especially in such a painful position.

"I told you about my heritage, and that I knew Conall. The reason he went mad . . ." he paused to gather his thoughts, "Conall was married, I told you. They were very much in love. They had been married for a few years, and his wife badly wanted to give him a child. They went to the priest, seeking help." Conall shifted his weight as his eyes bored into Bowen.

"There is a ritual. Pliny wrote about it. It's one of the only things about my people that has survived. The ritual of oak and mistletoe. It is a fertility ritual. The mistletoe was believed to bring healing. The high priest told them he would perform this ritual, so that a baby would be born. But then Conall's wife became obsessed with having a child. She also became very ill over time in a way I could not then diagnose. They came to me when Conall noticed she wasn't well. When I examined her, I couldn't explain where the fever and delusions came from. It was as though she had made herself ill. I gave her herbs to calm her, to help heal her condition. But I'm afraid it didn't do much good." Bowen looked regretful.

"Keep going, Bowen. I may not speak this new language, but I'm watching this woman's face and I'll know when you've told her," Conall smiled an evil smile. "It's one of the things I have lived for, Bowen!"

Bowen closed his eyes briefly, seeing himself there again. He breathed deeply and continued, "The herbs merely helped her sleep for a few days. Because of her illness the priest decided to put off the fertility ritual. He suspected she was no longer in her right mind. She started to have hallucinations, at first mild, but they increased rapidly. Conall had put all of his faith in me to heal his wife. He had become bitter with the druid priest order. He hated them for not going forward with the ritual. He believed if she conceived a child she would be well again. He came to me many times hoping I would try to convince them. I refused. One day he brought her to me to watch over while he went to work. While I was watching her, I was asked to visit someone else who was sick. I locked her in, thinking everything would be fine for just a short time. When I returned she had escaped. I couldn't find her anywhere. I didn't tell Conall. Instead I told everyone else I could find to help me search. It wasn't long before we found her."

"Say it!" Conall screamed as he looked back and forth between Catherine and Bowen.

"She must have gone straight to the sacred oak, where the ritual of oak and mistletoe is done. I believe she thought she could get the mistletoe herself and make the tea without the ritual. She was very delirious from the fever when I left her. She had been mumbling incoherently as she laid there barely moving. I didn't think she had the strength to lift herself. But she did, for she climbed that oak tree, into the highest branches. I assume she slipped. We found her body contorted and broken on the ground. She was dead." Bowen showed no sign of tears. They had dried up over the centuries. But the regret was palpable in his voice and the deeply pained look in his eyes. Catherine swallowed back tears of empathy.

Bowen went on. "Conall had heard the commotion and, worried, joined the search. He appeared beside me very shortly after we found her. No one had touched the body yet. He screamed, Catherine, a horrid blood curdling scream that I will never forget. It was so heart wrenching, it tore at my very soul. He laid over her, his tears mingling with her hair as he kissed her and held her. He pleaded with her not to leave him. Then he begged to go too. His face was sunken in and he became a man destroyed completely.

Conall had slowly became more and more unstable as he had watched her illness progress, the woman he loved withering away in front of him. Then, when she was completely ripped away from him, what was left of the Conall I knew disappeared. I saw him go mad with grief. He couldn't bear it. She shouldn't have been out in that cold, in her condition. It's true, I should have stayed with her, or gotten someone else to watch over her until my return. Though she was already on her deathbed, and he hated the priests who refused them, he blames me entirely for it all, their inability to conceive, and her illness as well as death. After he buried her he swore that I would suffer and feel his pain before he killed me. That's when he left home to rally his followers against our priests and create a violent divide. From that moment forward, he was the Conall you see now, torn and empty inside, consumed with his sorrow and writhing with hatred for me," he ended sadly.

Conall watched Catherine's face closely. When he saw the momentary flash of judgment in her face as Bowen admitted to leaving his sick wife alone, he smiled and felt a deep satisfaction. Much like when he killed Kathleen. He knew it was hurting Bowen somehow. Yet now Catherine felt Bowen's overwhelming pity for Conall as her body was still sprawled on the stone wall that burrowed into her back sharply. But she herself did not feel pity towards him. She still hated him, and wanted to inflict on him that which he desired for Bowen. She realized now she couldn't hurt him any more than he had already suffered, but she wanted to rid the earth of him. She wanted him dead, and his remains to be burned so the earth would never have to bear his weight again. Then it occurred to her—from the beginning why did Conall want to hurt *her* to get to Bowen?

As if Conall had read her mind, he hurried Bowen to finish with a threatening look. Bowen sighed, "He hates you because you matter more to me than anything in this world." Catherine didn't have a chance to digest his words.

Conall was suddenly distracted as bitter memories replayed in his mind, and he carelessly loosened his grip on the knife until his weight was no longer painfully pressing down on Catherine. This was her last chance to break free, she told herself for courage. She lifted her legs up from the ground and kicked hard at Conall's torso, bracing herself against the stone wall. Then she grabbed his wrist with the knife and pushed it as far away from her as possible. When Conall snapped back to her, the moving knife stabbed him in the face. He screamed, and blood dripped down on Catherine. She stood quickly as he pulled away and stumbled backwards, his hands grabbing at his bleeding face. His stone knife fell to the ground at Catherine's feet. Frantically, Conall smeared blood everywhere, searching for the wound. In his panic, he checked his eye since the cut went up in a slit, just missing his left one. He forgot about Catherine and Bowen as he screamed.

Bowen ran to Catherine, and swooped her over the short stone wall. They kept running. After a time, the echoes of Conall's mad ravings faded into the distance. They had survived once more.

As they bobbed and weaved through the thick grass, they managed to get across the field far enough so Conall couldn't hope to see them under the cover of the forested hills. They stopped at a paved road as dawn brought them some morning light. Breathing heavily, they stretched out on the grass beside it. The sun rose quickly. Catherine's body ached, her lungs burned inside her chest, and she only heard the loud thumping of her heart in her ears as she squeezed her eyes shut. Bowen's dislocated arm throbbed, and he was exhausted, but he kept his eyes on Catherine.

"Catherine . . ."

Catherine simply waved some fingers for acknowledgment.

Bowen stood, and looking determined he said, "I have to do something that you're not going to like . . ."

Catherine struggled to turn her head to look at him, confused. But before she could speak, Bowen turned away from her quickly. He walked over a few feet to a tall tree, suddenly rushing it on the last step, smashing his dislocated shoulder against the thick trunk. His other arm had been precisely placed on the limp arm to steady the impact. A very unpleasant grinding noise erupted, and Catherine cringed.

The impact of tree and bone were so blindingly painful that upon contact he lost control and the force threw him sprawling backwards on the ground. He lay still, and his eyes leaked tears as he breathed sharply through the pain. Catherine couldn't look away, silent with shock. Eventually Bowen sat up slowly. Checking himself carefully, he found the movement in his arm was back to normal, but would ache badly for days at least. He looked over his good shoulder to Catherine still laying on the ground. The corners of his mouth tugged at first in a grimace, but then he managed a small smile.

"Don't *ever* do that in front of me again," Catherine finally said.

Bowen nodded, and losing strength to hold himself up, he fell back to stretch across the grass again.

Despite herself, Catherine fell asleep. In her dream, she saw Conall crying over his dead wife. She wept for him. But then Kathleen appeared and Conall killed her. Catherine screamed and fell over her sister, rocking and holding her. When she looked up at Conall, he was laughing. This turned her pity to cold stone. Then everything vanished and she was standing under a stone figure of Bowen reaching out to her. Startled by this she backed away until she stumbled onto two tomb stones that read Kathleen and Catherine Green. She looked back up to Bowen but in his place was Danny with Conall. They both turned from her with hateful glares and walked away. Though they walked slowly, no matter how hard she ran after them she could not catch up.

Catherine woke up with a jolt. Her body felt weightless and warm. But she was jostled from the unnerving feeling of falling. She awoke at the precise moment she was lifted away from the warmth in mid-air and she returned to the waking world as she was being pulled back in Bowen's full grasp, his cradling arms around her.

"Sorry, I was trying to get us down that hill without waking you," Bowen motioned behind them. Catherine looked over his shoulder to see its steepness and shuddered to think how she might have woken up if he had dropped her.

"Where are we going?" she asked, feeling completely natural wrapped up in his arms.

"Back to town," he answered.

"Do you think Conall will come after us?"

"No, he got what he wanted for now. He's not done though . . ."

"Oh . . . I can walk now," she slipped out of his arms "thank you, Bowen."

Bowen winced at the movement of his sore shoulder, then nodded.

"Did you sleep well?" he asked, checking her wounds once more. He had no time to search out herbs he knew could help, but decided it would keep as long as they got to civilization soon to clean it properly.

Bowen seemed fidgety rather than his normal, steady self. He knew Catherine would soon talk to him about what happened. Would she be more focused on his past? Would she accuse him as Conall did? He tried not to think about it as they walked, and just admired the green surrounding them. His eyes watched the ground where he stepped. The rich colors helped him find peace briefly. His love of the Emerald Isle was often on his mind. He'd roamed this same patch of land hundreds of times before. He knew a great deal of Irish land. While cursed he was bound to it, but even without the curse he was connected to it. His people believed in such a thing, and even though he was taught it as truth, he knew it was truth for himself. He brought his hand to his chest over his heart and breathing deeply, smiled as he walked.

Catherine wasn't looking at Bowen for the moment, and didn't see him smiling. If she had she would have wondered why, as she always wondered what was on his mind. But she wasn't thinking of anything really. She felt as if she had been beaten up. She laughed under her breath. She *had* been beaten up. It wasn't funny, but it still made her chuckle. While she wondered if that was sane, Bowen nudged her shoulder. She caught his eye when she chuckled.

"Are you okay, Catherine?" he asked with a serious face.

Catherine ventured to guess that meant she mustn't look very well, "I don't know really."

"It's not too far away. We can rest when we get there. Now that you're awake I need you to stay awake. Carrying you will slow us down."

"That's fine, I'm not tired . . ."

Bowen shrugged, and absentmindedly combed a hand through his thick hair. He flinched through the pain in his sore shoulder.

Everything now flooded Catherine's mind at once, and her eyes locked on Bowen as she raised an eyebrow. "How did Conall know you loved me if you hadn't spoken to him since before I existed?"

"You're simply not an average woman, Catherine."

"What's that supposed to mean?"

Bowen laughed.

Catherine felt insulted. "What's so funny? My sister died, I've been attacked several times, and I'm being hunted down. I don't find anything about this romantic," she said haughtily.

Bowen's smile remained, "I suppose you're right. You're wonderful, and that makes you exceptional," he took a breath after stealing a glance of Catherine's flushed face. "The curse we were all under for centuries could be broken by you because you are the woman I love. The priest's daughter, I told you before, her name was Arlana. She told me she thought she loved me, and was upset that I didn't have feelings for her in return. Since she knew of my involvement in Conall's tragedy, she gave me the punishment of being the cursed one to watch over them in the caves." Bowen sighed. "Arlana was bitter. She felt I was incapable of love since she was considered to be very fair and of high station, she couldn't understand why I didn't want to be with her. So she made the rules of the curse be that the one who could break it would be a woman who was my heart's desire. She never thought I would fall in love. You were the one who broke the curse, because I'm in love with you. That is why I asked you repeatedly to leave Ireland." Bowen frowned.

Catherine paused thoughtfully, "How did Conall know I was the one though?"

"He thought it was Kathleen. His men found her near the area where you had been with me before when you obviously stepped past a marker stone which was the borderline before I saw you at the creek. Then when he saw both of you, he wasn't sure. He hoped he wasn't killing you so quickly, but he wanted to watch me suffer immediately. So he took a chance, and succeeded in killing your sister."

"But we both could have been just random people. He couldn't have known for sure."

"That didn't matter to him. If he was wrong, it was just another innocent stranger. At first this was probably more his thinking. However, when he saw my reaction to seeing you there in his grasp . . . He knew you weren't random women," Bowen explained.

An image of Conall and his wife pleading with the priesthood vividly flashed in Catherine's mind as she thought about their recent narrow escape from him. "Why was there such strong belief in the ritual of the oak and mistletoe?" she asked.

"The great oak brings life and power. And the mistletoe has

great healing properties. The two together make wonderful things happen," he stated.

Only a small smile came over Catherine's face in response. After having heard so much about this great oak tree, a part of her kept imagining Kathleen lying at the foot of it. She shook it off and stared ahead.

Bowen reached for Catherine's hand, and as she felt the tug at her fingers they wrapped around each other, palm to palm. She felt truly safe for the first time since she had lost Kathleen.

"But it can't heal the mind," Bowen said sadly. "I've never seen love like that, the way Conall loved his wife. I had never known it myself, until now . . ." Bowen looked into Catherine's eyes.

"Conall had a wonderful smile once," Bowen continued. "A real one, where happiness caused his whole face to light up. But then he lost her, and everything else. Against his will, he's empty of all things good. So you see, I can't hate him. Because it's not really Conall who we see now. It's the madness and evil that have complete control of him. But he's there, somewhere buried deep within. Because he's still hurting, and I bring it out of him in the worst way."

"I don't think you did anything wrong," Catherine remarked.

"Yes, well, you saw he blames me still, after all this time. Time, which you think brings clarity . . . instead, as history shows, it often brings more lies and gossip. But sometimes the truth is there, and so I hoped he would see the truth of what happened. But each time I checked on him, the madness grew. And he saw nothing but that."

Catherine grew silent, digesting everything. After that they stopped for a few moments so Catherine could relieve herself. She was nervous about being alone and away from Bowen, but couldn't see any way around it. So she hurried through it and returned to his side quicker than Bowen had expected her to.

They walked on in silence. The two of them were back in town before she spoke again. But it wasn't about the curse or anything related to them. The village centre was still bustling, and she looked around, remembering the dread she had felt here before. She was now amused to think of the old woman as part of Conall's many followers. Realizing her rather bruised appearance could attract unwanted attention and spark questions, she covered herself as best she could. She licked her hand to calm some of the mess that, no doubt, was her hair right now.

"No one is looking at you, it's okay," Bowen said.

"Thanks," Catherine grunted, as she noticed her dried blood on his clothes before turning away. She could see the car in the distance, and fantasized about sitting down. Catherine remembered they hadn't had a chance to get a place to stay yet, so her change of clothes was there too.

"How long was I gone?" she leaned sideways as she whispered to Bowen.

"It was only yesterday morning that we were last here."

"It seemed so much longer . . ." she blinked.

"Traumatic things often do," he said.

Pleased to see the car unharmed, with her things still inside as she had left them, she was eager for a place to clean up.

An old lady appeared in front of Catherine suddenly, and she stepped back against the driver's side of the car. Gasping loudly, her fear quickly vanished as she recognized the old woman.

"You!" she said pointing.

"How's the body? You looking for help?" the old woman said casually.

Bowen searched the old woman's face.

"Yes, we are," he answered.

The old woman no longer looked disheveled or menacing. In fact, she looked quite the opposite. She wore a blue blouse with small fake pearl buttons up the front, tucked into an old fashioned long black skirt that ended right below the knee. She wore cream colored stockings, and comfortable-looking shoes that were very obviously designed for seniors. With her white hair pulled back from her old but still elegant face, the old woman took her eerie gaze off of Catherine to look at Bowen when he responded. She lifted her bony chin as her eyes lifted to take in his tall and manly stature.

The old woman spoke to him. Catherine's eyes snapped from her to Bowen, she was speaking the ancient language. Was the old woman one of Conall's followers after all? One who had bothered to learn some English to trick her? But something wasn't right in her words. It wasn't quite the same. Bowen responded in his old Celtic language. The blue blouse shifted as she brought both her hands to her mouth, her eyes twinkling with excitement.

"It's you!"

"What?" Catherine said raising an eyebrow. Bowen walked over and put his arm around Catherine.

"Do you have a first aid kit? We can't go anywhere looking this way. This needs to stay discreet," he told the old woman.

She eyed Bowen's hand on Catherine's waist, "The curse is broken then . . ."

Bowen waited.

"Come with me then, and you may find the answers you seek," she said decidedly, then looked at Catherine. "You can call me Mary."

Catherine was not sure about this, but she trusted Bowen, "I'm Catherine."

Bowen didn't say anything. When Mary walked around the car, Catherine leaned into Bowen and whispered "Why didn't you tell her your name?"

"I already introduced myself," he whispered back before letting go of her.

"Wh—" Catherine stopped. She was surprised she didn't catch his name, even in the old language.

The old woman led them up a lane scattered with rocks to her small home a little out of the small town. They entered the darkly lit cottage, blinking as their eyes adjusted. Right away, Bowen was thrown a pale blue men's T-shirt that came from a laundry basket nearby. "Let's give it a wash," Mary said, gesturing for his bloodied shirt. Careful of his sore shoulder he pulled the worn black fabric over his head and handed it over.

Catherine was wondering who the borrowed shirt belonged to when she suddenly felt overheated as her eyes scanned Bowen's lean muscular torso. She was thankful he couldn't see the deep rose color bloom on her skin in the dim lit living room. The distraction was brief as Bowen covered back up with the clean shirt, though it stretched and clung too small on him in some areas. She managed to casually look away, breathing out slowly.

Next, Catherine was given an old worn towel to dab her wounds dry for a shower, and shown the bathroom she could use to clean up. After thanking Mary, she shut the door and stripped off her bloodstained dirty clothes. Eagerly entering a hot shower, she reveled in the warmth, every so often flinching from the resulting sting to her wounds. Stepping out of the steaming shower she dabbed and dried herself as best she could before searching in the store bag she brought from the car, containing her only change of clothes. After slipping on a pair of jeans, she was thankful she had chosen to purchase a loose fitting button up shirt to avoid brushing against the exposed wounds. Catherine was also happy this shirt was black. She worried for her future shopping choices if she were faced with these situations on a regular basis. Putting it out of her mind as she found Bowen, she first let him work on her head wound.

"Ouch!" Catherine winced.

"I'm sorry," Bowen breathed by her ear as he continued gently cleaning the wound caked with some newly dried blood. His breath was warm, and made goosebumps rise on her neck and arms.

"It's okay," she mumbled, still wincing.

"Sit down, it'll be easier for me," he said. His voice was gentle but serious and focused. Catherine assumed it was his doctor voice, and imagined him helping other patients. She thought of what the patients in his time must have looked like, and wondered what ailed them. Thinking better of it, she decided she didn't want to know. Catherine enjoyed Bowen's attention, especially on her body. His touch was soothing. Not just because of his healing well-practiced motions, but mainly because it was Bowen's touch.

She was sitting on a stool, and when his hand pressed on her shoulder or waist to turn her, Catherine realized she felt natural when he touched her now. She thought it was strange that she had so casually allowed this man to touch her. Like when he would reach for her, usually to help her in some way. But then she had done the same with him. Especially during times of crisis. She realized with him it was different than it would be with anyone else. It had always been natural.

Bowen worked his way through the wound on her head, her neck, and the slightly deeper gash on her back. He was relieved to find the bruising and soreness were the worst part. Confident that her wounds were already healing well, he sighed happily. When he was finished he squeezed her hand before cleaning up the area and leaving so she could get dressed. Catherine unwrapped her arms from around herself and sat up from leaning over her knees, swinging her shirt around her bare shoulders to button up. She found him in the front room with Mary and a young man with blonde hair dressed in gardening clothes who had just come in from the kitchen.

"This is my grandson, Kenneth. He's visiting me on his holiday. Kenneth say hello," Mary said patting him on the shoulder with a smile at Catherine.

Kenneth was an average sized man. His skin, though smudged on his cheeks and forearms with dirt, held a noticeable and natural tan, and his hair was platinum blonde. He looked at her with innocent baby blue eyes. Catherine smiled.

"Yes, Gran. Hello," he politely obeyed, taking off his gardening gloves to shake Catherine and Bowen's hands.

"They broke the curse," Mary said bluntly.

Catherine's face went from surprise to concern. Her insides cringed. She didn't trust easily, and she had no idea who this Mary was, or Kenneth for that matter. Bowen seemed unshaken by Mary's announcement.

"You've seen the ruins then?" Kenneth asked, looking up.

"Ruins?" Bowen said.

"Aye, the druid ruins. They're up that way, very close. You should go see it," Kenneth pointed up and to the left side of the house.

"Kenneth, I was just going to show them. They needed to clean up first."

"Oh, I'm sorry, Gran." Then he said "long trip, hmm?"

"You could say that," Catherine replied.

Kenneth looked at Bowen. "We're not quite the same size, are we?" he said, amused by seeing his shirt overstretched across Bowen's broad shoulders.

"Aye aye, I gave it to him while his is in the wash." Mary chimed in. "I'll buy you a new one for your birthday, hm?"

Kenneth shrugged. "Thank you, Gran."

"Now that my grandson has stolen my surprise, I'll show the ruins to you if you're ready?" Mary said.

"Thank you," Bowen nodded.

Mary took them outside, and led them down a separate rural

road. This road was very narrow and looked overgrown. It was more like a walking path that hadn't been maintained.

"An Garrán Oaken," Mary said with a thicker Irish accent.

"What does that mean?" Catherine asked.

"Gaelic for 'The Oaken Grove,'" Mary answered. "It's this way."

Bowen walked slowly behind, and Catherine kept in step with him. He whispered that he didn't want to be rude and over-run Mary. Occasionally Mary would turn and yell out "I'm the old woman here remember!" with a chuckle. They smiled to themselves, but didn't reply. "You can't hurt my feelings you know! The only person's time you are wasting is yours!"

Bowen and Catherine continued to follow as they were. They went up a bit, and then down and over, and around a bend they finally came upon the ruins. Kenneth was right, it was very close to the house. The three stood looking on at the wide field littered with the remnants of ancient history. The ruins were mostly giant stone. Catherine's hazel eyes lit up. She was amazed. The stones didn't resemble any pattern like the famous Stonehenge, but they were unique just the same. She walked through, eager to examine everything, but reverently. Mary stopped and eyed Bowen as he calmly took in the site of his old home. Catherine noticed that the ruins reminded her of a maze. As she zigzagged through the fallen ancient stone, she saw some protruding from the ground along with the ones on top. She grew more excited. After a moment of being caught up in her own world, Catherine looked for Bowen to express her excitement. He was still standing in the same spot as when they arrived. He placed his hand on one of the stones near him, his face solemn.

"Bowen?" Catherine walked back over.

"This is where we lived. Everything had changed when I woke up in a different place," he mumbled. Then louder he said

"I didn't think I would ever see the remnants of it. I was sure the earth had swallowed it completely by now."

"Feeling at home?" Mary asked from her distant perch on a short stone, perfect for her small size to sit upon.

"It feels different now," he said softly to Catherine, "too different," he answered louder for Mary's benefit.

"Is that why you look so sad?" Catherine took Bowen's hand, looking up at his face.

"This place was once filled with oak trees. They were old and glorious. Now they are all gone, uprooted and cut from the earth . . ." his voice grew quieter.

"A lot has happened in two thousand years, Bowen," Catherine said. "From what I've studied of the ancient druids, there wasn't much peace coming from other cultures and religions. Oak trees were very sacred to you, right? Didn't that come from the Greeks?"

"Yes, the oak trees are very sacred. They represented life to us, among other things. After that day, that day when Conall's life was destroyed before the oldest of oak trees in the grove, this place only represented death and sorrow to me," he looked deep into Catherine's eyes, then glanced up at one of the remaining stones next to him. He took his hand from it and then answered, "Some of our religion was connected to the ancient Greeks, yes. They too upheld the oak tree as sacred."

Catherine nodded, and tugged on his arm to walk with her. They looked for any clue, scanning with bird-like vision, but found nothing. Only stone.

Mary waited for them where she sat, too tired to walk. Sometime later, when they returned to her, she simply said, "Aye, I'm an old woman, I am," answering an unasked question, before turning around to begin the descent. The two companions exchanged looks and smiled. As they walked, Catherine wondered why it was so easy to trust her.

"Mary?"

"I can hear you, Caty," was her response.

Catherine made a face at the nickname, but continued "How do you know about the curse, and that we're involved?"

Mary opened her front door and let them into the empty living room before she securely locked it behind her. "Hmm," she said, gesturing for them to follow. She opened a door down the hall and they were hit with the smell of old books. The room was filled to the brim with yellowed and worn pages between battered covers, as well as rolled up documents. Catherine was the first to step in. She'd never seen so many books in one place outside of a library. A large wooden table was in the middle of the room, covered with old newspapers and other papers. Catherine raised an eyebrow at a mug half-filled with cold coffee, looking as though it had been there for a few days. Some of those rolled documents were on the table as well as a bench nearby. Catherine looked back at Mary in the doorway who was clearly enjoying watching them browse.

Bowen wasn't as fascinated as Catherine was. However, he did enjoy seeing her eyes light up at the relics, artifacts, ruins, and anything old. He wondered if Catherine liked him for that reason, that he was basically a relic. She certainly didn't seem to take to him when they first met, not outwardly at least. Then again, he had given her the wrong first impression. Even though she now knew he had done that only to protect her, he couldn't be sure what her true feelings were for him. Their journey had brought them closer. But how close, he couldn't tell.

Drawing out Catherine's positive emotions was like trying to get one sip from a thick ice cream shake through a thin straw. She did not disclose things freely. He walked around, in between the standing bookshelves, casually picking up a book to skim through. Bowen looked up through the top of a shelf and met Catherine's eyes. His heart felt on fire. She batted her lashes while blinking the moment away and turned around to page through another text. Bowen continued casually viewing trinkets placed on a windowsill, a tiny music box, that he didn't wind up, and a glass figure of an elephant. The elegant grace of the animal and design of the artwork itself made him smile. He stood upright and walked back around.

When Mary saw Bowen, she moved from her spot in the doorway. "I know about the curse because I read about it," she said looking at Catherine. "I've studied druids for a long time," she added, stepping into the room fully, "My ancestors were ancient druids. I don't know if they were descended from those here, but my family has lived in this town for as far back as can be traced. They passed on knowledge throughout generations."

"That's why the Gaelic you spoke to Bowen is different from his and the Gaelic spoken now? You learned it from them?" Catherine asked.

"Aye, what pieces of it that survived centuries of change," Mary said.

Bowen had already surmised all this based on their brief conversation earlier. "My people didn't keep records other than orally. Tell me, Mary, where did you read about the curse?" he asked.

She leaned a hand on the table for balance before she spoke. "If you go back to the circle ruins of your people, then walk a bit further, you will find a message written in the stone. I believe it is for you, Bowen."

Bowen looked at Catherine, and she gave his hand a squeeze before letting go.

He thanked Mary, and left the house. He rushed back the way they had come and searched. Thinking he had missed something, he was just about to go ask again when he noticed the ground further out was raised slightly. The years had helped conceal it, but walking over, Bowen realized it was the massive tree stump that was once the largest blooming oak tree of his people. He noticed many more such stumps now, and wept for the trees. He forgot how much he loved them.

Tracing his steps back from the largest tree stump, before he went too far, he found the engraved stone slab Mary spoke of. The ancient Latin script told the brief history of Conall and his followers. Eager to know more, he read in anxious haste. He looked closely and realized this was written by Arlana's father, the high priest. He read on to find that Arlana died shortly after she cast the curse, and her last wish was for her father to leave this for Bowen. Below that the text stated that if Conall should be freed, the one who freed him was the only one with the ability to seal him again. This made Bowen's mind pause. He had his answers now, but they were not the answers he wanted.

Bowen closed his eyes imagining the high priest, clothed in his white flowing garments, lifting his hands to seal the stone, knowing one day Bowen would find himself there. Bowen opened his eyes to see the gray sky above him, covered with clouds. Looking back at the stone, he thought of Arlana. It was her vindictive nature that had led to this. To put such burdens on the woman he would someday love. Bowen hated Arlana more than before. He squeezed his fists and hit his thigh hard, gritting his teeth in his chiseled jawline. Bowen decided he wouldn't let Arlana get away with this. Yes, Catherine would have to enact this curse, but she would succeed. He would not let her suffer any more.

He remembered the need to know how, and continued reading. The text told of the staff, now destroyed in the hunter's lair, but it also told of another item to use with it or alone.

"It can still be done . . ." Bowen exhaled.

He stood, fuming. The stone message seemed to have ended. He scrapped and kicked out some of his frustration to help reveal anything further down on the slab. But no more of the ancient script was shown. The enactment of the curse was up to Catherine now. Bowen breathed in deeply, taking in the crisp Irish air. It filled his body, and made his blood pump. He felt lightheaded as he thought of Catherine's possible reactions to this news. With everything he felt for her, he was not looking forward to telling her, or what would spiral from it thereafter.

CHAPTER SIX

Danny woke with a splitting headache, and soon realized he was bound to a stone fence. He saw strange-looking men and women everywhere he looked. Then he remembered his blind chase for Síne. He needed to find her quickly, to get back to his sister. He knew Catherine would be safe with Bowen, but he also knew she would be worried sick about him. He didn't like the way he left, but he needed Síne to lead them to Conall when they were ready to enact the curse. When he returned to his normal life, he needed her so he could keep his promise to the Gardai. But he couldn't find her, no matter how hard he tried. He couldn't be sure he was tracking her. Days and days with hardly any food or water and sleeping without shelter had left him shaky and unwell. The last thing he remembered was feeling relief when he suddenly spotted Síne and stalked her movements before she snuck up and clubbed him from behind.

Grimacing as he tried to shift against his binds, he bitterly regretted leaving his sister on this foolish attempt to recapture an ancient druid woman who was clearly more intelligent than he was.

Suddenly, noticing that Danny was awake, some men stopped in their tracks. They spoke in an unknown language.

The conversation ended abruptly and they came over. Danny tried to brace himself. But to his surprise they freed him. Still, Danny's hopes of escaping were quickly dashed when he realized there were too many of them for him to sneak around, even if he could struggle enough to remove himself from the men. He was too weak from hunger and illness to even try.

The men brought Danny to a clearing where what looked like an army of wild-looking men and women were gathered. They seemed to be separated into two contentious tribes. In the middle of the two groups stood three men, who were clearly unhappy with something. Danny couldn't hope to figure it out. His two captors carried him towards the middle, and waited patiently for a break between the three men.

A swift kick from one man to another caused an uproar from all around. The perpetrator gave a barbaric growl and sneered menacingly. He turned his angry glare on Danny.

The hateful man approached them, leaving everyone behind to wait. He looked Danny over like he was a captive animal to be surveyed. The men were clearly speaking to the man about him, and so he waited, hoping to be released. He suddenly spotted Síne in the crowd. She was walking towards them, apparently called on by this evident leader. An explanation followed.

The leader stood with one arm wrapped around himself, and the other propped so he could massage his cheek with ease. Danny felt uncomfortable, being forced to watch the man disrupt the healing process of a large cut near his left eye. Suddenly the leader punched Danny in the gut, and his legs collapsed under him. His weight fell completely on his two guards as he was carried back to the fence and bound alongside it against a tree. It didn't matter what happened now, Danny thought, as he lost all his strength.

* * *

Bowen had forgotten about that.

"Perhaps I can help?" a voice rang from around the corner.

Catherine and Bowen turned their heads to see Kenneth approach. Raising a hand, Kenneth said apologetically, "I didn't mean to eavesdrop."

"Well sure, if you think you can . . ." Catherine wondered how he could possibly help, but decided to wait and see what he had to say.

Kenneth held out his tanned arm to show a uniform draped neatly over it. Catherine leaned forward, and her eyes widened. It was the same uniform that the guards wore at the museum.

She looked at Kenneth, "Where did you get this?" she asked, her voice sharp.

"I work there a few times a week. It's near my flat," he explained.

"What shift?"

"It changes each week. I'm not permanent, even though I've been there awhile. I fill in when I'm needed."

"I—I don't know if I ever saw you before . . ." Catherine held her temple trying to recall, stepping back against the tree. No bells were ringing.

"I don't think you did. I saw you there," he shrugged, "a handful of times. You were very busy receiving and cataloging the artifacts. Your attention was rarely diverted to anything else," Kenneth responded.

Catherine didn't say anything, but she guessed Kenneth was right because she had no memory of any of the guard's faces. She only recognized this uniform. She wondered what he thought about her "death," if he even knew. Catherine traced her fingers in tiny circles on the tree behind her absentmindedly, pressing in hard. Her finger-tips lost the little color they had. She felt nervous. Finally, Catherine pushed off from the tree in a decided manner. "How can you help us?"

"I could get you inside, easily."

"You mean . . . to steal it?"

Kenneth held her questioning gaze without flinching.

"Why do you want to help with this?" Bowen asked.

"Because helping you would help my Gran. She's always wanted to be a part of that old druid legend." He gestured up the hill to An Garrán Oaken.

It was Bowen's turn to fall silent.

Catherine nodded awkwardly to Kenneth, as if to finish the conversation.

"I'll be going back late tonight," he said, and he turned to walk back towards the small house.

"Well, this just might work," Bowen said when they were alone again. He looked confidently at Catherine, who frowned. "It's perfect. Because you're dead, no one should suspect it's actually you. We may just be able to use that to our advantage."

Catherine disliked the idea of stealing the chalice, almost as much as she disliked being dead to most everyone she knew. But she had to stop Conall, and she had to find her brother. At her breaking point, she decided she would do whatever she had to do to finish this . . . *whatever* she had to do.

* * *

Mary had been told about their objective, without the details. Kenneth saw to that, and they didn't object. The less people involved in their crime, the better.

Catherine relaxed against her seat where she could, though her healing wounds made it almost impossible to do so at first. She hadn't slept much in the car when they left last night. She gazed out the window at the now familiar terrain. Turning to Kenneth she asked, "Are you close with anyone at the museum?"

"No, it's too erratic a schedule for that. The only other guard I talk to is a superstitious man who hates his job. He's always telling me he feels it's bad luck to have such old artifacts together in one place," he answered. After scratching behind his neck he added, "Though I hardly ever see him these days."

Catherine nodded before leaning forward a bit on her lap. The sun felt good against her back. She could almost sleep like this if it weren't for the swaying of the car. Drifting off alone in her own world of thoughts, she stayed like that for as long as it was comfortable, feeling calm for once. The potent fragrance of Mary's laundry detergent was still wafting off Bowen's black shirt, practically smacking her in the face. She soon reached to roll her window down enough for some relief.

Kenneth looked innocently at Bowen, his eyes full of curiosity. "How did you know you couldn't leave Ireland?" he asked bluntly. "Had you tried before?"

"Yes, I did try," Bowen answered, reluctantly remembering.

"What happened?" Kenneth asked, shamelessly intruding on the ancient doctor's privacy.

"I only seriously tried once. My body was stricken with some sort of invisible force that blocked me and seemed to pull me backward."

Bowen closed his eyes thinking of that day. He remembered how gray the sky had looked, and how far away the sun seemed behind the cloudy gloom. Standing on the edge of a cliff, looking down he felt the cold wind rushing up at him lightly sprinkled with mist. Fear didn't stop him; fear was pushing him. He wanted to end this torturous life. He had lived long enough, hundreds of years. Surely God would welcome him now, taking another small step. Yes, yes the end. Bowen remembered trying to move his leg in that last step. But it was stuck in mid-air. He could not hope to move it further. He stepped back instead. Tried again. Forced back. He put all of his weight forward, but somehow he was laying across the thin air. He could push back, or be pushed back. This time, he tried leaning only his upper body forward. He was pushed back upright. He moved faster and ran to jump, but he was thrown backwards onto the hard rocky ground. The invisible barrier had won.

"Damn! Why?!" he cried loudly striking the ground with his fist at his side, making imprints in the dirt. "Let me go!" he exhaled hoarsely, then gritted his teeth in anger. So this was his destiny, he thought. To live forever without happiness, love or the release of death. And if he were to find that happiness it would mean destroying others. How cruel.

Bowen sighed slowly, returning from his foggy state. He had always thought succumbing to love would be selfish. But now he understood it was not something he could control, for the fate of everyone here had been in his hands for centuries before they were born. Perhaps if he had never seen Catherine that first day, hadn't seen her glance around the busy Dublin street at the airport. Or seen her lovely curved smile, red hair blowing around her head like fire, the sunshine reflecting golden light to bounce off it . . .

"A powerful curse," Kenneth said, bringing Bowen back to the conversation.

"It had to be to keep so many people locked up for so long," Bowen remarked casually.

Kenneth didn't say any more. He spent the rest of the ride reading a magazine. Catherine switched with Bowen to take the wheel. Having listened to their conversation before, she pondered over his words and the pauses in between. Curiosity about Bowen's past led her to think of what his life must have been like before the curse. She imagined his home. She wondered what it looked like. She decided she would ask him after all of this was over, when they had time to spend together. Go on a real date maybe. A pang hit her as she realized that was impossible. If they did not succeed they would be on the run, or fighting for their lives. If they did succeed, she would have to leave her beloved Ireland, and the man who she had risked everything with. Concentrating on driving helped her stop thinking about it as she drove on. Ahead now, she saw the museum in the distance. She braced herself for the crime they were about to commit. She hoped they could pull it off.

Catherine stopped the car far away from the museum, so no one would suspect them. She was disguised slightly in case any previous co-workers used this route to walk to work. Her hair was pulled up in a loose bun stuffed into a knit hat she had borrowed from Mary, and thanks to the sunny day she had another excuse to wear Bella's sunglasses. Getting out of the car to stretch her legs, she walked further down the road. It was warm today. She didn't even need her light jacket, but she kept it on anyway. She walked back with her hands stuffed in her pockets, and took a turn around the car casually a few times, before getting back in. She stared ahead at the immense building in the distance and imagined herself a giant tearing through the roof of it. She continued on, and thought she could even see the pieces of debris falling from her hands while she grabbed the priceless skyphos and fled back to the country side, her giant figure shrinking back to her normal size with each step. Catherine's eyes refocused. Her chest expanded as she sighed.

"Catherine?" She turned around, pulling down her sunglasses to see Bowen next to her.

He smiled at her, though she thought he seemed uncharacteristically unsure of something. "We've got a plan," he said.

"I'm glad that's been established, since we're here and running out of time . . ."

Kenneth spoke up. "It was important we did this today for a reason other than that it's my shift. The museum's been going through a major upgrade of the lighting, fire, and security systems. Today is the day they're officially taking down the security alarm of the old system and switching it over to the new system in the main building, which means it will also be closed to the public for that time." He opened up a little map he had of the museum's layout.

"How long will it be down for before the new one kicks in?" Catherine asked, taking off her sunglasses to look at the map.

"They didn't exactly announce a time estimate, but they suggested only a few minutes during the last meeting. Later I heard my superiors say that it would be down for at least a half hour."

Catherine wrinkled her forehead, and she drew her eyes up to watch him finish speaking. Since meeting Kenneth, he had become increasingly bold. Outwardly he seemed a different person completely. He was almost outspoken. "Is that a problem?" he asked, interrupting her thoughts, fixing his eyes on her.

"A half hour, it's just . . . I'm not sure that's going to be enough. It takes time to handle something that old with delicacy. Not to mention sneaking around to avoid people." She looked worried.

Kenneth pointed to the map at the side entrance. "Here is where I can get you in. After that the only thing I can do is maybe cause a malfunction in the electricity system to prolong the system upgrade, but that's a huge maybe," he said while putting on his blazer jacket.

"If not, what then?" Catherine said half to herself.

Kenneth's tone grew aggravated, "If not, then we're going to need a distraction."

"Where is the skyphos now?" she asked. "The last I saw, everything was being reset for a new exhibition."

In answer, he pointed on a part of the map that was a little too far into the building than Catherine would have liked, but she nodded in acknowledgment.

"Bowen, where will you be, here in the getaway car?" Catherine asked, secretly laughing at the thought.

"I'll be with you of course," he said.

Catherine nodded again, this time suppressing a smile.

"I don't think that's such a good idea. It's best if we all split up," Kenneth said with a minor twitch in his hand that Bowen noticed, but Catherine did not.

"Will she be in any great risk?" Bowen asked casually.

"She'll have a direct way out," he said quickly, and snatched up the map before Bowen could see.

"Splitting up?" Catherine's voice was imploring. She felt uneasy.

Looking at his watch, Kenneth said loudly "We need to go now!"

"But I don't know how we're getting out yet?"

Kenneth hesitated, "When we split up you'll just have to go with my plan, and hope it moves smoothly. While we're inside, I'll assume you need more time and try to cause the malfunction, but remember I may not succeed, so get the skyphos as fast as you can."

"Right," Catherine replied with a sharp nod.

"What time?" Bowen asked calmly.

"It's going to happen at two o'clock."

"What time do we have now?" Catherine wondered.

"One thirty, let's go!" Kenneth said as he opened the car door.

Catherine felt nervous, but she knew she had to go through with this. Bowen grabbed her hand before she pushed away from the seat. Giving it a light squeeze he smiled. "Be careful," he said.

"I will," she breathed nervously. Propping her sunglasses back on, she got out of the car carrying Bowen's smile in her mind as she walked. She caught up with Kenneth, who had moved away from the car at unexpected speed, and kept pace with him. Catherine struggled with the urge to run back, and abort the whole mission.

"The main building is the one undergoing the security changes. The side entrance is still something we need to get past without anyone noticing. So stay close to me," Kenneth cautioned as they walked calmly through some alleys to get to the museum. The side entrance was located away from the main street and from any prying eyes for a reason. The crew for the security upgrade was already inside, as well as the guards. "Don't speak either, someone may recognize your voice," he added.

Catherine thought that sounded very unlikely, and slightly strange. "I doubt that, but I will be quiet," she whispered.

"Your voice rings out. Everyone will know it's you, so trust me, don't talk to anyone, and keep your voice low if you must speak," he said with finality.

Catherine shrugged. She never thought her voice was very pronounced, but then she supposed it wasn't really something you would know about yourself.

As they walked closer to the entrance ahead, the whole area was shaded from the sun. Catherine felt silly keeping her sunglasses on. She was glad she left them alone though for just then a lady with regular glasses, short brown hair, and walking in high heels emerged from the door they needed to get through without detection. Catherine recognized her. It was the intern, Sharon.

Kenneth readied his swipe badge in one hand, and grabbed behind him with the other for Catherine's hand. But she wasn't paying attention to Kenneth. Sharon wasn't too far ahead, and would pass by them soon. Catherine felt the whole plan blowing up before her eyes as she drew closer. She could hear the echo of the high heels clicking on the pavement of the back lot. She hoped Sharon wouldn't notice her. She certainly shouldn't be looking for her since she was supposed to be dead. Catherine stopped looking ahead, and kept her gaze down towards the back of Kenneth's legs so she wouldn't trip on him. The click clack of Sharon's heels grew louder. She held her breath.

"You should hurry, they were having a quick meeting for all the guards as I was leaving," Sharon briefly looked up from carrying paperwork, and smiled at Kenneth.

"Thank you, I will," he said quickly.

"Bye," Sharon said, behind them now.

Catherine kept her head down but glanced behind to see Sharon swish away, her nose in a large folder, distracted and unsuspecting. Catherine breathed easy again. Her presence didn't seem noticed at all. Relieved, she was thankful to be one step closer to this being over.

The door was directly in front of them now, and Kenneth swiped his badge, his hand covering one side of it entirely. Kenneth seemed agitated about something. She hoped he wasn't losing his nerve. They waited for the red light to turn green, and a noise announced the door could be opened. *Now into the fire,* she thought, and in they went.

The museum's familiar hallway was poorly lit, which Catherine never thought she would be thankful for until this moment. Though it was difficult to see now with her sunglasses, no one seemed to be around. It was very much deserted. Kenneth let go of her hand as soon as they were in, and motioned for her to keep up. She hurried next to him, watching all sides. A room with open doors wasn't far ahead, and another hallway which sprung off the one they were in. Catherine recalled the floor here, and how her own high heels used to feel clicking against it. She was happy she wasn't wearing loud shoes as they passed rooms which occasionally weren't as empty as they seemed at first. The employees only heard Kenneth walking by, and didn't bother looking up from their various tasks.

As the two drew deeper into that section of the museum, Catherine's nerves began to act up again. Kenneth found a small storage closet and he pushed her in and followed right after before someone from ahead of them could see. They waited in the closet quietly peering out through the cracked door. Catherine thought it strange that he hid as well, but considered it could be that he simply didn't want to be seen if he could help it. But why? Wasn't it his shift? Or was it that he actually wasn't supposed to be there that day, and if he was seen by someone then questions would arise.

Then it hit her. Kenneth was too eager to do this with them. And why was he unhappy at the thought of Bowen coming in? Suddenly Kenneth seemed incredibly suspicious.

"How did you happen to overhear your superiors talking about how long the system would be down?" she decided to whisper.

"Shh," Kenneth said keeping his eyes ahead.

"Did you just happen to be there at the right time?" she whispered again, after the man finally walked past the closet, blinking the light across their faces.

Kenneth turned around angrily and grabbing Catherine's arm too tightly, he locked it with his own, bringing her close to him. "Look, you're going to get me that cup, and a few other valuable things while you're at it," he growled.

"I will not!" Catherine gasped.

"You will, or everyone here will not only find you alive, but they'll find you caught by me," Kenneth opened the closet door and stepped partly out, "Who do you think they'll believe, a criminal or a member of security?" he asked while he checked for any more people. In the light she could see how he had changed so drastically. His anger made his once clear eyes look devilish. Kenneth had been manipulating them the whole time. Catherine now saw his true self.

She was furious, but too scared to think what to do. He was right. Her credibility would be shot in front of the others. They would believe whatever he told them. Catherine felt panic rise in her stomach. The idea of being caught and going to jail wasn't appealing.

Kenneth strong-armed her out of the closet, and she tripped over her own feet. She would have fallen if it wasn't for his violent hold. She noticed that even his walk was different than before. Before, he evidently was trying to appear timid, weak, but maintaining professionalism with his compulsive cleaning of his uniform and shoes. Now he unleashed his inner self without warning, and she regretted asking him the questions that led to this. She might otherwise have escaped him.

"What do you want with the skyphos?" Catherine asked as he pulled her along.

"I want it for myself of course. Don't act the fool, I know why Bowen wants it," he said.

"For the curse!"

"Wrong!" he said, then laughed under his breath. "You think he wants to really stop them, and give up such power?" he said looking back once as he strode ahead down the wide hallway. "Its magical abilities can give you whatever you want. He wants world domination just as the rest of them do. I swear I won't be under Bowen, Conall or anyone's thumb. I'll be *their* leader. Nothing will stop me once I get it!" His fingers dug into Catherine's flesh. She struggled to get him to loosen his grip, but he was too distracted.

"No more trivial jobs like these," he spit out the words disdainfully, "or of any kind. I'll be like a king in the end," he said with a triumphant voice as they took a turn and went through a set of doors.

"Stop it! You're hurting me! How will it look if they find me with your finger marks?" she said anxiously. He sharply turned his head to look at her, and glared before looking back. He didn't say anything but his grip loosened, which she was thankful for.

Everything was on the line for Catherine now. She figured he would somehow betray her further so she would take the fall entirely. It was just a matter of time. Catherine's thoughts were cut short when suddenly someone's arms wrapped around her and pulled her backwards sharply, squeezing the breath out of her. The knitted hat fell off, letting loose her waves of hair. She feared she would be torn apart, until Bowen came into view and swung his leg, kicking Kenneth in his lower back which knocked him straight into the wall. Catherine was set free. She fell backward off her feet, leaning on Bowen. His arms still held her middle and he lifted her back up quickly. Kenneth was about to recover when Bowen knocked him out completely with his fist, and he sagged down to the floor.

"Bowen?" Catherine found her voice.

"I knew something wasn't right about him," he said.

"How did you know?"

"He strongly resisted me coming with you. It seemed like a red flag to me." He looked forward and back to see if anyone was around, "and I just didn't feel right."

"But he was Mary's grandson, I didn't think to be wary until it was too late," she said.

"Everyone is someone's relative, Catherine."

"Ugh, I feel stupid I didn't see it." She picked up her hat which had slid down the hall.

Bowen shrugged "Don't worry, it's what manipulators do. But we must be more careful."

She nodded, "We've got to hurry, it's after two." She looked down at Kenneth's wrist watch that read two-oh-four.

"I know, I had to wait until then to get in," he said.

"How long do you think he'll be out?" She slipped the leather banded watch off his wrist, and onto her own.

"We should assume not long. Let's go!" he grabbed her hand and they took off.

They went down the remaining portion of the current hallway and through less industrial-styled doors. The lighting was at its lowest setting since the display rooms were closed to the public. Both of them leaned forward slightly and squinted. The room seemed frozen in time as items from centuries past stared back at them. Catherine imagined the items knew why they were there, but quickly shook the thought away.

"Do you know where it is?" Bowen asked in hushed tones.

"Yes," she answered, partially out of breath. Her heart was still beating wildly from her struggle with Kenneth. But her answer wasn't entirely true. She guessed the skyphos was most likely already on display, but if it was being cleaned or there was a special exhibition out then it could have been moved to a different position than the one originally planned.

"It would be just ahead and to the left!" she said a little louder than she meant.

"Would be?" he asked, but Catherine wasn't listening.

She came to a sliding stop on the slick floor. They stared for a second. There was a medium glass display case holding pieces of an ancient Viking ship. Catherine admired the carvings for a moment, before frantically looking around to figure out what the museum might have done in her absence.

"You don't actually know where it is?" he said, searching her eyes like a hawk.

"It was one of two places, Bowen. How can I be positive?"

Bowen tried to help, and looked around again. "I guess I would just like to be told, for next time," he flashed a smile.

"Next time?" she mumbled.

Bowen took Catherine's hand and led her in a different direction. Before them was another cluster of glass displays, but this time they held different kinds of ancient Greek pottery. She breathed a sigh of relief, "Oh, thank God!"

"We're not done yet . . ." he looked around, finally pointing at the skyphos, a glass case away. "Hurry and get it so we can get out of here," he said.

"Right," she reached in her pocket and pulled out a small pouch with a drawstring.

"What is that?" Bowen asked curiously.

"It's a bag," she said.

"Oh . . ." Bowen was doubtful.

She pulled the drawstring loose and unraveled it to reveal a large carrying bag. She held it out for Bowen to see, and looked up at him.

"Very inventive," he raised his eyebrows. "Now hurry."

Catherine calmly opened the glass casing with one of her keys. She carefully took the two-handled wine cup in her hands. Even in the dim lighting, she could make out some of the different animals she now knew symbolized the night sky. A bull, hare, lion and snake. Then she placed the chalice inside the large bag. The bag was too big, so she wrapped it around the fragile cup several times for extra protection. She quickly re-closed the case and left it unlocked. Holding the wrapped skyphos close to her chest she covered some of it with her jacket as she did so.

"Okay!" she said, and they were off.

"What time is it?" Bowen asked as they ran.

"Two twenty six," she said glancing at her wrist.

Bowen stopped abruptly in front of her. He turned to face her just in time to keep the delicate skyphos in one piece. She let out a loud breath, relieved she didn't drop the ancient cup.

"What the—" she stopped when Bowen shook his head sharply in one quick motion, his eyes telling her to hush. A distant noise could be heard in the direction they were headed, the only direct way out to the car.

Two men walked down a hall with wire and tools hanging from their work belts. They were walking casually through, one with his eyes focused on his phone, and the other taking in the artifacts.

"Oi, I should bring my kids here next week, they really like this sort of thing," the shorter of the two men said in a gruff voice.

The other peered up from his phone to look around, "'This sort of thing'? *You* don't much care for it though, yea?"

The short man nodded, "I'll enjoy it with them though," he replied.

Catherine could hear the smile in his voice. The two men finally passed where they hid behind a replica Viking boat that took up quite a bit of room. Their voices trailed off and faded as they continued. Bowen peeked around the other end of the boat to look for their exit where he saw many more men were passing by. He carefully crept back next to Catherine who was closely clutching the skyphos, resting her cheek on it.

"We need to find a different way out," he whispered close to her ear.

"I'm thinking," she said, holding her head with her free hand. She leaned down, crouching further over the skyphos to keep it secure and covered her eyes to block out the dim light. Her head throbbed from the stress. Bowen wondered if she was having a panic attack, as he craned his neck to see which way was clear.

Suddenly they heard yelling from the hallway.

"Either they've found Kenneth, or he's awake," Bowen said.

"Damn it!" Catherine said.

"We don't have time to think of a plan," he said, his voice hoarse from whispering.

"I know . . ." she said to herself.

Bowen looked up over the ship and saw the remainder of workers and security speed in the direction of the commotion. The way was clear at last.

"Now!" he said and pulling Catherine up on her feet they darted off in the other direction.

As they passed countless artifacts, it felt like they were running blindly through a labyrinth of glass and pottery. The layout of the museum was definitely not built for easy getaways. Whoever made the plans certainly did a great job, Catherine thought. She watched her every move so as not to cause an accident and draw attention to their location. She had to grip with her toes to keep a hold on her slippery flats. They were becoming more uncomfortable with each stride.

"Do you know where we're going?!" she panted.

"To the nearest exit of course!"

"How do you know?" She didn't know where one was herself based on memory. Everything looked different.

"I'm guessing!" he said and grabbed her hand to help her as she struggled with the skyphos.

Suddenly, Catherine stifled a yelp as she nearly fell, but regained her balance on Bowen's steady arm. "Take those off," he gestured to her feet.

Catherine stopped to bend down but found she couldn't manage to reach her flats. Bowen stooped down and roughly removed them, while Catherine hopped on one foot at a time. He stuffed the shoes in the waist of his pants against his back, and the two continued. No longer afraid of slipping, she felt her feet grip the smooth granite floor, and they picked up the pace.

As they moved from hallway to hallway, Catherine began to get her bearings. She knew where another non-fire-alarmed exit was.

"No, this way!" She tugged at Bowen's arm when they stopped abruptly at an intersection.

At the end of the corridor was the door to their escape.

Catherine could see it just ahead, though the way was long. She never imagined she would look upon a door with such joy. Bowen flashed another smile at her as they shared mutual relief in a quick glance. Both of them were drained of energy, if not from the endurance of the run, then by the mere pressure of the situation. They were close now, only a few strides away. The shirt she wore under her jacket was pasted to her body with sweat. A cramp in her gut reminded her of a reoccurring New Year's resolution she made to exercise regularly. She now bitterly regretted never sticking to it.

A man dressed in jeans and a T-shirt and wearing a bright red baseball cap suddenly stepped into their path. He gripped a rolled up magazine in his left hand that he had been swinging a moment before. He stared at their sudden approach in surprise.

At first Catherine was terrified that he might recognize her, until she realized he wasn't dressed professionally like any of the museum staff. They came to a halt and she used her elbow to press firmly against her cramp for relief as she stood.

All three of them seemed to be at a stalemate. Catherine knew they had to be the first to move or it was game over. *Not yet!* Not when they were so close to the finish line, when all of Ireland's future was at stake. Sweat trickled down her spine in apprehension. She was suddenly very aware of her jeans sticking to her legs. She wanted to get out of her clothes, and into a freezing cold shower. Catherine longed for relief from the heat, the sweat, for the end of this entirely. The exit door loomed not far from where they stood, and her eyes rolled back to the stunned man in view. She longed for the Irish cold breeze and mist outside, for that fresh air to touch her face and neck. Remembering the feel of cold water trickling down her spine instead of the hot sticky sweat that was residing in the small of her back now, she was even more determined to get through that door. This man was the last obstacle.

Catherine thought of speaking to him, of reasoning with him, but she thought better of it and said nothing. Her throat was parched from all the heavy breathing, and she knew she needed the cold water waiting for her somewhere on the other side of that magnificent door ahead.

Finally, Catherine made a decision. Clutching the wrapped skyphos in her arm, she lunged for him and used her forearm to shove his chest. Then pushing her arm up in a flash she knocked his chin. He stumbled backwards into the narrow hallway from which he had come.

Bowen was startled to see such a reaction from Catherine, but they made it to the exit, and out the door they went. Disoriented, they frantically tried to figure out where the car might be.

"It's this way!" Catherine was looking to her left and took Bowen's hand again, but he resisted.

"No, Catherine, I moved the car when you left with Kenneth," he said quickly.

"Why?" she asked, her eyes narrowed in search of the car.

"I thought it best to do if I was right about him," he said.

"Oh, good idea, where then?"

"Come with me," he said, and they went through some tall shrubbery. Bella's car was ahead, in all its yellow glory, parked behind the museum on a tiny unused road that would be better described as a slightly oversized paved bicycle trail.

He pulled the car key out and gave it to Catherine who was eager to put great distance between them and the museum. She kept looking in her mirrors for any sign of pursuit. When they passed the city limits, her grip eased on the wheel. Bowen could see the relief pass across her face.

"I wonder what happened when they found Kenneth?" she said with a knit brow, pulling off her hat.

"I don't know. The commotion may have been something to do with the security system," he said with a thoughtful tone.

Catherine looked for her sunglasses, then quickly remembered she wore them inside the museum. They must have fallen off somewhere along the way. She shrugged, then glanced at Bowen with a smile. "We made it," she stated.

"Yes, we did," he smiled back.

"Thank you for coming in after me."

"I'm thankful I found you in time," Bowen said.

Catherine kept her eyes on the road but she nodded in agreement.

Bowen held the bundled skyphos in his lap securely with one arm, "We escaped this disaster. Now we have to avoid the next one." He looked down reluctantly.

"When do I get to find out how the skyphos is going to help us do that?" she asked.

"Soon," was all he said, and looked down. It was almost as if he was afraid to unwrap and admire the ancient piece of art.

After a while Catherine began to fear the idea of casting a curse of any kind. She tried to think of other things. She thought of their narrow escape at the museum, the encounter with the innocent bystander, and Kenneth lying there on the floor unconscious. A shiver went up her back when she recalled the devilish glare he gave her. She wasn't worried about leaving him, not only because he was an awful person, but because if he was terribly injured his relatives would be called. Her eyes widened when she thought of Mary; and here they were driving back to her now. What if she blamed them?

"Should we go back to Mary's house? She could have been in on the whole thing with Kenneth," Catherine asked cautiously.

"Yes, we have to. At least to the druid ruins, if not to Mary's house," Bowen answered. "I don't think she was involved, though it's certainly possible," he paused. "But thinking back, Kenneth made sure nothing was discussed around her. He was obviously trying to hide our plans," he said.

Catherine nodded when she remembered Kenneth abruptly hushing them when Mary approached. At the time she thought it was merely Kenneth trying to be considerate and not bother his grandmother with worry.

"You're right," she said slowly as it became clearer in her mind, "but if you suspected from the start, why did you have us go along with it?" she looked curiously at Bowen.

Bowen leaned back in his seat and turned to face her. "I didn't know for sure, and we needed the skyphos," he answered.

"Why didn't you tell me at least?"

"I didn't have a moment alone with you after that, not long enough to discuss it without fear of being overheard. I couldn't take the risk," he took a deep breath, "I made sure I could be there to protect you, as I promised I always would," he shrugged.

"Next time, if it's safe to, please do tell me," she said, and quickly added, "Though I hope there is no next time!"

"I will. Agreed." He shifted the skyphos in his lap.

When the pair arrived at Mary's house, they were greeted with unexpected congratulations by the small old woman. They glanced at each other, both startled, as Mary neglected to ask about her grandson's whereabouts.

"You did it! I knew you would," Mary playfully elbowed Catherine in her side.

"You knew?" Catherine asked.

"Aye, and don't concern yourself with my foolish grandson. He's been trying to steal artifacts and information from me for years," Mary explained.

"Why didn't you warn us?"

Mary looked over at Bowen. "I knew you would be fine," she answered Catherine, and turned back with a motherly smile.

Bowen chuckled as Catherine shook her head in disbelief.

Mary suddenly became very serious, and took Catherine's

hands in hers, "It was the least of the problems that lay ahead for you, Caty," she gave her a warning look.

Catherine's heart grew heavy when she heard Mary's frightening tone. It reminded her much of Uncle Mickey's warning voice, which now rang in the back of her mind. "Is there something you haven't told me?" she asked.

"You're the one to cast the curse, you know that, dear."

"Yes, well with help . . ." Catherine looked at Bowen questioningly. Bowen folded his arms, his face stern. "Right?" Catherine looked back down at Mary.

After a quick exchange of glances with Bowen, Mary lifted her hands and placed them on Catherine's face, pulling her down to her height. "It is you alone who has to do this."

"But how can I? I thought we were going to use magic, and recite something together?" Catherine realized she may have gotten that idea from a book or movie.

"No . . ." Bowen sighed.

Catherine waited.

"Caty, you were the one chosen to break the curse, not just by Bowen, or Arlana, but by the great oak tree."

"What do you mean?"

Mary sighed and released her.

Bowen walked over and took Catherine's hand. "The oak tree where Conall's wife died, the one which the priesthood and all my people held sacred," he explained.

Catherine twisted her face in confusion, "I thought the ancient druids held all oak trees sacred, not just one."

"Yes, we did. However, this oak tree was believed to select and give power to whomever it chose. When Arlana made the curse, she chose you with evil intention. But the oak is good, and meant it for good. The oak granted you ability because it knew who you were going to be," Bowen said.

"It knew all that was meant to be," Mary added.

Catherine felt the swelling ball of anger quake inside her, "My sister was not meant to be killed," she spoke coldly.

Mary was taken aback, "No, of course not, dear girl," she said quickly.

Bowen said nothing, for he knew the subject needed to be dropped to stop Catherine from breaking down. The ball inside her calmed to a steady steam again, and she pulled her thoughts back to him.

"I don't understand this ability you say I was given. I've never seen any sign of it in my life. How am I supposed to cast this curse?"

"The oak's power lay dormant until you freed those under the curse. That moment set your destiny, Caty. If you never had come to Ireland, Bowen would never have seen you, and your power would have remained unknown for the rest of your life."

Catherine shook her head, "But that doesn't explain why I haven't noticed anything since," she said frustrated.

"You probably have stronger emotions? Everything feels elevated to extremes?" Mary suggested gently.

Catherine thought about it. She was always pretty emotional, but perhaps it had been worse lately. She must not have noticed given the traumatic events following Conall's release.

Mary saw the realization cross Catherine's face, and nodded. "I think you need to accept what's happened in your life now, and use it to stop the evil that will spread over this country if you don't," she said firmly.

Bowen watched Catherine carefully. She was a strong woman, but he feared madness would creep in on her as it did for Conall.

Catherine nodded, then thought of something. "Does that means I'm able to cast other curses, like Arlana?"

"Arlana was a very powerful priestess. She had to be to cast the curse," Mary remarked.

Bowen shifted his footing, "She could cast many curses." he answered.

"You too have potential to be just as powerful, if not more. Your will is strong," Mary added.

"Without the right training, how can I reach the level I need to be to do this? Who can teach me?"

Mary touched her cheek in thought. "Come with me, Caty."

Catherine cringed inside at the nickname again, and scolded herself for not having the courage to tell Mary not to use it anymore. She let her crossed arms fall in defeat and followed Mary.

Mary led Catherine back to the room filled with scattered books and documents. Upon entry, Mary immediately set to searching for something through the mess on the table, and among the books stacked everywhere. Catherine waited by a wobbly wooden chair that looked at least a hundred years old, deciding not to risk sitting. She noticed Mary's briefly combed hair was rather wild again, though it was still pulled back in a barrette decorated with pearls and other tiny gems. *Pearls must be her favorite*, Catherine randomly thought, remembering her blue blouse. The strands around Mary's face, however, were quite loose. Mary pushed them back in a huff.

"Aha!" she said after a few minutes of shuffling. "I found it," she announced, as she stepped from a windowsill where stacks of aged books were piled on top of each other. The pile almost covered the window entirely.

Catherine walked over to the table as Mary brought an old book over to lay carefully flat. The book was so ancient and worn that the pages were no longer bound. She motioned for Catherine to stand close. Mary's glasses were on the tip of her nose as she traced the inked page with her finger.

"Look here," she pointed.

"I can't read that . . ." Catherine said after taking a look. The page was filled with merely scribbles and runes, and what appeared at first glance to be Latin in certain sections. If in a language she could read, she would have loved to have her old reading glasses back to study it.

Mary chuckled at her forgetfulness, "I'm sorry, I forget. It says here," and she traced her finger to translate word by word "that when teachings are forgotten, dead, and buried, one must go to the wee folk," she looked up from the book to see Catherine's startled face.

"The wee folk? That's . . . fairies?"

"Why, yes, dear," the old woman said matter of fact, without a glimmer of surprise.

"But . . . so . . . they exist then?"

"Well, you don't expect all myths to be false, do you?"

"I suppose not," Catherine replied, her eyebrows still raised on her forehead. "Aren't they thought to be scary, even evil, creatures?"

"Aye."

"Oh . . ."

Mary chuckled, "No need to be afraid, Caty, no not one bit." She put her glasses on her head.

"Why ever not?" Catherine said becoming agitated.

"If you seek them, they will welcome you and do as you request," Mary said.

"Why would you think that?" Catherine said confused, and tapped her forefinger on the table, ridding herself of the blast of nervous energy.

"I know. They won't harm you specifically. You're one of precious few in the world left who can harness their powers. If you do this, they will be stronger for it," she answered.

"Enacting the curse is their power?"

"No, no it's *your* power you're using, but its force will bring them strength. They connect and feed off of it. That, and the cosmos dear," Mary said reflectively.

"The cosmos . . ."

"Yes, the moon, the stars. Everything is connected you know. The moon gives our women strength too," Mary said.

Catherine blinked a few times before saying "And to men?"

"Oh no, not to men. No, men get their strength from us . . . the good men anyway," she added, nodding to herself.

Catherine shook her head quickly, "How do you know all of this?"

"Read Caty, read."

Catherine sighed. "How do I find the fairies then?" she asked, defeated.

"The wee folk dear. Some of them don't like to be called 'fairies,'" Mary warned.

"Oh, okay, well how do I find them?"

"Your inner spirit will guide you."

"Mary, what does that mean?"

"It means you need to go search for yourself. I cannot tell you where to find them, just that you need to," Mary answered.

Catherine gave a confused slight nod in response, and with a tight jaw she turned away.

"Be warned, you must go alone. Do not take the druid boy with you," Mary said as she swept her forefinger through the air in one motion for emphasis.

Catherine looked back at her shakily. She tried to smile unsuccessfully before leaving the room.

CHAPTER SEVEN

Catherine stood alone in the cottage's small living room, leaning against the wall. Trying to relax she closed her eyes and thought about the day. How could she possibly find the wee folk alone? She stepped into the sun, which made her feel warm and cozy. Her mind wandered to her childhood house with the surrounding gates, and her family name in bold capital letters 'GREEN.' She could remember the sound the gates made when swinging open, and the smell of the freshly cut grass in her nose.

But then her thoughts shifted to fields of green, how they seemed to go on and on until they disappeared into the horizon. She remembered running through and the smell of the overgrown grass, brush, and trees. The mix stayed with her, and the green made her feel safe. Bowen's eyes were green. They pulled her in. A deep color that reminded her of the ocean depths, and the vibrant green fields she loved. When the ocean was calm, it was light and still. When a storm came it grew darker in alarm. The green fields were the same. Rhythmic. His green did not match any one green. She had never seen it before.

Catherine heard the rain pattering against the house and the window. Thinking of Bowen, she longed to see him. As she opened her eyes, she gasped. Bowen stood right in front of her, staring. He smiled at her funny reaction. She didn't say anything but glared briefly back.

Bowen's deep and mesmerizing eyes looked like a calming pool of liquid green. She blushed, remembering her daydream, though she didn't feel awkward as she usually did. The chemistry they shared was something she couldn't resist. They both had strong personalities, and clashed on occasion, but that only brought out more of the connection they felt to each other. Catherine felt she could be herself with him. She boldly reached out to run her fingers through the curly soft locks on his head. Bowen slipped his hands around her waist and pulled her to him.

Catherine sighed happily. But doubt and fear still plagued her. Bowen saw her expression change, and tensed his shoulders. "What is it?" he asked.

"I never want to lose you," she answered.

Bowen's shoulders relaxed. "You'll never lose me. You have all of me. You've always had me, even when you didn't know it," he said leaning down slightly, his nose touching hers.

"I never didn't want you," she said. "But how do I keep you?"

He took her hand away from his shoulder and put it on her chest where her heart beat steadily, "In there."

"But the curse, it'll take you away. I'll have to leave here and never see you again," she said, her brow wrinkling with anxiety.

Bowen didn't want to dwell on that while he could still see her. "Don't think about that now . . . I've waited for you to let me hold you like this for a long time," he said softly. Catherine went on the tips of her toes and kissed Bowen lightly on the cheek. He held her there and tentatively brushed his lips over hers. When she didn't resist, Bowen kissed her tenderly, and he felt her give into it.

Bowen was like air to Catherine. She needed him.

The pattering of rain stopped, and soon Mary's voice was heard from the garden outside. "I've got fresh cucumbers ready for brunch, you two!"

Reluctantly they pulled away from the kiss, and both smiled at each other before going to meet Mary in the kitchen.

* * *

Catherine was about to go outside when she saw Bowen standing by the front door, his back to her with his hands in his pockets. Stuck, she swirled around, closing her eyes tight in frustration. She didn't like the idea of leaving without Bowen, but she didn't really have a choice in the matter. Knowing Bowen, she guessed he would insist he come along for her safety. Fighting all her instincts, she opened her eyes and left out the back door, cutting straight into the woods.

Eventually she reached the road that led her to the ruins of the druids. She stood there amidst the tall stones. She didn't know why she was there, or what she was going to do. But this was the first place she thought of to start.

Walking along, she eyed the stones, and then her eyes fell on the raised ground where the oak trees once stood proud and tall. She stopped at the largest stump and gazed down reverently.

Suddenly, the tree stump expanded upward, and grew tall, branches blooming fully while spreading and covering the sky above her. Catherine jumped back, gaping at the magnificent oak tree in awe. It was just as it had once been, full and strong. In that moment she could understand why they'd been held sacred in ancient times. She revered the giant in front of her, and shut her eyes as she soaked in the beauty of it. But to her astonishment when she opened her eyes the oak stump was back, and gloom hovered again in the air.

Catherine squatted down and stared at the stump. Burrowing

her eyes into the ancient wood, she waited, almost as if expecting the tree lines to tell her what to do with their years of wisdom and knowledge. A tree sees all around it, she thought. She ran her fingers carefully along the lines, feeling the ridges. Her legs were becoming numb so she stood to return blood flow and walked to the stone message. She stood over it and stared as well, but this time she allowed herself to fall into a kind of trance.

Though unable to read the message, Catherine somehow felt connected to it. She wondered what the old man looked like who wrote it, Arlana's father, the high priest. Touching the engraved letters with the tips of her fingers, an image of an elderly man flashed before her eyes suddenly. He was dressed in white with sparkling eyes. The priest? Somewhere deeper, in a gut feeling, she knew she was right. Catherine knew it had to do with her untapped potential trying to come out at last. This place, or her mindset was triggering it. Or was Mary right—had she been experiencing it since Conall's release, and didn't know it? Catherine feared what kind of abilities she could have in the future. How far could it go? She desperately did not want this burden to control what could happen to countless of lives. And then to be left with this uncontrolled power all alone?

Catherine turned to walk away, and was momentarily terrified to see Bowen standing in front of her perfectly still. She let out a stifled scream.

"Stop doing that!" she shouted.

"I'm sorry . . ." he said calmly, but with a blank face.

"What are you doing just standing there anyway?" she asked irritably.

"Why did you feel the need to sneak away from the house to come here?"

"Wha—?"

"You were avoiding me at the house, so I followed you here," he explained. "Now why?" his face was stern.

"I don't have to tell you, Bowen," Catherine didn't want to get into a feminist debate right then, but if that's what he wanted . . .

"Yes, you do!" Bowen was furious, his eyes blazing with green fire.

"I don't see why! How dare you!"

"How else can I keep you safe? How can you expect me to protect you if you don't stay with me, or tell me where you're going? Damn it all! It wasn't enough that we both could have died when we were separated before?" Bowen's face was stricken with worry.

Catherine didn't say anything. She could hear the fear behind his words. She felt guilty. Their eyes hadn't left each other. Both were filled with angry fire, but Catherine was the first to cool. Bowen saw it happen instantly, but it didn't matter. He was too upset.

"Bowen, I'm sorry I ran . . ."

"Where were you running away to?"

"I need to find the wee folk, Mary told me they can teach me how to wield this power I have," she said.

"That is incredibly dangerous, Catherine," he put his hands on her shoulders "do you understand?"

"Yes, as a matter of fact I do know that it's dangerous, but only if I don't go alone!"

Bowen let go of her shoulders.

"The last thing I want to do is leave you, Bowen, believe me," she sighed.

"Mary told you to go alone?" he asked.

"Yes," she said simply.

"Then she must think they will welcome you instead of taking you."

"Take me?" Catherine was alarmed.

"Yes . . . you haven't heard of the folklore?"

"Yes of course, but I didn't think about that. I was only listening to what Mary read from the book," she answered.

"Mary meant you no harm. It is true they will not harm a druid," he said.

"But I'm not a druid," she stated confused.

"They will see you as one," Bowen folded his arms.

"Oh, I suppose that's good then . . ."

"Yes, it is, very much so."

"If they won't harm a druid, then why can't both of us go together?" Catherine wondered.

"They have rules. If you come in numbers often it's for shenanigans. If you disobey the rule you are inherently disrespecting them. They will ignore you or harm you depending on their mood . . . the wee folk are fairly mercurial," he said in a matter of fact tone.

Catherine doubted more and more that she could do this. She longed for her normal life, and thought suddenly of Danny.

"You need to be direct with them, and stay calm with a kind voice. Don't alarm them or their shape shifters will try to intimidate you," he said.

She snapped her head up. "Wha—? I've read about the wee folk turning into the people they've taken, it's all true?"

"To some extent, yes," he answered.

"Have you ever met them before?" she asked, a bit shaken.

"Yes, once, but it was different for me. They ventured out to speak to my high priest. They are normally very private creatures and would rather wait for human audiences to find them or be completely alone in the woods for them to lure away to their realm."

"Do you remember why they went to him?"

"They were concerned about their future. I suspect they

foresaw the massive change coming, and wanted to get as much energy from the druids as they could before it was too late . . ." he said, his expression thoughtful.

"Before Christianity arrived," Catherine finished.

"Exactly," he said, leaning on a large smooth rock.

"Bowen?"

"Yes?"

Catherine sat down cross legged on the ground next to him, and looked up. "Knowing everything you do, after all this time you've been alive, what do you believe?"

"Ancient druids believe in an ultimate being, and I still do," he said.

"And nothing has changed?"

"My belief in a higher power? No. While under the curse I was never able to become too familiar with others until now to seek out details of such things," he said forlornly.

"Now you can," she stated.

"Not really, I'll be back under the curse in no time at all," he remarked. He straightened his back, and had a far off look on his face. "And that's just what we have until then: no time."

Bowen obviously dreaded the idea of being cursed again, Catherine thought, trapped forever in so many ways. She still didn't want that for him. She wanted him to live freely, to be allowed a real life, to seek out and learn everything he could possibly want. To be fulfilled in mind, spirit and body. As it was, he would be stuck forever, long after she died. The thought scared her. Upset now, she pushed it from her mind, shaking it off as she stood up.

"I must go find the wee folk. Do you know where they live? Mary told me to just search. Helpful," Catherine said sarcastically.

"They loved the woods, which is why so many legends speak of people disappearing in the forest." He brushed his hand through his hair in thought, "Some enjoyed abandoned areas, like these ruins, and to be near us, the druids. They may be just over there waiting for you to come," he pointed to the woods a distance away from the great oak's remains.

"Just over there . . ." she said quietly to herself, looking far off.

Bowen came closer to her, and she looked up at his approach. She was reminded of his lips on hers, and the warmth emanating between them. "It will be fine. They won't harm you if you remain respectful and calm," he soothed.

Catherine shook her head, refocusing her thoughts on the word calm.

"I won't follow you this time. It would mean death for both of us."

She nodded gravely.

"Now go," he said, and pushed her gently off in the direction of the woods.

The sun was bright, though the woods were thick with leaves. She trembled at the thought of passing through the dark interior. She feared wandering too far and getting lost. She thought of Conall finding her there, and pursed her lips in agitation. Without the use of her power, Catherine knew for sure she would not survive another encounter with him alone. She felt incredibly thankful for Bowen. She turned and saw his shrinking figure standing in the ruins where she'd left him. He was watching her. This brought her comfort, though she knew he couldn't come rescue her if she needed him this time. She prayed she wouldn't for once. Pausing at the tree line, she felt the bright sun on her forehead, how it heated her fiery hair. She exhaled, and taking a step forward she entered, leaving possibly the last sunlight she would ever see and feel behind her.

In the woods she walked on for what felt like hours, but it was probably only twenty minutes. Twigs snapped under her feet and made her heart jump. She passed countless trees in the dark, snagging her hair or clothes on their branches. She rolled her mane into a thick red twist and put her jacket hood up. She looked around constantly, watching her surroundings, all the while trying very hard to walk in a straight line. The alarmingly overgrown vegetation made her paranoid of insects and creatures possibly creeping and crawling around everything. Her imagination was getting the better of her, and she tried to ignore thoughts about lurking shadows, hidden creatures and the like behind each tree.

The shadows in the woods made her think of when she met the large bear. The memory of Conall stirred up dark thoughts again as she walked along in a dark place. Now that she had power, maybe there was hope for justice. Maybe she actually could kill Conall, instead of locking him away again. Catherine knew she would have to keep it from Bowen. He would never condone it. But for all she knew, her power might not even be strong enough to cast the curse yet. She desperately hoped she would be able to save them from Conall.

While Catherine tried to convince herself there was nothing to worry about, something suddenly moved to her left, and stopped in an instant. She snapped her head, too late to catch a glimpse. She waited for a moment. What looked like a rabbit's shadow ran across the path behind her. Catherine turned around watching it, making a full circle. She relaxed her tense shoulders slightly as she thought of the peaceful rabbit living somewhere in these woods without being eaten by a terrifying fairy.

As Catherine walked deeper into the dark woods, she realized there was no turning back. If she dared to try, the wee folk would likely attack, perceiving the move as an offense. There was no escape for her, and so with each pensive step she kept her slow pace.

Catherine kept wishing Bowen was next to her, or Danny. But such thoughts were pointless. If she was going to die, then she might as well just do it. So she walked faster, with deliberate strides. They carried her past more trees, passing other skittering animals of the dark woods. If they weren't afraid, then she wouldn't be either.

Faded sunlight pushed past the thick matted leaves above. Catherine stepped into the dappled light, and noticed a tiny bulb that appeared from thin air. Its circular form looked illuminated from the outside while somehow getting fainter in its core. It twinkled, as if to wink at her.

As Catherine stood still, amazed, the light grew uncomfortably brighter. The miniature star lit up the woods, and Catherine squinted as she cowered down to protect her eyes from sudden blindness. Finally she adjusted and looked up. The light was strange, not like anything she'd seen before. Not like a light bulb of any wattage, not the powerful light of fire from the sun. It wasn't even like the moon at its fullest, as she expected in connection with fairies after all. No, it was more like starlight, yes that was it, that distant and dull white fire. As if a star in its marble shape was in midair before her, somehow maintaining its distant appearance and illuminating a place where no light had been for centuries at a time. The ball shape had rings of brightness. The inside was faint, the first ring surrounding that a bit brighter, the next ring brighter than the last, and so on. It seemed to grow with intensity, drawing her in. Catherine imagined it shone from another universe. If it were here, then its fire would consume her.

Nothing happened at first, as the ball of light floated. Catherine was not afraid, for once. But she was beginning to be uncomfortable as it lingered. Was she supposed to do something? Speak to it perhaps? She opened her mouth to speak but stopped herself when she contemplated that this might be considered too forward. Respectfully she waited; patiently she stood.

Suddenly the light flashed out and the woods went black again. Then suddenly they were unnaturally bright as though blanketed in blindingly white snow. But Catherine's eyes were not blind. Looking down at her hands, she saw they blended impossibly with everything else. She grabbed her hair and pulled the twist out to look at it. It too appeared white as snow. The eerie starlight consumed and melted into everything. Amazed, she looked around her and found everything had lost its color and seemed to be flowing, reverberating, as though she could actually see them living. The plants, the trees, the very ground all had an ever-so-slight tremor about them, their own kind of breathing. Though strange it was at first, but only because she had never seen it before, it quickly became normal to her, as if it was always there and she had only to notice.

"You seek us?" Catherine heard an eerie voice speak behind her and spun around.

The voice came from a sleek creature of small build. It was incredibly fair, matching the starlight. The appearance in the face was feminine, but she couldn't be sure of the gender, simply that their features appeared gentle, like that of a small girl. Sleek and thin, too thin to mistake for human. Beautiful kind eyes looked out of the narrow face that was framed with long hair. This was not what Catherine had imagined when picturing the wee folk. Definitely not the size that you could hold in your palm, nor the Norse tall standing kind. But this being seemed like a child.

"Yes," Catherine answered as steadily as possible. She wrapped her arms around herself to control her shaking body. She hoped desperately it wasn't noticeable to the creature.

"You are a druid," the eerie voice was almost melodic, a kind of echoing perhaps. Catherine told herself she would find out if she survived this.

"No, I was given the ability of a druid," she stated honestly.

"You are a very young, human woman, how is it you have this power? The druids have been gone since long ago."

"There was a curse, and I was the one to break it. The great oak tree gave me power to recast the curse," she answered as plainly as she could.

The fae creature rolled its head oddly, then nodded in reply. "Why have you come?"

"I have to protect innocent people. But I need help to use the power first. For that I was told to find you. Please, will you help me?"

"Humans are not innocent," the creature quietly remarked, and searched Catherine's face with a frightening stare.

The creature was dressed in translucent garments that looked as frail as a spider's web. She waited and gazed at the gorgeous figure before her. Though the creature was kind, and beautiful, she felt somehow it could all go sour rather easily, and therefore was still holding onto that bit of fear in the pit of her stomach.

"Our knowledge is precious to us. We do not share it with others. There must be something equally precious that you must give of your own free will," the fae said, breaking the silence.

"Equally precious?"

They nodded.

"How can I judge that?"

The creature looked over Catherine, and she felt its eyes moving across her. They stopped. "Your hair."

"My hair? You want my hair?"

"I can see it is important to you, though not for vanity."

"How can you know that?"

"Your hair is a part of you, and you are alive. Therefore, I can see it."

"You want all of my hair?" Catherine asked anxiously.

"No, only a lock."

Catherine nodded slowly. "May I ask, what you will do with it?"

"That is not your concern."

Catherine hesitated. But what choice did she have? Without their help it would take too long for her to learn enough to enact the curse, and Conall would overrun them. No, she had to do this, they didn't have any time to spare. Perhaps it was already too late. Also motivating her was her deepening concern for Danny. She had to keep taking action, she couldn't get stuck and lose momentum. She blinked back the urge to cry when she thought of him, but told herself inwardly that he was still alive, she just needed to hurry.

"A lock of my hair is yours," she said, palms up in submission.

"I see you are very strong. There is great power within you. More than what was given to you. Do not think it is another's power you use. It is yours alone." The creature walked a few paces over, all the while gazing at Catherine with an eerie air surrounding their body.

Stepping close to Catherine, the fae creature grew taller and leaned over her. It gave off an overwhelming fragrance, a combination of fresh fruit and springtime after a rainfall. She felt feeble and lightheaded as breathing became a minor struggle. It reached its hand close to her neck, and she felt a small tug on her scalp.

The fae looked pleased then, and said, "It is done." They stepped away from Catherine. She could breathe normally again.

"As promised," it said, and waved an arm in front of them. The starlight ball reappeared out of thin air at the creature's command.

"To help you hone the necessary skills, I give you this to

bring them years ahead," the fae spoke, and the circular object holding the light of distant stars floated to Catherine, who couldn't help but lean away at first.

"Place your hands under it." Catherine did as she was told. It hardened and crystallized in form, as it descended into her palms. It felt warm and somehow comforting.

"Take this. It has been bound to your will. Be warned, starlight cannot be contained forever, it will eventually return to its place of origin. It is your tool now, use it as you must." The creature moved away as Catherine tore her gaze from the hardened bulb. "Heed our words, we warn you, it will increase your power by years but without the discipline that comes with time and practice." Suddenly, the creature disappeared.

Catherine swiveled around to find it hovering behind her. Relieved the creature hadn't left and yet terrified at the same time, she realized she had difficulty swallowing. Her throat was parched. "How do I use it?" she asked through a scratchy throat.

"It cannot be told; it must be felt. You will know when you try. Now go from this place." The fae disappeared again. This time no sign of them remained.

"Thank you. I will treasure and use it as you say," Catherine said, hoping they had heard.

Catherine turned back and walked along with the warm bulb cradled in both hands. After a while she realized the forest's brightness dimmed dramatically but it wasn't as dark as before. It was still slightly infused with the eerie light. She wondered if the wee folk had lit her way. Looking back, she saw that the light was slowly dissolving as she passed through. When she neared the edge of the wood, thankful to see normal light and colors ahead, the darkness quickened. Just as she stepped onto the green grass the light disappeared completely, and darkness fell like a curtain behind her.

Seeing the black forest now made her feel like she had

stepped in and out of time. Relieved that she had survived and that it was over, she walked back to the ruins. Pulling her hair around, she saw less now where the lock of hair had been cut. She was thankful it was easily hidden under the rest of her hair. Remembering how alarmingly white it had looked in the strange light, she was thankful to see color returned to it, as well as everything else. Once more, she glanced back at the forest and hoped never to go there again.

The sun was still high in the sky and she reveled in it, letting her skin and hair absorb every ray. Bowen was in the distance, waiting in the ruins. He spotted her soon after she saw him and ran to meet her. He reached for her with both his arms.

"I'm so glad you're back at last!" he said happily, obviously relieved.

"It wasn't so long as all of that, but me too," she said smiling.

"A full day isn't very long to you?" he laughed.

"But the sun hasn't moved that much," she said, gesturing a hand upward.

He squinted up for a moment then back, realization striking his face. "You didn't know?"

"Know what?"

"You went into the woods yesterday, Catherine."

Catherine pulled the star bulb tightly against her chest. "But how? It was only a couple hours, tops," she said astonished.

"The wee folk must have known you were coming and enchanted your path to watch you," Bowen speculated.

"But I don't feel tired, or even hungry!" she said, then remembered her throat was parched and grabbed above her collarbone.

"It was not uncommon for the women who went missing for a time to have no idea how long they were gone when they returned," he answered.

"Oh my, Bowen . . ."

He hugged her over the bulb and pulled back to look into her eyes for reassurance, "It's okay now. They returned you safely. Though—" he stopped short and pulled away looking puzzled, "you seem different somehow. Did they do something to you?"

"They gave me this," she moved to show him the star bulb.

"Hmm, no, it's something else . . ."

"No? Different how then?" she touched one of her cheeks quickly.

Bowen looked her over momentarily before his eyes widened as he saw it. "They took your hair," he said, reaching for the shortened piece tucked behind and sticking out from under her ear.

"Yes, they did, they wouldn't tell me why they wanted it."

Bowen contemplated as he ran his long fingers through her hair. "Was it purely payment, an exchange for this orb?"

Catherine held out the warm bulb, "I think so," she answered.

Bowen's eyes glowed as he examined it. He raised his eyebrows as he quietly gasped at the beauty. "The light from distant stars," he said, as mesmerized by it as Catherine had been when she first saw it in the woods.

"Yes," she answered, and pulled it back to keep her chest warm again. Even though it was sunny, the wind was cold on her skin and made her shiver. Bowen shook his head and looked at her.

"I'm relieved they didn't do anything else to you," he said.

"What do you mean? I thought you said they wouldn't do anything to hurt me?"

Bowen's mouth twitched, "They wouldn't break their oaths. But if they really wanted to, they could have found a loophole without having to actually harm you themselves."

Catherine cringed. Absentmindedly she moved her thick waves behind her shoulders. "Why do you think they wanted some of my hair, Bowen?"

"You seem worried," he said.

"Well yes, it seems like voodoo."

Bowen chuckled slightly. "Yes, well. I can't say I know for sure why they wanted it. But it may simply have been the only way they could make you different upon your return. To take something forever away from you. It's what they do with humans. Every woman who returns does so in worse condition than when they were taken."

"Since they couldn't harm me, they took some of my hair?"

"So it seems," he said looking ahead as they walked slowly together.

"You know, some of those folk stories, I don't believe were women being taken by the wee folk. I'm pretty sure they were being abused by men." Catherine said conversationally.

"I know," he said.

"You know?" she asked.

"Yes, some the wee folk took and returned. But some men preyed on the superstitions of their village in order to hurt or kill women for whatever purpose. Sometimes it was their wives. It happened a lot over the centuries. I stopped a few from happening. It was such an evil thing. Another reason to avoid superstition. Religion and its branches become corrupt; people can't be trusted," he said.

"You trust your ultimate being?" she asked.

"Yes, *our* God. Belief, and devotion is our place. Not human religion and superstitions. Very few of my people believed that. Rituals, and tradition without reason is man's obsession," he said, his eyes searching the ground as they walked on. He seemed far away in thought.

Catherine imagined he had many reasons to feel the way he did. Seeing history repeat its own horrors would certainly be depressing and upsetting. Being forced to watch, helpless, must be a terrible thing. She felt the same way, as someone who tried to solve the mysteries of the centuries for a living.

Catherine stopped walking, and kept her eyes on Bowen. Bowen felt the tug on his arm and turned to face her. "The wee folk . . ." she said.

"Hm?" he said, mildly interested.

"There was only one."

"That they let you see . . ."

"She-they looked nothing like I imagined," she said, her voice quiet.

"There are many different kinds of wee folk, the same as humans," Bowen said.

"The one I saw, she, or he, I don't know which, they seemed lonely. Do you think they live all alone in that big wood?" she asked.

"They do have both genders, but it isn't something humans can easily decipher. Both are startlingly beautiful." He paused for a moment, "I don't know if you encountered only one of them. The others may have been around you, but only one showed themselves. You see, they need each other to maintain long life," he explained.

Catherine shivered when she considered she may have been surrounded by them, camouflaged in the eerie light.

"The ones with wings, the ones that can stand on your palm, I wonder if they exist," she said as they set out again.

"I've been told they do. The ones I saw were not like that," he said.

As the two neared the old cottage, Mary emerged from her back garden, running towards them. "You've done it!" she exclaimed.

Catherine smiled at the old woman, and showed her the glowing crystal between her palms. Mary was shocked to see the eerie, yet lovely object. "Why, Caty!"

Catherine realized in that moment she no longer minded the nickname, as long as Mary was the one to say it. She laughed out loud, and hugged Mary tightly. "Thank you," she whispered in her ear.

Mary winked happily in return. "I knew you would find them, my dear. They didn't hurt you, yea?" she asked.

Before Catherine could answer, Bowen interrupted. "We need to prepare," he said, his jaw set.

"Aye, of course, you two go. Take this." Mary handed Bowen a small basket filled with sandwiches and water bottles. "I'll be in the house if you need me," she said.

Catherine spotted the water and guzzled one down completely. After the two ate the delicious sandwiches, they prepared for what was next.

"What did the wee folk say?" Bowen asked, looking at the star bulb.

"They said they couldn't tell me, that I must feel it myself," Catherine explained.

He looked curiously at her. "You've experienced some of the power now, haven't you?"

Catherine sighed. "Yes, but I don't know how it happened. I don't understand it!"

"When did it first happen?"

"I—I'm honestly not sure," she answered. She couldn't be certain whether it had been her overactive imagination, or if it had been the power leaking through the whole time. "But it happened for sure before I went into the forest."

"What did?"

"I saw the great oak tree alive and tall above me, among other things," she answered, reluctantly thinking of Conall and his wife.

"Have you experienced any other heightened senses?" Bowen wondered.

Catherine thought about it, and couldn't think of anything different besides her heightened emotions. "Just my moods really, but that could be from all that's happened," she said.

"Yes, you're right . . ." he gently massaged his shoulder. The soreness was gone now. All that remained was an occasional ache. "Catherine?"

"Yes?"

"Has anything become a need for you?"

Catherine wrinkled her nose, "What do you mean?"

"Like something you absolutely *must* have, and once you do you feel better instantly? Almost like an addiction," he replied.

Catherine hadn't noticed anything like that, but she went over the last few days, or even weeks. She shook her head in answer, and while Bowen continued to think, Catherine watched the green grass, enjoying the sunlight flicker across it. She imagined what it would feel like to bathe in a pool of sunlight. She felt re-energized. Then it hit her.

"The sun . . ."

Bowen turned in attention, "What about it?"

"I've been very aware of the sun, at least since that day Conall was released." Saying his name made her want to vomit, but she continued on. "It wasn't so much at first, but it's been getting more aggressive. I *crave* it. All I could think about today in the forest was the sun. Every light inside drew me to it," she stated.

Bowen didn't say anything at first, just stood in thought for a moment. "What happens when you stand in the sunlight?"

"I feel good, strong and satisfied. As if . . ." she looked around as if literally searching for the word, "as if it gave me actual energy," she said.

"I think then, you should concentrate on that," Bowen decided.

Catherine stood with the orb in her hand, enjoying the

warmth it gave her. She tried to think of how the sun felt and imagined spreading the warmth throughout her body. "Okay," she looked at Bowen, "How do we perform the curse?"

Bowen lightly clapped his hands together, "The skyphos will need to be present. It connects old with new, the cosmos with us."

"Do I have to recite anything?"

"No, it's more like the curse, as such a powerful one, remembers itself. Arlana attached it to you, so you'll find it just fine."

Catherine was doubtful. "Try again," he assured.

Catherine held her arms out, and looked again. All she felt was the warmth resonating from it. She closed her eyes to block out the external distractions, and remembered the great oak tree shooting out of the ground. Thinking of its power, she recalled the jealous priestess who harnessed it. Her thoughts took a dark turn and Catherine was reminded of her buried anger. The hateful image of Conall appeared, and she trembled with rage.

Bowen waited patiently, watching her small twitches of discomfort.

Catherine remembered seeing Conall in the field, Kathleen captured next to him. She wanted to stop then, but her mind pushed forward. "No," she mumbled at first, "I don't want to see it again!" she shouted.

Bowen grew uneasy as he helplessly watched.

Catherine saw Kathleen die again before her eyes. She lost all control of her connection with the star and jumped away, causing it to fall from her hands and roll in the grass. Bowen went to her side and put his arms around her shivering shoulders. She wept uncontrollably. "Bowen, I can't do this," she cried, "not if it's going to bring it all back!"

"It showed it to you because it's your reason for doing this, your driving force. But you must let it go; it only makes you vulnerable," he explained.

"I know that!" she said harshly, "But I can't let it go." She shrugged him off her.

"Why do you keep pushing me away? I tell you multiple times that I love you. You never say it back, but you care what happens to me. Have I been wrong to believe there's more, Catherine?" Catherine turned away. Bowen grabbed her arm gently but forcefully and stepped in front of her. "Let me be with you, Catherine. Talk to me! Let me help you, I just want you to be happy again. What can I do? No more silence! What on earth is happening?"

"I don't know, Bowen! What do you want from me? You love me? Do you want to know who it is you claim to love, who I really am? Fine!" she ripped her arm away from him. "Will you still love me when you hear that I hate myself, that I hate you, and everyone! I'm filled with hatred. It's burning me from the inside out. But if I quench it I'll have nothing left. I'll lose my mind. And the fear, oh there's so much fear! I hate even Kathleen for this," she paused and looked up at Bowen through her tears. He stood still, quietly weathering her outburst.

"I hate her for going back there without telling me. I hate her for dying and leaving me alone!"

"You can't blame Kathleen for being gone, Catherine," Bowen reasoned.

"I know it's madness, but I feel like she should have been able to stay with me even after death. You can't understand," she sobbed.

Bowen said in a calming voice, "I know what it's like to lose a family member. I told you I lost everyone in mine—"

"That's terrible, but you *don't* know! You *can't* know what *this* is like for me. Losing someone— losing your literal other half. I can never be whole again, Bowen. You can't fix this for me. No one can." She wiped at her face profusely.

"Stop this hatred, Catherine, you must stop it! You'll destroy yourself! I can't lose you, especially not like this, please. Conall suffered such a loss, and—"

"Don't!" Catherine interrupted, glaring at him. "Don't you dare try to defend him to me," she practically spit the words out.

"Even after knowing what he went through. That he's insane. It doesn't matter. I have no pity for him. He still did what he did! He still killed my sister!" Catherine fell where she stood and sobbed viciously in the palms of her hands, gulping for air.

Bowen sat down and put his hands on her shaking shoulders. He held her closely, his nose in her hair, and closed his eyes trying to soak up the sorrow. He wanted badly to relieve her of this suffering. It tore at his heart to see her rage and weep in such a way. She had finally poured herself out to him. Bowen didn't know if she could ever heal, but he hoped she would let him help her.

The two returned to the house, and Catherine fell into a deep sleep. Bowen stayed in the room with her, sitting up with his back against the wall, watching over her.

The next morning Catherine awoke early at dawn feeling rested, but emotionally dry. She was alone. Lifting her legs up and over the edge of the bed, she stood and walked out of the room.

"Oh!" she yelped as she bumped into Bowen's broad chest.

"I'm sorry," he smiled down at her.

"What were you just standing at the door for?" she asked, rubbing her face.

"I was about to come back in when you opened it," he answered, laughing.

"I see."

"Did you sleep well?"

"Yes, I think so. You?"

"I couldn't," he said.

Catherine felt a pang of worry, "Why not?"

Bowen shrugged. "Catherine," he led her backward to sit on the bed, "Mary gave me this," he held out a piece of paper.

Catherine took the folded paper and opened it. The contents revealed a message asking for help. It was signed—her heart stopped—by Danny. Conall had him. Her head snapped up, "Where did this come from?"

"Mary said it was left at the door. They must have delivered it in the night," Bowen answered.

"Danny," she said slowly, and eased herself back down, wanting to cry. She recognized the handwriting now. They must have forced him to write something.

"They know where we are," Bowen said. Catherine felt goosebumps crawl up her arm.

She started to ask how, but thought better of it.

Bowen couldn't bear to watch her face crumble any longer. "I'm going to leave for a bit."

Catherine nodded absently. Danny was captured and was somewhere in the woods with an army of ancient druids and the madman who killed their sister. She tried to convince herself that he would be fine, but she couldn't manage to believe it for longer than a few seconds.

The front door closed, and she snapped out of her thoughts. "Bowen?" she said. She rushed out to find him. Bowen turned when she caught up with him. "Where are you going?" she stood defiantly.

Bowen hesitated. "I have to do something that you're not going to like."

"You're not going to run into a tree again, are you?" she asked, remembering the first time he said that to her.

"No, I'm going to turn myself over to him," he replied. Bowen was completely serious.

Catherine froze. "To *him*?"

"Yes. If I can get through to him, I'll tell him that I'm giving up. I'll tell him you're dead so he won't come after you, and he may even let Danny go. You can cast the curse while I'm distracting him. The army won't leave without him."

"Are you crazy? I can't do this alone! Conall will see through you. He will only torture Danny in front of you before he tortures you," she said.

"Yes. But if there's a chance I might be able to stop all of this with my life, shouldn't I try?"

"No," she said angrily, clenching her fists at her sides. "We're in this together. Don't go off trying to make heroic gestures! I can't lose you too, Bowen. I won't survive it."

"So you do love me?"

"Yes, I love you! You're so stupid!" she burst out, and Bowen smiled. She bit her lip.

With a yearning look, he stepped in and swooped his arm around her waist firmly as they released in a passionate kiss. Catherine ran her hands wildly through his hair and down his neck. She longed for his touch, and let herself bask in their embrace.

"I deeply love you, Bowen," she whispered when their lips were satisfied. Bowen was blissful, and caressed the side of her jaw. Her full lips made him want to kiss her again, but he stopped, remembering their dire straits.

"They're coming today, Catherine. Can you do this?" he asked gently.

Catherine somehow knew they were coming today without him telling her. Her usual warning signs where she could feel the chills on her arms, and the bad feeling in her stomach, were there and going strong. The message from Danny was the red flag.

"I'll have to," she answered, giving a doubtful smile.

Bowen reached down and locked his hand in hers. "We'll be together either way," he said, and Catherine squeezed his hand.

CHAPTER EIGHT

THE SUN ROSE over the horizon behind the cover of gloomy clouds. Catherine wondered if the weather was marking their impending doom.

Mary rushed to the door and yelled for them to come back into the house just then. She shut the door behind her. "Keep the gloom away, my dears!" she encouraged.

"Mary, they're coming," said Catherine.

Mary looked from Bowen to her, "Save us then, Caty. I'll be here willing you to find the strength."

Catherine simply smiled.

Bowen left the room briefly and returned with the star bulb and skyphos in hand. "Keep in the house, and don't come out until we return," he told Mary firmly as he handed the bulb to Catherine.

"Aye, you won't see me cross the threshold, old man."

Bowen nodded affectionately, "Take care," he said.

"Mary, thank you for believing in me," Catherine said as Bowen pulled the door shut after them.

Leaving Mary safely in her cottage somehow made Catherine feel better, at least for now. Bowen led her to the ruins where they sat on the ground, waiting. Catherine tried to practice using her power, and strengthening her mind to push past her unstable anger, while Bowen watched for the coming army. He returned from a long surveying walk, and rested his legs next to her. It was noon by now, and they had seen no sign of their enemies.

Catherine took a break and watched Bowen resting his head beside her. His brown curls covered part of his face as he hung his head between his propped up long legs. Maneuvering herself to see him better, she watched as he sprang up when her hair brushed the top of his hand.

"Hm?" he gazed at her happily.

"How can you be happy right now?" she asked.

"Because I'm with you," he answered.

"Yes, but we might be waiting for our death to come . . ."

Bowen didn't let this phase him. "At least I'll die with you," he said. Then he took her forearm and looked her closely in the face. "When the curse is cast, don't worry about me."

"What will happen to you?"

"It will be like before, stifling. But I'll be happy knowing you're going to live," he said with a small smile. "I would marry you if I was free."

Catherine blushed, but her heart was heavy. She secretly decided that even if it was risky, she wasn't going to leave him. Curse or no curse. But Bowen could read it on her face.

"No, you must leave," he said firmly, and she was speechless.

"Catherine, my love, I need you to live. Live on after all of this, and live well for both of us," he said, his eyes sorrowful. He caressed her face, then ran his hand through her silky hair, sending shivers of pleasure through Catherine.

"Even though I walked this earth for centuries before you were born, now I can't imagine a world without you." He paused and smiled down at her. "I've always loved you," he half whispered.

Tears welled up and began to fall down Catherine's cheeks.

"Even when you didn't know me?" she chuckled through her sobs.

"Yes, even then. Because you were always meant for me. I happily give my freedom as the price to pay for your future."

"But if we can't be together . . . what makes you think I want a future like that? What if *I* can't bear it? What am *I* supposed to do?"

Bowen furrowed his brow. "You'll live without me, just as I will without you. The only difference is you will have a happy life, and die a peaceful death. I won't have that luxury. I will live on until the end of times when all of this is burned up. But I'm keeping my sanity together because you're still here in front of me."

"I don't think I can do this without you," she cried.

"You aren't doing it alone, I'll be standing next to you the whole time," he said reassuringly.

"No, I mean I don't think I can move on without you, knowing you're somewhere here suffering. Knowing I could still see you." She slumped over, feeling overwhelmed, "What if I choose not to go through with this? Will you hate me?" she looked up at him with pleading eyes.

"I could never hate you, Catherine. If you chose it, I would fight with you, and die with you. I only want to be with you." he replied, keeping his gaze set on her. "Don't give up now."

"No," she said simply as Bowen wiped her tears away. She took a deep breath and released it. Bowen's face was mere inches from her own, and she eagerly leaned in to taste his lips just once more. Catherine didn't hold back, and completely melted when he responded with matching fervor.

After a few moments, she pulled away. "Bowen, I want to memorize everything about you, every little thing. Your features, your mannerisms," she told him.

"I want the same. I've sealed so much away already. The

way you laugh, or how your cheeks blush when I catch you off guard." He smiled, and Catherine didn't shy away. "Everything, so when the time comes, and I find myself alone and hidden away from the rest of the world, I can imagine what you would say to me, not just remember the things you have said to me. I can keep you with me. I can hold you in my mind for the rest of time. I want to remember everything Catherine, the scent of your hair, the way it falls down and touches your face and shoulders. I love everything that is you. The ground you walk on. I spent years watching you before we met, longing for you, and I've enjoyed every second being in your presence. If it were possible to be absorbed by you, I would be. Each random and deliberate touch we've shared, they will all stay with me, and help me live through forever."

Bowen stopped and looked around. "It's time to go meet the army. You can do this. We will succeed, and all will go back to how it should be, no regrets, no sorrow. If you're happy, I'll be happy," he said with a sweet smile that Catherine hoped she would always remember.

She stood then, and Bowen took her hand to lead the way. They walked through the ruins and abruptly stopped when they spotted something. Catherine stared at the dark mass of men and women spread across the field and distant hills. Amazed and terrified, she stood in awe. The armies seemed to be in three large groups, like ants lined up in formation.

"There's something wrong," Bowen observed.

"How do you know?"

"They should be one, but they're not. Today is the day, but they're not coming for us just yet, they're arguing amongst themselves."

Catherine thought she could see a lone figure, Conall. She breathed in deeply and reassured herself with the thought that Kathleen would be avenged soon.

"We need to do this now," Bowen said.

Catherine nodded, and turned her body to face east precisely as Bowen directed. Looking far out at the gloomy day, she longed for the sun, feeling cold and weak without it. Then she took the bulb of starlight and held it closely to her face. The warmth moved from her palms and down into her bones. It touched her chilled cheeks. The light from the bulb was small at the moment, but strong. She closed her eyes and concentrated. Somewhere deep within her she pulled a string. Something clicked. She pulled another string and continued. With each pluck the light grew brighter. She could feel the heat rising, and saw some of it leaking in through her tightly shut eyelids. Her fingers clasped against the crystal which rapidly became hotter with each string she pulled. She was getting closer.

"Catherine, they're fighting," Bowen said. Conall's armies had clashed. The violence was barbaric, and Bowen felt the old pull to help the wounded.

Catherine heard but didn't respond. Perspiration dripped from her forehead.

She pulled the final string. Suddenly the bulb burned red hot, and shone bright white light through her fingers. She opened her eyes and saw the power in her hands. Pushing down her fear, she tried to focus on the energy soaring through. Just when the burning was no longer tolerable, the bulb began to shake uncontrollably, which caused her to drop it. But instead of falling straight to the ground the star bulb catapulted itself a distance away, and the incredible light she witnessed in the black fairy woods spread for an instant to form into a single streak, then dropped and shed into millions of sparkling crystals on the grass. With a loud noise, the freed starlight shot out like a cannon ball up to the clouded sky. The noise lingered, seemed to grow louder for a moment, then ceased completely. Bowen and Catherine uncovered their ears as they drew their gaze back downward. Catherine was sure her fingerprints were gone, and she looked at her burned hands with worry.

Bowen looked ahead. The three factions must have been disrupted by the bulb's noise, and fell still. Conall yelled madly at the masses, enraged at their disobedience and betrayal. "You fools! All of you! We shouldn't be fighting against each other. Have you forgotten we have a common goal?" he shouted.

"You mean *your* goal!" someone shouted back.

Conall sneered. "No! *Ours*!" he shouted slowly for emphasis, then twirled himself around with outstretched arms. "For all of these centuries, who was the guard who mocked us outside the caves?"

A murmur of agreement rose from the crowd of warrior men and women.

"Here we are because of this man now, and he wants to put us back in those caves, locking us away forever so he can mock us again. *That* man," and Conall swung his arm, pointing at the distant Bowen. "And his puny woman."

The armies stirred, angered by the notion.

"Our common goal was to rule over ourselves in the old world, free from the priesthood's oppression. These two are the remaining oppressors!"

Shouts of agreement flew from all sides.

"We shouldn't be killing each other!" He gestured to the dead at his feet. "We should be killing *them*! Let us *destroy* them! Then let us flood over this land and take it back from the descendants of our oppressors! Let us once again, UNITE!" Conall screeched.

Bowen watched closely. "They're coming now." The three armies melded into one giant mass. Catherine's heart sank and her eyes grew wide in panic.

Bowen had been holding onto the skyphos, and now placed

it on the ground. He reached over and gave Catherine's shoulder a small squeeze. "The curse," he said quickly, nodding his head.

Catherine wanted to plead with him, but she knew she had to do this. Without the star bulb's help, she didn't trust herself to succeed. How was she supposed to enact the curse? Catherine had no idea how to use her power. She could only *feel* her power. She wished she could freeze everybody in place, or run away. But she knew she couldn't escape this. Then suddenly she remembered seeing the great oak tree spring from the ground. She had called for it to grow, and it did, but because she didn't believe it the dream remained a dream. *That's it!*

Catherine shut her eyes again, and tried to picture burying the armies in the caves. She imagined stone surrounding them, and not a drop of light. The images began to falter and fade, so she concentrated harder. The feet of the army could be heard now, and she was weakening from exhaustion. Once again she longed for the sun. She started whispering to help herself keep the images in her mind.

Bowen stood next to her, helpless. He kept looking at the skyphos, expecting it to give off a visible energy projected from Catherine. He saw the skyphos begin to have an aura of pale light, and he held his breath. It grew brighter, and he waited, expecting any moment to wake up far from here, days from now, cursed again.

Catherine's whispers grew louder. "The caves, caves. Stone, stone, STONE!"

Just then the skyphos rattled and broke in two. She had failed. Shocked, Bowen looked over at Catherine. Her eyes were still shut, but her face was strangely calm now and she seemed otherworldly, as if she was apart from reality. Her body now gave off the pale light.

"Catherine?" he whispered.

Though her eyes were shut, she saw Conall's army approaching in her mind's eye, they were close enough to see their faces through the light.

Catherine heard the words coming from her lips, one after the other. Something else clicked within her, and a surge of great power arrived and fell still. It felt like she was frozen with it. She couldn't move. Suddenly the power grew and burst. Her eyes snapped open. The power was unbelievably great. She realized now that she had been wrong. She didn't have to learn to control her own power, she had to learn how to *trust* it.

Thunder cracked the sky, and strong winds came. Catherine raised her arms as if to direct the wind. She blew the clouds away and the sun emerged triumphant. When the sun rays hit the land, she felt the power within her reach its peak.

All of a sudden, something like the power of God came down from heaven and engulfed her entire body into a living flame. Terror struck everyone who saw it. So powerful was it that the ground rumbled and shook when it hit her body. Some of the men too close went instantly blind, or caught on fire and burned alive.

Then there was another tremble deep in the ground. The whole army stopped. A sudden wave of darkness appeared from thin air and swept across the masses of people. There was a buzzing noise, like a mosquito that was too tiny and quick to see or catch. It grew louder and louder. Slapping their ears to make it stop, eyes squinted in pain. Bowen hunched down.

Suddenly piercing screams rang out and the buzzing stopped. There was a flash. Before Bowen's eyes, the armies turned to stone!

Bowen stood undamaged and stared at the scene in amazement some feet away behind Catherine's body of fire.

Conall had let the army go ahead of him. He beheld his legacy frozen in stone. He screamed wildly, startling the stragglers remaining next to him. In an instant, the stone druids crumbled and disintegrated into dust, blown away by the last of the wind. Conall was stricken with horror.

Catherine released herself from fire and light, and returned her body to its natural state. Bowen pulled her in an embrace, then jumped away with a yelp. "You feel like a kiln!" he said, gazing at her singed finger tips. The drizzle falling on her now turned to steam, creating a mist around her form.

"I don't *feel* hot to the touch," she said, curiously examining her frayed hair. She noticed the added burns to her fingers, and sighed.

"You almost burned me . . ." he mumbled. He waited until her body cooled down, and tested touching before he went all in on holding her. "Are you all right?" he said with a desperate voice muffled by her hair, his face buried tightly in her warm neck.

Catherine had seen what took place within the flame, but she stood there in Bowen's arms astonished at what she had done. "Yes, Bowen, I think so," she replied.

He pulled away. "You did it!" he exclaimed happily.

"I didn't cast the curse, Bowen," she reminded him, stepping back. She looked over at Conall, disappointed that he hadn't been trapped in stone. Though when she turned back she was visibly relieved to see Bowen moving and alive, breathing heavily.

"No, you did something far better . . ."

Before Bowen could finish, a figure suddenly swept across the field and threw itself at Bowen. She looked over with shock to see a wild bear. *Conall!* The ground trembled and shook beneath them as Bowen was thrown around. Luckily, Conall's blind rage caused him to lose his bear form rapidly after reaching them. The man, Conall was now struggling to pin Bowen.

"You took everything from me!" he screamed. Catherine realized suddenly that she could understand his words.

Conall was strong and powerful, but so was Bowen. Both men fought relentlessly. Bowen fought for his life. Catherine tried to help, throwing herself in the mix and she managed to stop Conall's grip from Bowen's throat by a swift knee to his side. But he elbowed her back.

When she managed to breathe again and sit up, one of Conall's remaining followers, a woman, raced toward her. Her hair was wild, teeth bared as she glared with piercing eyes, wielding a spear. The woman lunged. Catherine rolled just in time to avoid being run through. However, she got the full brunt of the woman's much larger body. Something clattered, then Catherine saw a dagger fall to the grass. She didn't have time to reach for it because the woman lunged at her again. Catherine wrestled with her to release her grip on the spear. The woman pushed Catherine on her back, pinning her down, holding the spear high in the air. Stunned, and seeing the end of the spear about to plummet, Catherine's adrenaline surged. She pulled her hand from under her, and with the dagger firmly in her grip, she stabbed. But the woman moved too quickly, and grabbed her wrist with mighty strength. The spear dropped.

Catherine struggled to keep her hold on the weapon. Knowing time was not in her favor, she took a risk and pushed with all her might to set the woman off balance. Then she reached for the spear, jabbing the sharp end in the woman's exposed side. The woman screamed, and fell awkwardly to the ground where she squirmed, dying in a pool of blood.

Catherine snatched the dagger and rose to her feet. With the weight on it, her ankle gave a sharp pain and she almost fell. She caught herself but was forced to kneel. Both her hands were on the ground as she recovered from the pain. It was useless to her now. But Catherine couldn't lose Bowen. Not him.

"Get out of here!" Bowen's voice boomed loudly through the scuffle.

Catherine looked at Conall with intensity, wanting to burn him or turn him to stone. He deserved a death much worse than all the people he had murdered, worse than Kathleen's, and for the suffering thereafter. Catherine wouldn't let him take Bowen, she wouldn't allow that to happen. She screamed out loud, her eyes shut tight as tears streamed down her cheeks.

Suddenly her eyes shot open. From her outstretched fingers the mist rose again. Filled with power, trusting it again, her eyes unclouded.

The last of Conall's men came to stop her. She was much stronger now, her blows equal to his. Her body had skill she never knew it had developed. Catherine dodged the man's futile attempt to grab her, and attacked with a jump. Gripping his head she snapped his neck in one motion. His body went limp and fell.

Catherine turned to see Bowen standing with the upper hand, and Conall now on the ground in agony. Conall rose slowly, and looked ready to pounce. In another fit of rage, he lurched forward, screaming madly.

Bowen managed to push Conall off him. Catherine's heart leapt up into her throat at the thought that Bowen could finish him off now. But he had been hurt somehow. Catherine couldn't tell where. Conall had backed away from him, so Bowen looked down at blood running down one of his arms. Catherine's eyes grew large.

Bowen was still looking down when Catherine saw the madness peak in Conall's eyes, and he charged. She knew if Conall got to him he would kill him. The pain inside her was unbearable. Bowen had to live.

Livid with anger and desperation she intercepted Conall, ignoring the immense pain of running on her pained ankle.

Conall saw her at the last minute, and they collided as Bowen fell backward. Conall's arm was bent crooked and his other palm pushed against her stomach hard. They separated breathlessly, noses inches apart. Conall's evil eyes stared into Catherine's. She suddenly saw why Bowen was saddened. She could see now that he was small and lost. Dagger still in hand she thrust it deep into Conall's chest, shoving it to the hilt. She felt the blood soak her hand, and heard the tear of fragile human flesh. Conall's eyes cleared in a flicker as the life faded out of them.

"Catherine!" Bowen shouted, and rushed over.

Conall's legs buckled and he slipped down. She pushed him away from her with disgust. Wringing her hands, she stood over him, both feet standing firmly.

"It's done now, Kathleen," she said over Conall.

Catherine walked a few steps away before her legs collapsed from under her. Her hair hung around her head wildly, still slightly damp from the earlier drizzle. She looked at her burned and bloodstained hands in a daze.

Bowen crouched in the wet grass and leaned over Conall's lifeless body. Catherine was relieved, and horrified. She had killed him at last, and claimed her revenge. It felt terrible. But Bowen was safe.

Managing to come out of her trance she saw that Bowen was crying softly. The green eyes, normally vibrant, clear and happy, were now clouded over. She hated to see him unhappy. She wanted to hold him until he could hurt no more. But she knew that Bowen had seen enough hurt in the world that she could never erase that from him, no matter how much she wanted to. He had seen such unimaginable horrors, and all manner of evil. Breathing in the damp air, she realized he had also seen much love in that time as well. She exhaled.

Bowen wiped his cheeks. "Be with her now, Conall," he

whispered, then laid a hand over the empty eyes to close them carefully.

Eyes closed, Catherine continued to breathe deeply. Bowen walked over and crouched down beside her.

"Can you walk?" he asked.

Catherine opened her eyes to see Bowen drenched in sweat, his curls pasted to his head and lovely face. She was about to answer no, when she found she could move her ankle without pain. She quickly looked down to see that her injuries were all healed, her broken ankle, and the burns on her hands. She checked her hair. The damage had mysteriously vanished, and her hair returned, lush and red as ever.

She looked up at Bowen in astonishment. "I can!" she said, quickly standing.

Bowen smiled, but winced when she grabbed onto him. "Oh!" she pulled back slightly, "He hurt you badly?"

"Nothing serious," he replied, holding his ribs.

"Are your ribs broken?" Catherine could see his face was bruised, and found the cut on his arm.

"No, bruised, maybe cracked."

Catherine wondered why her wounds had disappeared. Bowen could see what she was thinking.

"It's your power," he explained.

"But how?"

"You willed yourself to heal, so you could save me. Thank you for that, by the way," he chuckled.

Catherine gave a little smile in answer, but her curiosity took over again. "You mean I was healing in the act of fighting?"

He nodded.

Catherine was in awe of her power. The power to destroy, and to heal. "Can I heal you?" she asked hopefully.

"I doubt it. You're incredibly powerful, but not all-powerful," he said between checking his wounds over and coughing.

The clouds returned then and brought with them a light rain, which sprinkled on their happy faces and the green grass. The sun shone through, so Catherine enjoyed the refreshing mix. As she wiped her wet hair from her face, pushing it back, she suddenly remembered something. *Danny!*

"Bowen, it's not over! Danny!" she said, as her breath hitched.

"Let's go!" Bowen declared, wasting no time.

* * *

Danny's eyes crept open. He could see the tree branches above, and the bright sun's rays shining through the clouds. It hurt his eyes, so he shut them again. His neck was craned back, with the top of his head leaning against the tree. His throat was dry, and he needed food, but his stomach ached too much to want it. At times he thought he heard Catherine's voice, or saw Kathleen on her phone sitting next to him. He knew he had a fever.

Waiting for death to come, he prayed his sister would survive him. He could let himself die, if he knew she was going to live. In and out of consciousness, he remembered Bowen was with her, and that he trusted him now to take care of her.

Danny's lips felt wet, and cold water filled his mouth. He choked heavily. His body was pushed forward to help him swallow the water remaining.

"Síne . . ." he said looking up. She was hunched down with a bowl of water in her hand.

Síne said nothing. She seemed displeased having to help him, and almost happy that he choked. She pushed Danny harshly backward against the tree, and stood up after casting the bowl aside.

Danny was able to hold his eyes open and watch Síne's erratic pacing. The place was empty of all other druids. They were alone. The armies of druids must have gone for battle at last. He quickly realized she must be angry being left behind to watch him. He worried about Catherine again. For all he knew, the battle could have been days ago, and Catherine gone.

Suddenly, Síne tripped forward on her hands and knees painfully. She shot an accusatory look at Danny, and he involuntarily flinched. She seemed to blame him for her fall, and finally tired of guarding him, she snapped back up and took one of the ropes tied to him.

Danny cringed. *This is the end,* he thought.

Síne pulled the rope tightly around his throat, and something in him gave him the strength to try and struggle against the strangling. But it was not enough. It was almost over, and he almost wanted to give in and let it be.

Just then the bushes rustled, and something shot through the air past him. The pull of the rope stopped, and Síne flopped backward onto the ground. Danny turned, violently coughing and rubbing his neck, to see an arrow sticking out of her. Upset, his eyes quickly grew in fear. He recognized that arrow.

"I couldn't have her killing you before I could, after all," the hunter boomed.

Danny spotted him as he emerged from hiding in the thicket, and glowered at him watchfully.

The hunter's brow furrowed in confusion. "What? Can't you speak anymore?"

"Why?" he managed hoarsely. Danny hadn't used his voice in over a week, and with his parched throat it was barely audible.

"Why am I going to kill you?" the hunter guessed. Danny nodded weakly. "Because you destroyed my relic," he said flatly.

Danny was trapped, and at the mercy of another lunatic. He didn't want to die, let alone at the hand of his uncle's murderer. But he could barely move. He was defenseless, and no one would know what happened to him. He started to think about what his life could have been, what he wanted from it. How foolishly he had lived before Kathleen died. He'd wasted so much time.

The hunter leaned over, resting on his knees. "Is your life flashing before your eyes?" he asked in an amused voice.

Danny just glared in return. The hunter chuckled. "Well, it'll be over soon."

Danny watched him put another arrow in his crossbow's slot. He squeezed his eyes shut in preparation. The hunter took aim.

But before the hunter could pull the trigger, Bowen rushed at him and pulled his arms upward. Noticing he wasn't shot yet, Danny opened his eyes and gasped.

Bowen and the hunter scuffled with the tug of war they were in. As they struggled, Catherine burst through the trees.

"Catherine!" Danny said, his throat burning.

"Danny! Oh thank God, you're alive," she exclaimed, relieved though alarmed by the sickly state she found him in. She had to get him out of there.

Meanwhile, Bowen was struggling with the hunter. The hunter had the upper hand more times than Bowen was comfortable with. His hand still on the trigger, he kept trying to knock Bowen off him, or at least free his hand long enough to shoot. Danny was still in the hunter's target view. When Catherine came to him, he tried to push her away so she didn't get caught in the crossfire should Bowen fail.

Just then, Bowen tripped, but tripped towards the hunter. The hunter pulled his crossbow up and accidentally hit the trigger. The arrow left its hold and shot up, tearing leaves and tiny twigs as it went.

Bowen was knocked back off his feet, as the hunter pushed him. Catherine stood and reached out a hand in front of her, wishing to stop the hunter's breath. The hunter dropped his crossbow and stopped in his tracks as if she willed it to happen. She watched him closely as he grabbed his throat in fear. He was choking, and he hunched over, fading fast. The noise of far off leaves rustling made them think someone else was coming, when suddenly the traveling arrow returned and shot down into the hunter's back, straight through his heart. His expression went blank, and his eyes glazed over. The hunter stayed on his feet for half a second more, then fell to the ground, face in the dirt.

The three, reunited at last, looked around and breathed heavily. Bowen rose from the leafy ground and went to help Catherine carefully pick Danny up. "How did you do that Catherine?" Danny struggled to ask.

Catherine pushed Danny's long bangs out of his face, and looked curiously at him. "What are you talking about?"

Zapped of energy, Danny just gave her a knowing look. Catherine hadn't had a chance to realize what did actually happen until now.

". . . I don't know how, but I think I was choking him," Catherine said as the three started walking, arms interlocked to support Danny's limp body. But Danny had already passed out from the exertion.

"We need to get him back to Mary's cottage," Bowen stated. Catherine agreed, and they left as quickly as they could.

* * *

When Bowen returned to the battlefield the next day to bury Conall's body, he found it disintegrated beyond recognition. It looked like it had been lifeless for years. Bowen suspected it had something to do with the curse. He moved the body as best he could and covered it with dirt and whatever rocks he could find nearby.

Bowen returned to Mary's home to find Catherine sitting next to her brother's bed where he slept soundly. "He's safe now, his fever broke last night," he said softly, careful not to wake him.

Catherine let out her breath. She had feared the worst

until that moment. Bowen smiled and leaned down to help her out of the room, leaving Danny to sleep. "You don't have to be such a gentleman and help me wherever I go, you know. You're injured," she said, gesturing to his bandaged ribs, and shoulder.

"I'll be fine, I'm healing already," he said, and waved his arm emphatically as they walked through the house.

Mary was cooking in the kitchen and they settled at an old wooden table. "He's going to live?" she asked without turning from the stove.

"Yes," Bowen said with confidence.

Mary glanced back at Catherine, "I'm glad to hear it, Caty," she said.

Catherine leaned on the table with one elbow, and looked through the newspaper. Bowen simply enjoyed sitting and watching normal life continue. Catherine's eyes moved across the large page, from one inked word to the next.

"Bowen?" she said.

He came out of his daze. "Yes?"

"Where do we go from here?" she asked.

Bowen looked confused, "What do you mean?"

"I can't go back to my old life," she said, "I can't be the Catherine Green that I was before."

"Why ever not?" he shrugged.

"Because you don't fit into that life, and I can't go back without you."

Bowen smiled.

"So what do we do?" she asked again.

"I hadn't thought about it. I've simply been trying to get used to the idea of no curse. It's nice," he trailed off.

Catherine continued reading.

Bowen's eyebrow twitched, "What are you looking for?" he asked.

"A place to live . . ."

Mary finished the dishes, and drying off her hands with a towel she turned to them. "And jobs? Unless you plan on being on the run?" she asked.

"Job, yes," Catherine answered, still looking through the paper.

"You're welcome to stay with me," Mary offered. "And well, I own a few of the shops in the village, if one of those suits you. I could use the help. My employees won't give you any trouble about where you're from or anything."

Catherine looked up from her paper, swinging her red waves behind her shoulders before she stood and hugged Mary.

"Won't Kenneth be unhappy we're here when he comes to visit?" she asked, pulling away.

"Caty, don't you worry about my grandson. He got himself in a bit of trouble when he betrayed you two. I don't think we'll be seeing him for a while."

"You're not upset?"

"Oh no, dear. It's nothing we can do anything about. He's got to pay his dues. Maybe it'll teach him a lesson finally," she explained.

Bowen stood, his head brushing against the tiny kitchen's ceiling. "Thank you," he said to Mary.

"I'll never grow tired of hearing your accent," she said happily to him.

Bowen and Catherine looked at each other and laughed.

* * *

Some days passed, and Danny's health improved steadily. With Bowen's doctoring, and Mary's homemade meals, he was well on his way to being one hundred and ten percent. Catherine was relieved as she checked on him day to day.

She knew it was time to return Bella's car to her, and Danny offered to drive it there since he wanted to return to Dublin. First Catherine bought herself and Danny a prepaid mobile with no names connected to it, and called her friend. She told Bella everything—well mostly. Bella didn't know about Catherine's power. Catherine thought that was best for now. But Kathleen's death was difficult for Bella to take at first.

"I'm so sorry, Cathy!"

"Thanks."

"Kathleen's at peace now," Bella said, and Catherine believed her.

When the call ended, she went over plans with Danny. Knowing he would be leaving to return the car the next day, she reminded him that he might be wanted by the Gardai for Síne's disappearance, as well as questioning about both her and Kathleen.

"I'll keep out of sight for a while," he said.

"Really? What will you do for money?"

He shrugged. "Odd jobs. I'll find tons around the city." Danny wanted some things to go back to normal, but he was going to be different this time. He just had to figure out how. Seeing Bella again would be a nice step to normal, he thought.

Catherine wasn't too sure about his plans, but let it go.

In the early afternoon, Bowen opened the door to Mary's book shop in the village centre and saw Catherine putting a large leather bound book away. She turned when she heard the door open and smiled at him.

"Just a sec," she said and disappeared behind a door in the back with a small cart.

Bowen skimmed the titles nearby. Catherine soon reappeared with her jacket and a sash purse in hand. They left the small book shop and as they reached the borrowed compact car, Bowen opened the driver's door for her.

"Where are we going?" he asked as she drove them from the

town they now called home. "I hope it's not another adventure," he added.

"Very funny . . . It's a surprise. I wanted to do this before I gave the car back," she said without taking her eyes off the road.

"I hate surprises," he mumbled irritably.

"I know, but not this one," she said, chuckling to herself.

Bowen watched Catherine as much as he could. Catherine looked vibrant. He loved seeing her this way.

"Bowen?"

"Hm?"

"Do you really think I brought the sun out that day?" she asked.

"I know you did. It explains why it was usually sunny in the days leading up to the battle. Somehow you call it out with your power, and it fuels you."

"I bring sunlight," she said quietly to herself. "When Conall attacked you during the battle, I understood what he said . . . but I don't think he was speaking English, was he?"

Bowen looked surprised. "No, he wasn't . . ."

"Then how could I know?" she wondered.

Bowen shook his head; he didn't have an answer. "It wasn't your power," he remarked.

Catherine nodded in acknowledgment. She told herself she would let it go, just like everything else. Catherine realized shortly after Conall's death that she would never be completely healed, never be whole again without Kathleen. But in her brother's safety and happiness, and with Bowen by her side, she found her bliss.

They soon reached their destination, and exited the car to see rolling hills, small mountains, and waving grass winking at them in the breeze. The sun was high, and warm. Across the way, the empty land was speckled with trees and hundreds of flowers. The flowers turned their faces to the sun, trying to soak in every ounce, and Catherine did the same. She led the way as they walked hand in hand.

Bowen saw it before Catherine could say anything, and he stopped to keep it in full view.

"I read this is one of the oldest oak trees in Ireland still standing," Catherine said, "I thought you would want to see it. Maybe it'll bring you hope for our future."

Bowen squeezed her hand and smiled. They walked closer, and stopped once more. Bowen's neck stretched as he looked high up at the layered branches and thickly grown leaves against the remarkably blue sky above. He breathed in the fresh air, feeling full of life. He smiled, remembering the times he'd spent playing around the brothers of this tree as a child. He gently touched the bark and felt Catherine give him a small squeeze.

"The oak is beautiful. Its life force is indeed old, but still very strong. Thank you for introducing me," he said smiling happily. Catherine nodded and smiled back.

"I want to live happily ever after with you Bowen," she said.

Bowen reached for her and pulled her into a deep kiss. Catherine wrapped her arms around him and surrendered. He pulled away slightly to look into her deep eyes and held her tightly to him.

"Can we be together forever?" she asked, wrapped up in Bowen under the majestic oak.

"Yes, forever and all of time."

The End

ACKNOWLEDGEMENTS

THIS BOOK WOULD not have been possible if it weren't for my loving and supportive family, and friends. I want to thank my husband and children for all their understanding, comfort, and love. You have been my rock and helped me stay focused. Thank you to my grandmother who encouraged me, supported me, and was a friend when I needed her most. Thank you to my aunt and mother who were excited to read it upon release.

Jayne, Chiara, Roksana, Janai, Linnea, Elisa, and Andy—Thank you to my dear friends whose kindness and support have kept me going.

K.P. Stewart, Cassie James, Elise Kova, Karen Tomlinson, and Katelyn Anderson—Thank you to my fantastic author friends who generously had a hand in helping the publishing and media process, as well as helpful writing critique and advice for this book. You guys are amazing!

Thank you to my wonderfully kind and extremely talented cover artist Mélanie Delon. You plucked Catherine's image from my mind perfectly and made her real in another exciting way. I am forever grateful, and already ecstatic to see the cover for the sequel.

Thank you to the editor Kiele Raymond for her hard work, helpful views, and writing advice.

Finally, thank you to my awesome and efficient publisher.

I'm incredibly thankful to everyone who helped me in one way or another to make this book a book and known to readers.

ABOUT THE AUTHOR

J.Z.N. McCauley resides in lovely New England, where she loves wearing jackets and boots in the unpredictable weather there. She is a wife and mother who enjoys life to the fullest. Also, being a nerd across many genres is something she expresses openly.

McCauley spends most of her spare time writing, drawing, or reading. She loves archeology, mythology, history, music and many other forms of art as well. Always having a variety of interests and talents, she could never pick just one. When the chance pops up to travel to any of her favorite places, she takes way too many pictures. Otherwise, she is exploring a mystical land in a daydream. Which all provides fuel to her immense joy of writing. She is the author of the novella A Bell Sound Everlasting as well as the fantasy novel Oak & Mistletoe. She is currently writing The Oathing Stone (Fall 2017), a sequel to Oak & Mistletoe.

Visit her Online at
www.jznmccauley.com
Twitter (@JZNMcCauley)
Facebook.com/JZNMcCauley
Instagram (@JZNMcCauley)

You can also subscribe to her monthly book newsletter for news on releases, appearances, and giveaways at www.jznmccauley.com/subscribe